THE BAYOU BULLETIN

Senator's Granddaughter Charged With Murder!

Nikki Gideon, 17, granddaughter of State Senator Philip Delacroix, has been formally charged with the March 29 murder of Steven Boudreaux, 19, a cook at Rick's Café in Bayou Beltane.

Appearing with Nikki Gideon in court today for the bail hearing were her mother, local attorney Joanna Delacroix Gideon, and a New Orleans attorney, Logan Weston III, who

"I don't care how lucky he is," an angry Flora Boudreaux, Steven's mother, told *The Bulletin.* "That fancy lawyer Delacroix hired won't get the murderer of my baby off! Chief of Police Jake Trahan has an eyewitness who saw Nikki driving away from the scene of the murder. And he has her fingerprints on the murder weapon!"

Although Chief Trahan has refused to comment on the evidence

the case against the accused is a strong one.

Could it be that Logan Weston's luck is about to run out and a member of the powerful Delacroix family will be put behind bars for life?

Don't miss an issue of *The Bulletin* as this important case unfolds in the months ahead!

luckiest
Louisiana."

M.J. Rodgers is acknowledged
as the author of this work.

ISBN 0-373-82567-6

OVERRULED BY LOVE

DELTA JUSTICE

Overruled by Love

M.J. RODGERS

Harlequin Books

TORONTO • NEW YORK • LONDON
AMSTERDAM • PARIS • SYDNEY • HAMBURG
STOCKHOLM • ATHENS • TOKYO • MILAN
MADRID • WARSAW • BUDAPEST • AUCKLAND

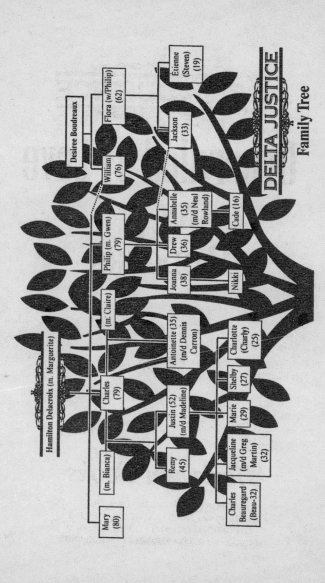

DELTA JUSTICE
Family Tree

Hamilton Delacroix (m. Marguerite)

Desiree Boudreaux

Mary (80)

Charles (79)

(m. Claire)

Philip (m. Gwen) (79)

William (76)

Flora (w/Philip) (62)

(m. Bianca)

Justin (52) (m/d Madeline)

Remy (45)

Antoinette (35) (m/d Dennis Carron)

Joanna (38)

Drew (36)

Annabelle (35) (m/d Neal Rowland)

Jackson (33)

Étienne (Steven) (19)

Charles Beauregard (Beau-32)

Jacqueline (m/d Greg Martin) (32)

Marie (29)

Shelby (27)

Charlotte (Charly) (25)

Nikki

Cade (16)

CAST OF CHARACTERS

Joanna Delacroix Gideon—Bayou Beltane lawyer. She's ready to make whatever sacrifice she must to help her daughter—even if it means giving up the chance for the love of a lifetime.

Logan Weston III—New Orleans lawyer. He's about to face the toughest case of his career—for both his client's life and his heart are on the line.

Nikki Gideon—Joanna's seventeen-year-old daughter. She made a disastrous choice in a first love—a mistake that may end up sending her to prison for the rest of her life.

Senator Philip Delacroix—Joanna's father. He's not above using fair means or foul to get what he wants, but this time his meddling could cost Logan the case and Joanna's daughter her freedom.

Taille Arbour—Prosecuting attorney. Dynamic, determined and deadly. She's using this case against Nikki to settle an old score with Senator Delacroix.

Flora Boudreaux—Mother of the man Nikki is accused of killing and Senator Delacroix's discarded mistress. Her plans for revenge on the Delacroix are now directed at Joanna's daughter.

Dear Reader,

Well, here it is, book seven in the exciting DELTA JUSTICE series! You've been introduced to its heroine, Joanna Delacroix Gideon, in the earlier books. Joanna is Philip Delacroix's oldest daughter, that gorgeous attorney who was widowed two years ago and returned to Bayou Beltane to make a fresh start for herself and her teenage daughter, Nikki. It hasn't been easy for Joanna. It's going to get harder. Fortunately, Logan Weston, a true Southern gentleman and stalwart Sir Galahad, is about to make a timely appearance in Joanna's life.

As you may realize, this story had to be integrated with the other stories in the DELTA JUSTICE series. I have to admit, dear reader, that was a new challenge for me. But working with the other authors turned out to be great! What a wonderful bunch of gals they are—smart, funny, full of creativity and wisdom.

And while I'm on the subject of wisdom, you should know that another person who made this project so enjoyable for me was its wise editor, Marsha Zinberg. Marsha is kind, competent, a true and dedicated professional. And, trust me, her ability to keep the facts straight through these twelve books is a magic act that not even David Copperfield would have attempted!

There's another reason I found writing this book so rewarding. Over the years my stories have taken place in many different states, but never before in Louisiana. I find Louisiana to be a very special place—a unique place. Its rich backdrop of culture, climate and culinary temptations is unbeatable for inspiring the senses. In this sultry, sizzling locale, a story about love and the law can't help but take on a flavor as sinfully delicious as its homemade hot gumbo and sweet jazz!

I sincerely hope you enjoy *Overruled by Love*.

PROLOGUE

JOANNA GIDEON AWOKE abruptly. She sat straight up in bed, open-eyed, instantly alert as the black night swallowed the final wisps of her disjointed dream.

The French doors to the upstairs gallery rattled violently against the advance of a fierce wind. Cool air swirled around her bare shoulders. The damp, earthy smell of an impending storm seeped into her bedroom.

Joanna was used to southern Louisiana's sudden spring storms and the resulting rattling and creaking of her old house in the wind. What had awakened her?

A violent fist-to-wood knocking erupted, vibrating the floorboards beneath her bed. She had her answer. Someone was at the front door.

Joanna pulled the bedcovers aside and slid her feet into her slippers. She grabbed her cantaloupe-colored robe off the chair and thrust her arms into its sleeves.

Her heart was beating high in her chest, fast. She knew such a strong summons coming in the dead of night could only be bringing bad news. Aunt Mary had already had one heart attack. And Joanna's father and uncle were equally susceptible to the heart disease that ran in the family.

Joanna clamped down immediately on her runaway speculations. She had learned long ago that wild, unsubstantiated worries did nothing but torment the soul. She would not anticipate what the bad news would be.

Whatever awaited her behind that insistent banging, she'd face it when she faced it. Not a second sooner.

Joanna stepped out of her bedroom and padded down the hallway, seeing her way by a small night-light as she headed for the staircase. Her hand glided along the banister as she descended. She was halfway down when a brilliant flash of lightning burned her shadow on the staircase wall.

And the shadow of someone directly behind her.

Joanna swung around, her heart pounding in rapid unison to the rumbling thunder that vibrated the wooden stairs beneath her feet.

"What's all the banging about?" her daughter asked, switching on the blinding hall light.

Joanna clung to the banister and exhaled a relieved breath, as her leg muscles turned to mush in the aftermath of their adrenaline bath. She hadn't expected the banging to awaken Nikki. Her daughter normally slept the sleep of the teenage dead.

"Shall we find out?" Joanna asked, projecting a calm she did not feel. She saw no reason to communicate her sense of foreboding.

"When are we going to get a doorbell like *normal* people?" Nikki asked.

"Our next renovation project," Joanna said as she turned around on the staircase to continue her descent.

Whoever was at the front door had stopped banging. Joanna realized that the person must have seen the hall light come on and knew someone was on the way.

"It could be a burglar," Nikki said.

"I rather doubt a burglar would knock, don't you?"

"It could be a serial killer who's going to pretend he has car trouble," Nikki said, changing mental gears as she began to follow her mother down the stairs. "Don't open the door," she warned.

Joanna sighed, then smiled. The older Nikki got, the dumber she thought Joanna to be. Still, Joanna counted her blessings. At least for the moment Nikki was talking to her. Pulling even a casual conversation out of her daughter lately had become tougher than getting a hardened criminal to confess.

"When was the last time you saw me open the door to someone we didn't know?" Joanna asked, trying to keep her tone light and nonconfrontational. Every time she said anything to Nikki she felt like she was stepping around eggshells.

"Someone we know would have called first."

"Good point," Joanna conceded as they reached the bottom of the stairs. "Unless the winds from this brewing storm have blown down the telephone lines. Go check for me, will you?"

Nikki didn't actually say she would. Agreeing to do something her mother asked had been beneath Nikki for some time now. But she did disappear into the dark living room, where the closest telephone was located. Joanna let herself hope for the best.

With Nikki, she did a lot of hoping for the best.

Joanna turned toward the door. She switched on the outside light, keeping the foyer in darkness. She peered through the peephole. When she saw the familiar face of the man standing there, his brown hair blowing in the strong wind, she immediately unbolted the security lock and swung open the door.

A hefty gust of moist, fresh air whirled through the open doorway, whipping back Joanna's hair and robe.

"Jake, come in before we both get blown away."

Chief of Police Jake Trahan stepped into the foyer, hat in hand. Joanna used her shoulder to close the door against the strong wind that seemed determined to join him. She switched on the foyer's antique chandelier to add a little more light to that supplied from the hallway above.

Jake stood before her, his face shadowed, his stance formal. He was wearing his uniform, his jacket spotted with twigs and leaves that had hitched a ride on the wind heralding in the storm.

Jake had recently eloped with Annabelle, Joanna's only sister. He was family now. Still, Joanna could tell her new brother-in-law had not come to see her in that role but in the performance of his job duties.

Joanna faced him squarely, steeling herself, knowing that

whatever he'd come to say, it would be best to get it said quickly.

Nikki emerged from the darkness of the living room and stepped into the foyer.

"Phone's okay. Hi, Jake."

Joanna watched as Jake turned to nod solemnly in response to Nikki's greeting. When his dark eyes remained on her daughter's face, a wave of unease swelled in Joanna's stomach.

"How about some coffee, Jake?" she asked.

Jake's eyes remained on Nikki as he answered, "A cup would be welcome. It's been a long night."

Joanna quickly led the way to the kitchen. When out of the corner of her eye she saw Nikki following, she halted, turned, faced her.

"You have school tomorrow."

Nikki cinched the belt of her red flannel robe tightly and glared at her mother in a way that Joanna found all too familiar. "And you have work. I'm not a child. I won't be sent to bed."

"It's Nikki I've come to see, Joanna," Jake said quickly, forestalling any protest Joanna might offer to her daughter's flat refusal to leave.

Joanna's initial swell of unease crashed like a cold, icy wave through her stomach. She turned and mutely led the way into the kitchen. She flipped on the light and walked over to the coffeemaker.

Jake and Nikki sat at opposite ends of the small kitchen table. Joanna turned her back to them as she concentrated on making the coffee.

Outside, the wind whipped the shutters and howled through the eaves. Lightning slashed deep holes in the sky. Rivers of roaring thunder rushed in to fill them.

Inside, Joanna's own personal storm tore through her body and scraped her nerves raw. *Keep calm!* she told herself.

The graceful, steady hands of the antique gingerbread kitchen clock pointed to midnight. Joanna painstakingly arranged and rearranged three cups on a serving tray, willing her own hands to steady. She poured sugar into a bowl and fresh cream from the refrigerator into a pitcher.

And all the time her muscles ached with the effort to stay calm.

The coffee gurgled and spit as it filled the pot. The rich aroma wafted through the kitchen, mixing with the raw scent of the coming rain, which sifted through tiny cracks in the old house.

Joanna carefully filled the blue-and-gold porcelain cups. She picked up the serving tray and carried it to the kitchen table.

Jake shed his jacket, draped it over the back of his chair. He took the coffee, sipped it gratefully, silently.

Joanna had always liked and respected Jake Trahan. He was a good man—honest, trustworthy. He was wonderful for her sister, Annabelle. It had taken Jake to finally help Annabelle see what Joanna had been telling her sister for years—that their father was a fallible man, not the god he pretended to be.

Joanna would always be grateful to Jake for that.

But she had a feeling she was not going to be grateful to him for tonight.

Jake returned his empty coffee cup to its saucer. He looked directly at her daughter. "Where were you tonight, Nikki?"

"Why, Jake?" Joanna asked. The words were out before she could stop them.

Jake kept his eyes on her daughter's face. "I'll get to that in a minute, Joanna. First I need some answers from Nikki."

Jake hadn't said the words unkindly. Joanna caught their warning nonetheless.

This was an official inquiry. She had to be quiet and let Nikki answer. Joanna's self-control was an absolute necessity at this moment, just as it had been at all the most tearing and heartbreaking moments of her life. She held on to it. It was all she had to hold on to.

"Nikki?" Jake prompted.

Nikki was stirring sugar into her coffee. Her head was

bent, her face covered by the thick drape of her nut brown hair. She didn't look up when she answered, "I was here."

"You didn't go out?"

Nikki's second response was even longer in coming. "Earlier."

"What time?"

Nikki raised her head. Her large walnut eyes darted momentarily to Joanna's face.

She has her father's coloring, the shape of his features, even his nose, Joanna thought. *Every day she looks more and more like Richard.*

The sweetness of Joanna's thought turned to sadness when she saw the cool defiance on her daughter's face. Richard's features had never worn such an expression.

"Ten-fifteen," Nikki said.

Ten-fifteen? Joanna felt a sudden constriction in her chest. So Nikki had sneaked out again after she had gone to bed. Joanna had thought that particular problem to be over. Apparently, she had thought wrong.

"Where did you go?" Jake asked.

"To see Steven."

Nikki's tone turned even more defiant. Joanna knew the emotion was directed at her, not Jake.

"Did you see Steven?" Jake asked.

Nikki pushed back from the table and whipped to her feet. She flipped her hair back with a toss of her head and shoved her hands to her hips.

"So that's why you're here!"

"Would you care to explain that, Nikki?" Jake asked, his voice quiet, even.

Nikki's lips were tight, her brown eyes overbright. "I'm not sorry for what I did. He got what he deserved."

"Did he?" Jake asked, his voice so cold and so much a cop's that a tight fist grasped Joanna's heart and squeezed.

She leaned forward, no longer able to keep silent.

"Jake, *please* tell me what's happened."

Over the erratic beating of her heart, Joanna became aware that the lightning, the thunder, even the wind had ceased.

It was suddenly, eerily still.

Jake slowly turned toward her.

"Steven Boudreaux is dead," he said.

A hard rain exploded onto the roof like machine-gun fire. Joanna was seized by an involuntary tremor.

Steven Boudreaux *dead*?

An inarticulate cry came out of Nikki, a sound like nothing Joanna had ever heard—or ever wanted to hear. Her eyes swung to her daughter as chills chased through her body.

Nikki's mouth was a huge hole in her face, her eyes dark, empty pools. She stumbled back, her shoulders hitting the wall with a loud clap.

Joanna rose quickly to go to her daughter's side and gather her in her arms. But Nikki's next words nailed Joanna's feet right to the floor.

"I did it," Nikki cried. "I did it!"

CHAPTER ONE

LOGAN WESTON SIPPED coffee as he read his morning paper. Sunlight poured into his upstairs kitchen window. The curtains lifted in a soft southwest breeze. The leaves of the giant oak that shaded his front yard sighed in appreciation. The rustle of the tall stand of banana trees echoed the sentiment.

The series of spring storms that had washed through New Orleans during the last couple of days had blown northeast, the tail end of them now harassing the folks up in Mississippi. Here in the Big Easy it was going to be a warm and sunny spring day.

For the first time in more years than he cared to remember, Logan had finally cleared his law practice calendar sufficiently to take a vacation.

He had no plans. He intended to follow his whim of the moment and let the day unfold. It was something he had always promised himself he would do. When he had the time.

Today he had the time.

Logan stretched leisurely. He was still in his robe and slippers despite the fact that it was after nine. He was feeling lazy, slothful, decadent, damn good. He intended to go right on feeling that way.

The phone rang. Only very special people had his private number. Logan leaned back in his chair to retrieve the portable phone off the kitchen counter. It was going to be a pleasure to talk to one of those special people without work cutting the conversation short.

He had barely said hello, however, when a clipped, emphatic, unfamiliar male voice boomed in his ear. "This is

Senator Philip Delacroix. I must see you on an urgent legal matter."

Logan's forehead furrowed into an immediate frown. A lot of questions were running through his mind, not the least of which was how this man had gotten his private number.

"Senator Delacroix, I am on vacation," Logan said politely but firmly.

"Time is of the essence, Mr. Weston. I will be ringing your doorbell in exactly thirty seconds."

The telephone line went dead. Logan flipped the phone closed and replaced it on the counter. He stood and leaned over the kitchen windowsill to look out.

On the street below, directly in front of the wrought-iron fence surrounding his house, sat a long black limousine. A chauffeur held open the passenger door. A slim, silver-haired man emerged from it. The silver-haired man pushed through the gate and approached the house in a long stride. Thirty seconds later, the front doorbell rang.

Logan leaned back from the window. He had heard a lot about the Delacroix. It would be hard to be a lawyer in Louisiana and *not* to have heard a lot about them. Particularly State Senator Philip Delacroix.

The man's power and money—not to mention his position as legal counsel to many of Louisiana's heavyweight corporations—were legend. So, too, was the man's habit of throwing around that power, money and position.

It was beginning to look like the legend had a firm basis in fact.

Logan was tempted to let Delacroix cool his heels on his doorstep indefinitely. The man had shown up without an appointment and without any acknowledgment of the fact that Logan had made it clear he was on vacation.

Logan considered himself to be an easygoing man. But even an easygoing man came up against some things he could not abide. Bad manners was one of those things high on Logan's list.

Yet Philip Delacroix had obviously made a determined

effort to seek him out. Why? For the moment, at least, Logan's curiosity overcame his resentment.

He took his time descending the staircase to answer the front door. He never hurried for want of a very good reason. He didn't consider the fact that he was keeping Philip Delacroix waiting to be any reason at all.

When Logan finally opened the front door, he found himself facing a pair of very deep blue, irritated eyes.

Philip Delacroix was quite obviously a man who did not like to be kept waiting.

Delacroix stood erect, surprisingly tall, only a couple of inches shorter than Logan's six-four. His silver hair was full, the skin of his late-seventyish face obviously weathered as much by a willful temper as time.

Delacroix stepped quickly inside, not waiting for an invitation. He had a lean, youthful energy about him that belied his chronological age by at least two decades.

Logan stepped over to the door that opened into his law firm's offices. He led the way through the reception area. When they reached the inner chamber of his private office, Logan flipped on the overhead light and closed the door behind Delacroix. Logan gestured toward a chair as he circled around his desk.

Philip Delacroix did not sit.

"I trust you will forgive my appearance under the circumstances," Logan said, gesturing toward his robe.

Delacroix waved aside the subject of Logan's attire as unimportant and beneath his notice. Despite the opening Logan had just given the man, the senator made no apology for appearing without an appointment and demanding Logan's time.

Logan rather doubted this man apologized for anything he did. Common civility appeared to be something Philip Delacroix also considered beneath him.

"How may I help you?" Logan asked, making himself comfortable in his chair. He saw no reason to stand just because Delacroix chose to.

"I want you to represent my granddaughter, Nikki Gideon."

Logan leaned back in his chair and looked up at the formidable man who stood glaring down at him with such force. Delacroix's energy emanated out of him almost like a warning.

"Why does your granddaughter need a lawyer?" Logan asked.

"The Bayou Beltane grand jury indicted her last night for second-degree murder."

Delacroix's words raised even more questions for Logan.

"Bayou Beltane is the major part of your senatorial district in the North Shore, is it not?"

"It is."

"Does your granddaughter live with you there?"

"She lives in Bayou Beltane but not with me."

"Who is the deceased?"

"Steven Boudreaux. A local man."

"Where did Steven Boudreaux die?"

"On my property in Bayou Beltane."

"Senator, the alleged crime took place in Bayou Beltane, and both the victim and accused are residents. This is clearly a local matter. You have access to a large staff of attorneys who are familiar with the courts and peculiarities of your district. Why are you coming to me?"

"My practice is geared to corporate litigation, not criminal defense."

"Your brother's firm specializes in criminal defense," Logan said.

Philip Delacroix showed no surprise at Logan's knowledge of the Delacroix family's legal enterprises. On the contrary, he seemed to expect it.

"There is only one attorney at my brother's firm who has both the track record and expertise to handle this kind of a case. She can't do it."

"Why can't she, Senator?"

"She's Nikki's mother."

Yes, Logan could see that would be a major problem. No

matter how qualified, family should never represent family in *any* legal action.

He'd learned that lesson the hard way.

Logan had satisfied his curiosity as to why Delacroix had come to see him. Nothing he'd learned warranted his giving up his much needed vacation. This wealthy and powerful man could certainly find himself another lawyer.

And he was going to have to.

Logan rose. "I can't help you, Senator. If you want me to recommend someone else, I will be happy to do so."

Philip Delacroix pulled a cashier's check out of the breast pocket of his hand-tailored silk suit coat. He slapped it down on Logan's desk. Logan blinked. The check was made out to him. It was for a million dollars.

"Your retainer," Delacroix said.

This man obviously thought he could buy him. Logan didn't know whether to be angry or amused. At least he had to admit the offer hadn't come cheap.

Logan looked up at Delacroix and smiled. He was going to enjoy saying this.

"Sorry, Senator. I can't help you."

Delacroix's brow creased in a deep frown. He leaned forward, his knuckles scraping the edge of Logan's desk.

"Listen to me, Weston. You don't have to work twelve-hour days for the rest of your life or wait another ten years before you can take a measly month's vacation."

"Excuse me?"

"You have the smarts, style and solid litigation record of a winner. Take this case and I'll back you with the kind of political clout that will catapult you into the Attorney General's office."

Logan knew his reputation as a laid-back lawyer and his seemingly effortless, consistent wins had earned him the nickname of the "luckiest lawyer in Louisiana." Very few people knew that Logan worked twelve-hour days to insure that "luck." Even fewer knew he hadn't had a vacation in ten years.

Philip Delacroix had obviously made it his business to find

out a lot of personal information about him. Logan cherished his privacy. He was not pleased at this arrogant, willful man's invasion of it.

Logan let his question roll lazily off his tongue with the deceptive ease that had caught many an opponent off guard. "Mind telling me how you gained access to my private number and this information about my personal life?"

Logan watched the intense light in Philip Delacroix's eyes as the man answered. "We have mutual friends at *the* krewe club."

Delacroix's answer brought Logan straight up in his chair. Those words were as close to a secret handshake as one could get. The city's many krewes were Carnival organizations—on the surface. But *the* krewe club Delacroix referred to was made up of the crème de la crème of New Orleans—the powerful, unnamed, unseen men who ran the city.

Delacroix might be from the North Shore, but he had just demonstrated his considerable presence in the Big Easy. Logan was struck with the realization that this man had made no idle boast before. If Delacroix put his mind to it, he probably *could* put Logan in the Attorney General's chair.

It was not a comfortable thought.

Still, for all Philip Delacroix's influence and contacts and their *mutual friends,* the man had missed the big picture when it came to understanding Logan. Missed it entirely.

"I'm not your man, Senator," Logan said, straight into eyes that were trying their best to stare him down.

A look of disbelief flashed over Delacroix's face. He leaned back, planted his feet on the carpet, crossed his arms over his chest.

"What do you want, Weston?"

"My vacation," Logan said unhesitatingly. He stretched his arms over his head. "As you say, it's been ten years. You can take your pick of a dozen excellent attorneys."

"You're the pick, Weston."

"I appreciate the accolade. However—"

"I'm not flattering you! I flatter *no* one! I'm stating the facts. Would you hire less than the best if she were your daughter?''

His daughter charged with murder? The idea was horrific, unthinkable. Logan refused to allow himself to entertain it for a second.

He looked at his watch with deliberate intent. "Senator, as I said, I am on vacation, so if you will excuse—"

"You have to take Nikki's case!" Delacroix interrupted, his voice climbing suddenly to a ragged peak. A feverish flash of color flagged his sallow cheeks. He unfolded his arms and stomped in jerky steps toward Logan's desk, his bony hands opening and closing tightly.

Logan was once again stunned. This sudden change of demeanor did not fit in with anything he had heard about the proud and impervious Philip Delacroix.

The senator stopped his pacing abruptly and glared at Logan. "Weston, for God's sake, she's only just turned seventeen!"

Delacroix's granddaughter was only seventeen? That made her the same age as Logan's own daughter.

For the first time Logan saw a desperate light flickering in the man's eyes. Delacroix's erect shoulders and facial features were tight with strain. That youthful energy that he had emanated earlier now seemed to have been drained from his body. He looked old, worn, tired—every bit his age. His voice was harsh, biting.

"Name your price, Weston."

Logan was certain that Philip Delacroix was a proud, arrogant man who shamelessly used his influence and power and money to buy him what he wanted, sparing no regard for the feelings or needs of others.

But Logan could now see that he was also a very worried grandfather desperately fighting in the only way he knew how to help his young granddaughter.

The first man could never have hired Logan.

The second man just had.

Logan picked up the cashier's check off his desk and stuck

it into his pocket. There was no triumph on Delacroix's face—only relief.

"When is the bail hearing?" Logan asked.

Delacroix checked the platinum Rolex on his wrist. "In less than an hour."

And it was at least a forty-minute drive around Lake Pontchartrain to the North Shore. Logan had not even showered or shaved. He started for the door leading out of his office, untying his robe. He took the stairs up to his living quarters two at a time.

JOANNA WAITED at the defense table in the courtroom, her nerves pulled tight and thin.

The bail hearing was supposed to have started five minutes before. The bench was still empty. Judge Victor Melling was not known for his promptness.

Joanna knew the drill by heart. She had sat in countless bail hearings over the years as a criminal defense attorney. But this was the first time that she was unable to remain the dispassionate player she must be in the role she was about to perform.

Because this time it was her own daughter's bail she would have to negotiate.

She shouldn't be doing this. She was too upset, too closely involved to be the impersonal advocate a defendant needed. But today she would do it. She had to. She was all Nikki had.

She had been so sure that Uncle Charles would agree to represent Nikki that she hadn't even thought to ask anyone else.

But Charles had declined. He had been burned by his brother when he'd agreed to represent Joanna's mother in her divorce from her father. Philip had never forgiven Charles for doing that. He had warned him to never, ever, even *think* about representing a member of *his* family again.

It wasn't that Charles was a weak man. It was more that he was a peace-loving one. He didn't want any more confrontations with his brother, confrontations that always upset everyone in the family. Crossing Philip Delacroix was always a guarantee of pain.

As Joanna well knew. She'd crossed her father several times herself. Philip Delacroix used his money and power and position to bend people and the law to suit his own selfish desires. He did not take kindly to opposition.

She'd left her father's law firm the year before and had gone to work for her uncle Charles precisely because she couldn't live with Philip's less-than-ethical practices another second. And she had told him so.

Nearly every conversation they'd had since had ended in an argument. Her father would never know how much it had hurt Joanna to say what she had, to do what she did, to face the fact that he was not the honest, ethical man she longed for him to be.

But what hurt most of all was that despite what her father was, Joanna still loved him.

Love was never a light load to carry. She'd accepted and lived with that truth for many years.

But now she knew that when you loved someone whose actions you could not respect, the weight of that love was almost too much to bear.

"Morning, Ms. Delacroix."

Joanna spun around at the sudden, unexpected greeting. Her heart sank as she looked into the dark, eager eyes of Gator Guzman, the owner and chief reporter of the *Bayou Bulletin*. He was sitting in the first spectator row, his big mouth open in a gratified grin.

She should have known he would be here. Gator always surfaced, his hungry news jaws snapping, whenever a member of the Delacroix family was in trouble.

And now it was her daughter. Nikki's arrest and grand-jury indictment had been the top news story in that gossipy rag Gator indulged himself by calling a newspaper.

"My name is Mrs. Gideon," Joanna corrected him, in her most formally cool and controlled tone. "It has been for eighteen years."

"Still, once a Delacroix, always a Delacroix," Gator said,

still grinning. "I hear tell that you're going to be representing Nikki yourself on this charge of murder. That so?"

"I'm not going to talk to you about this matter, Gator. So you might as well save yourself the embarrassment of having your questions ignored."

Joanna refaced the front of the courtroom.

"No reason to get all riled up at me, ma'am," Gator said, sounding both whiny and wounded. "Just trying to do my job."

Joanna hated this pitying act Gator was putting on. Selling newspapers was more than a job to him. Everyone knew Gator liked snooping into other people's business. *Really* liked it. Particularly when he could snoop into the private life of a member of the prominent Delacroix family.

Joanna's attention quickly shifted as the side door opened and a uniformed female officer of the court brought out her daughter. Nikki looked tired and pale. Joanna's chest ached. She stood, holding precariously on to her outward calm as she saw Nikki being marched forward like a criminal.

Joanna laid a comforting hand on her daughter's arm the moment she was beside her. "It's okay, Nikki. I'm here."

"I thought Uncle Charles was going to represent me," Nikki said.

Joanna tried not to take her daughter's words as a personal rebuke. She reminded herself that even she knew it would be better if Charles were the one standing beside Nikki now.

"He couldn't make it," she said, in as calm a voice as she could muster. Disappointment flashed in Nikki's eyes before she turned away. Joanna withdrew her hand, silently emitting a deep sigh.

The prosecutor, Willard Melling, took his place at the other table. Joanna had gone up against him many times. She had no respect for him. Willard never argued his position on the basis of the law, but only on the basest of emotionalism.

Joanna always thought that Willard had missed his true calling as a hell-and-brimstone, Bible-thumping preacher.

An officer of the court announced the arrival of the judge. Victor Melling, Willard's second cousin, took the bench.

Joanna was reassured by the fact that Victor wasn't all that friendly toward Willard. It seemed Willard had made the very big error of going to law school "up North" somewhere.

On the other hand, Joanna had gotten her law degree in California—not a point in her favor.

Plus which, Judge Victor Melling had a reputation for setting ridiculously high bail for minor offenses, and in the case of a capital crime, refusing to grant bail at all.

Joanna knew it was critical that this bail hearing result in Nikki's release. The idea that her daughter could be kept in jail another second was tearing her up inside.

"The *State of Louisiana versus Nikki Gideon*," the bailiff announced.

"Let's hear your recommendation on bail, Willard," Victor said.

Joanna was well aware that Judge Victor Melling did not have a very long attention span at these bail hearings. She hoped Willard would drone on with his usual Bible-quoting bilge. As soon as it got boring, she knew the judge would tune out.

"Your Honor, this crime is the most serious one of murder," Willard began. "Neither the state nor I—as a God-fearing man—could sanction the unholy release of this most serious of sinners on bail. *Thou shall not kill!* the Bible commands us. Nikki Gideon killed."

Willard pointed at Joanna. "Returning this defendant to the harmful home environment that spawned her heinous behavior would be an offense against every law under God!"

"Excuse me?" Joanna said, unable to believe what she was hearing and seeing, even from Willard.

"Now, just hold on there, Ms. Gideon," the judge said. "You can have your say in a minute. Let Willard get it all off his chest first."

"Thank you, Your Honor," Willard said, making a ridiculously dramatic bow in his cousin's direction before continuing.

"The State of Louisiana asks that the defendant, Nikki

Gideon, be held in custody—for her crimes as well as for
the protection of the good people of Bayou Beltane—while
awaiting the trial that will decide the rightful punishment of
her perfidious misdeeds."

Normally Willard's incredibly stupid posturing would
have amused more than angered Joanna. But his nasty words
and implications came far too close to home today. Matter
of fact, they were directed dead center at *her* home.

"Now you can have your say, Ms. Gideon," the judge
said as he turned his face to her.

Joanna fought back her anger at Willard's personal attack.
She had to find the cool words and countenance that would
allow her to defend Nikki, not herself.

But this was hard. How could she defend Nikki's right to
be released into her care without defending herself as the
caretaker? Willard was in rare form today, his speech both
abridged and biblically abusive.

Joanna was searching her thoughts, trying to decide how
best to begin, when suddenly a voice spoke from behind her.

And what a voice. Overlaying its growly cougar cadence
was the distinctive, refined drawl of a Southern gentleman.

"If the court please, I would like to be heard on this matter."

Joanna turned to see the man behind that remarkable
voice.

He stood alone at the back of the courtroom, wearing an
impeccable three-piece suit and an authoritative air. There
was a relaxed stillness about his tall, powerfully built frame.
A briefcase hung from one hand. The overhead light painted
pale streaks through the dark gold of his short, thick hair.

"Approach, sir," the judge said.

The stranger strode toward the front of the courtroom with
a disciplined, deliberate slowness that spoke of an effortless
inner control. He had a clean-featured face, made even more
attractive by the lines of experience and self-awareness
etched into it.

"And who are you, sir?" the judge asked.

"Logan Clayton Weston III at your service, Your Honor.

I have just been engaged by Senator Philip Delacroix to act as Miss Nikki Gideon's attorney in this matter before the court.''

Logan paused and turned to Joanna as he stepped up to the defense table. "Providing Ms. Gideon has no objections, of course?"

Despite his slow advance, the look Logan flashed Joanna was intense and sharp and spoke of a very quick intelligence beneath that deceptively laid-back manner.

Joanna knew it was typical of her arrogant father to take it upon himself to engage Weston without so much as a word to her. But she wasn't fool enough to let her personal pique at her father's actions interfere with Nikki getting the best legal representation possible.

And Joanna had a very strong feeling that the best legal representation possible might be standing before her right now.

She had heard of the consistent wins of this New Orleans defense attorney. She was not surprised that her father had selected him.

She was only surprised that Logan Weston was asking her permission to take over as her daughter's counsel. Philip Delacroix and those on his payroll weren't known for asking permission from anyone. For anything.

"I have no objection to Mr. Weston taking over as the defendant's counsel in this matter before the court," she said.

Logan moved to Joanna's side and set his briefcase on the defense table. In doing so, his arm brushed against hers. It was the smallest of contacts, yet it sent a strong, alarmingly sweet quiver through Joanna.

Her sudden intake of breath startled her as deeply as her elemental feminine response to being touched by this attractive stranger. Logan turned to look directly at her.

He towered over her by a full seven inches.

His eyes up close were a deep bronze flecked with pale gold. Pure male vitality poured out of him. Joanna's heart began to race. She suddenly found it increasingly hard to catch her breath.

"Looks like you have yourself a client, Mr. Weston," the judge said.

Logan returned his eyes and attention to the bench. "Thank you, Your Honor. Now, if the court pleases, I would like to address this subject of bail for my client."

"You may proceed," Judge Melling said.

"Have a seat," Logan said in a low voice to Joanna, before stepping from behind the defense table to the podium positioned in front of the bench.

Joanna understood Logan wanted the judge's full and complete attention. It was a good move, considering Melling's short attention span at these hearings. She put aside her erratic reactions to Logan and sat down, motioning for Nikki to do the same. Seeing them sit, Willard had no choice but to follow suit.

Although he did not turn around to check, Logan seemed to know the exact second that he was the only one still standing in the courtroom.

"Your Honor," he began, his deep baritone soothing, almost a purr, "sometimes we forget that the only reason to set bail is simply to insure that a defendant shows up for trial. The theory is that if sufficient money or collateral is at stake, the defendant will not want to lose it by fleeing.

"I respectfully call Your Honor's attention to the young lady who sits before you today." Logan turned around to smile at Nikki before continuing. "Nikki Gideon is no flight risk, Your Honor. She has only just turned seventeen. She has no money of her own. She could hardly escape this court's jurisdiction."

Logan's eyes returned to the judge's.

"But even more important, Nikki wants—no, not just wants—Nikki is *eager* for her day in court. She has never been in trouble with the law. She is a member of one of Bayou Beltane's proudest and most prominent families. She wants to show her friends and this community how false the accusation is that has been brought so hastily and unwisely against her."

Logan stopped to point his index finger at Willard Melling.

Joanna heard a new note in his voice when he resumed speaking. It sounded more like a growl than a purr.

"This prosecutor spoke as though Nikki had been convicted of a crime for which bail should be a partial punishment! Nikki has not been convicted of a crime. She comes before you today innocent under the law. That *is* the law, something that seems to have completely slipped that man's attention."

Logan redirected his eyes to the bench as he dropped his hand. "This prosecutor also made a slanderous personal attack on Nikki's counsel. I know you are as appalled as I to have been a witness to such unprofessional—and ungentlemanly—conduct in *your* courtroom. That it comes from a representative of the State of Louisiana makes it even more unconscionable! Such callous disregard for fairness! I cannot believe that a Southern law school could have graduated that man!"

Logan paused again, this time to shake his head as if he were ashamed to be in the same room with the prosecutor.

Joanna saw Willard Melling flush. It wasn't often a defense attorney could get through his thick skin.

Logan was good, all right, and obviously well coached. His well-modulated voice returned to that deep purr that stroked the ears.

"Your Honor, Nikki's concerned mother is before you now, by Nikki's side, determined to be with her every step of the way through this terrible ordeal that she is so bravely facing."

Logan stopped to look at Joanna. He smiled. Joanna told herself he was only performing his role. But that didn't stop the quiver skating across the surface of her skin.

"You know Joanna Delacroix Gideon. She is an officer of this court, a pillar of this law-abiding community. Nikki could have no better example, be in no better hands, as she fights for her reputation against this scandalous charge."

Logan turned his smile on the judge.

"I appeal to you, sir, not just as the judge who sits before this court, but as a true Southern gentleman who understands that the welfare of our womenfolk must always be our first duty. Send Nikki home with her mother where she will be safe and protected. Thank you.''

Logan slowly turned to retrace his steps to the defense table. He sat down and calmly looked up at the bench.

Joanna could see the gleam in Judge Victor Melling's eyes as he looked first at Logan's confident face and then at his second cousin's still flushed one. One thing was for certain. Victor had not been bored this morning.

"Bail is set at fifty thousand dollars," he said.

Willard jumped to his feet. "Fifty thousand dollars? You crazy, Victor? You made it seventy-five thousand for that case last week, and it was simple car theft!"

Victor rapped his gavel and then pointed it at his cousin. "You will address me as Your Honor in my court, Willard Melling."

"But—"

"No buts. Weston's right. You have not been behaving the way a Southern gentleman behaves himself. You might as well just plaster that Northern law degree over that disrespectful face of yours. Court's adjourned."

Joanna let out a sigh of pure relief. She turned to Nikki, wrapping her arms around her daughter in a heartfelt hug. Nikki's body was stiff in her embrace.

"I'll make bail and get you released just as quickly as I can," Joanna promised as she drew back.

A deep and unmistakable voice boomed from behind Joanna. "It's already being handled."

Joanna rose to her feet and turned to face her father.

Philip Delacroix was staring at her with eyes that held no warmth.

"Thank you," Joanna said simply, sincerely.

Her father ignored Joanna's remark as his eyes swept to his granddaughter's face. He offered Nikki neither a hug nor reassuring words. Physical and verbal shows of affection were not Philip Delacroix's style. But the fact that he had gone out of his way to get Nikki the best attorney he could told Joanna of his concern for his granddaughter.

As usual, Philip Delacroix's tone was a command, not a request when he addressed Nikki. "I told you to stay away from Steven Boudreaux. You wouldn't listen to me. Now you'd better listen to Weston."

Delacroix did not wait for a response from his grand-daughter. He turned and quickly left the courtroom.

Nikki's sharp exhalation was full of defiance.

At that moment, the weight of Joanna's love for both her daughter and her father had never seemed so heavy.

CHAPTER TWO

"WHEN DID MY FATHER hire you?" Joanna asked Logan as they stood in the jail's outer alcove, waiting for Nikki's papers to be processed so she could be released on bail.

Logan's eyes dropped to his watch. "Ninety minutes ago."

Joanna shook her head in disbelief. Her rich, dark brown hair folded around her shoulders like soft velvet.

Logan had thought he was way past the age when just the shake of a woman's head could turn him on.

He had thought wrong.

Joanna Delacroix Gideon was a classic beauty—tall, slim, sophisticated, with eyes more startlingly blue than a spring dawn and a voice like a ream of pure raw silk. Every time it unraveled in Logan's ears, he felt his stomach muscles tightening and his pulse pounding. Like now.

Logan had been around attractive, sophisticated women all his forty-three years. None had ever put him on such an immediate and full sexual alert before. What was it about Joanna Gideon that was having this effect on him?

Coming up against reactions he could not explain logically upset Logan. He liked to think he lived by logic. Lawyers had to, or they weren't lawyers for long.

Still, he knew it was the woman in Joanna—not the lawyer—who had stared at him in that courtroom with uncensored approval in those cobalt eyes. And it was the woman's sharp intake of breath he had heard when he had lightly—but oh so deliberately—brushed up against her. She was feeling this, too.

Joanna turned to face him fully. He caught her subtle

scent, warm as spring, elementally female, with just a whisper of something that reminded him of the fragrance of a pale pink rose.

The look she gave him was clear, cool, free of even the smallest hint of flirtation.

"You handled the judge exceptionally well, Mr. Weston."

Logan felt very certain that Joanna wasn't making small talk. Her straight stance, her straight look…everything about the lady struck him as straight. As an arrow.

Too straight? Could it be the combination of her stunning looks, her obvious attraction to him and that far-too-solemn, too-sensible air of hers that was raising this havoc inside him?

He captured her eyes with his and smiled into them, lowering his voice to an intimate caress. "It was my pleasure, Joanna."

The growing approval in her eyes came to a sudden and complete halt. She turned away. He watched as she slowly inhaled a deep, silent breath and let it out. In spite of—or maybe as a defense to—the natural honesty that seemed to emanate from her, Logan could tell that Joanna was a woman who was used to being in control of herself. And attraction or no, she was in control of herself now.

Logan admired her self-control. And was disappointed by it. It was a bit disconcerting to admit how much he wanted to test these interesting responses to her, with her. He wondered what it would take to get this woman to lose her cool. He recognized it could take a lot. That it could take *him* was a thought so seductive that he almost succumbed to it.

"I don't know what my father has told you about Nikki," Joanna said.

Nikki. Her daughter. His client. The reason that had brought them together. The reason that was going to keep them apart.

A lawyer who let himself become personally involved with his client, or with his client's mother, committed the cardinal professional sin from which there was no absolution, no redemption. Just an eternal, personal hell.

Logan deliberately poured an enormous mental bucket of ice water over his rampaging reactions to Joanna.

"On the way here in the senator's limousine, I concentrated on learning about the judge and prosecutor on Nikki's case," Logan said. "Why don't you tell me now about your daughter."

Joanna hesitated. Logan sensed she was thinking about how best to begin to tell him about Nikki. He knew the relationship was not what it should be. Joanna's spontaneous hug when she realized Nikki would be released on bail had been warm and heartfelt. But Nikki's lack of response spoke volumes about the underlying friction that existed between mother and daughter.

Logan also hadn't missed the subsequent interaction—or lack of it—between Joanna and her father. A thick tension existed between these family members.

"Nikki is an intelligent young woman, Mr. Weston," Joanna said, "despite some of her…inappropriate choices as of late. Up until a couple of years ago, she was an excellent student."

Joanna had not rebuked Logan openly for using a personal tone with her earlier. But her cool voice and emphasis on his last name now were both clear indications to him that she considered their relationship to be a professional one and expected him to behave consistent with that expectation.

It was the subtle, graceful way a lady handled an unacceptable overture from a man.

"What happened a couple of years ago, Ms. Gideon?" he asked, letting her know just as subtly that he had received her message and would comply.

It was the way a gentleman handled a lady's retreat.

"So many things," Joanna said. "Her father died. Adolescence hit full force."

"And her grades now?"

"The only subjects she gets As in are those that are heavy into computers. Her interest in other subjects has waned considerably."

"What about out-of-school interests?"

"They are in the music, clothes and subculture that kidnap all American teenagers from their families and turn them into another species at this time in their lives."

Logan noticed that Joanna's voice had not lightened with the observation. This was all very serious business to her.

"What's your viewpoint as a lawyer?" he asked.

"Nikki won't be easy to represent, Mr. Weston. She hasn't talked about what happened that night when Steven died. Not to me. Not to anyone."

"Normally, the people I defend have already talked too much by the time I get them," Logan said, sending Joanna the kind of smile he hoped would put her at ease. "Nikki's sounding good to me."

"Then I've already misled you," Joanna said, no returning smile on her lips.

"In what way?" Logan's lips straightened in anticipation of what he could tell was going to be bad news.

"Nikki all but admitted to Chief Jake Trahan that she had seen Steven on the night of his death. And when Trahan told her Steven was dead, Nikki said she did it."

"When was this?"

"Three nights ago."

"And she's said nothing else since?"

"Nothing."

"How did Steven Boudreaux die?" Logan asked.

"The medical examiner said he drowned right after receiving a blow to the temple."

"The blow by itself wasn't severe enough to result in death?"

"No. But it appears to have rendered him unconscious, causing him to fall into the lake and drown."

"What lake?"

"Moon Lake. It's on my father's land."

"Do you think Nikki was the one who hit Steven?"

Logan noted the darting shadow of sadness in Joanna's eyes that belied the cool, even control of her voice. "I don't know what to think."

She was facing this, handling it exceptionally well, but he could see it was taking its toll.

"What was Nikki's relationship to Steven?" he asked.

"They started seeing each other several months ago. She was only sixteen then. Steven was nineteen. He was far too old for her. I tried to stop it."

"How?"

Joanna rolled her shoulders as if trying to shift a heavy weight that lay upon them. "In all the wrong ways."

"Meaning you tried to reason with her."

Joanna's eyes drew to Logan's face. "You sound like you know about teenagers, Mr. Weston."

"My daughter, Shari, is also seventeen," Logan admitted. "How did Nikki respond when you tried to reason with her about Steven?"

"She informed me that she was no longer a child and she was picking her own friends. She added that it was her life, and she was going to live it her way."

"Yes, those phrases sound all too familiar," Logan said. "I assume you pulled the favorite parents' line that goes, 'While you're under my roof, you'll live by my rules?'"

Joanna almost smiled at the teasing note he'd put in his voice. Almost.

"I held off for days before resorting to it. First I did my best to explain to her that dating someone that much older could lead her into doing things that were too adult for her."

"Which naturally made anything Steven might lead her into doing immediately irresistible."

Joanna did smile this time. "You do understand teenagers."

She had a great smile. It traveled up her face and flickered like a blue flame in her eyes.

"So what happened then?" Logan asked, forcing his mind back to the business at hand.

"I asked her to bring Steven to the house for supper. I wanted to meet him, to sit face-to-face with him and let him feel my presence in Nikki's life. But Steven wouldn't come to supper."

"Of course he wouldn't. His intentions weren't honorable."

"Precisely what I said to Nikki when she told me he had declined the invitation. Unfortunately, Nikki stopped listening to me long ago."

"Your father told me Nikki hasn't been in trouble before."

"She's never been in trouble with the police before."

Logan didn't miss the equivocation of Joanna's answer. "But?" he said, letting his voice rise to invite elaboration.

"I suspect she smoked and drank when she was on those dates with Steven. I also suspect she was intimate with him. Steven's reputation wasn't good."

Logan wondered how he would have responded if his daughter had taken up with the likes of a Steven Boudreaux. On second thought, he realized he'd better not even think about it.

"Tell me what else you know about this Steven," he said.

"He was a cook at a local café called Rick's. He grew up here in Bayou Beltane. He had that kind of dark, brooding demeanor and swagger that made him look like a cross between a member of a street gang and a rock star. Apparently, the combination was irresistible to girls."

"How did he meet Nikki?"

"At the café. It's a hangout for the under-eighteen set here in Bayou Beltane. Those eighteen and over frequent the places where liquor is sold."

"Were Nikki and Steven ever in the same school?"

"No. Nikki attends a private high school in Covington. It's only when she's here in town that she socializes with the local crowd. That means whoever walks into Rick's."

"Or works there like Steven did," Logan said.

"Yes."

"So what did you do when reasoning with Nikki didn't work?"

"When I found out Nikki was determined to see Steven despite my disapproval and warnings, I neither condoned her decision nor made it easy on her. I refused to buy her a car.

I gave her a curfew. She met it or she didn't receive her allowance."

"All this to no avail, I take it?"

Joanna nodded.

"When did she see him?"

"At night after I'd gone to bed."

"How did you find this out?"

"I was awakened by a wrong number around midnight a few months ago. I went down to the kitchen to get something to drink. I caught Nikki sneaking back into the house. She reeked of alcohol and cigarettes. She wouldn't tell me who she'd been with, but it wasn't hard to guess."

Joanna paused before going on. Her soft, throaty voice remained unemotional, but not the look in her eyes. "I couldn't lock her up. She has to be given the freedom to make her own decisions, her own mistakes. I know that's the only way she can grow and learn. But there's still so much she doesn't accept as important. She doesn't understand that a wrong decision now could ruin her future."

And now she's made that wrong decision.

Joanna didn't say the words, but Logan knew she had been thinking them. She'd been faced with the age-old dilemma so many parents came up against at some time.

What did a parent do with a teenager demanding to be allowed to behave as an adult, but who was neither an adult nor fully cognizant of the far-reaching results of adult behavior?

Logan had defended several "good" teenagers from "good" families who had been taught right from wrong, but who had ended up making the wrong decision when peer pressure came into play. Nikki's behavior did not surprise him.

"Did Nikki continue to sneak out to meet Steven?"

"I asked her to give me her word that she wouldn't. She refused. I withheld her allowance. When I noticed that the keys had been moved, I suspected that she was taking my car after I went to bed. I hid the keys after that."

"What about the night that Steven died?"

"The police seem to think she drove my car to see him that night. They impounded it for forensic examination."

"I thought you said you were hiding the keys?"

"I left the keys out that Sunday night. I thought Nikki and Steven's relationship had ended."

"Why did you think the relationship between Steven and your daughter was over?"

"Because a couple of months ago something happened between them that made Nikki stop seeing Steven on her own."

"What was it?"

"I asked her, but, as usual, she wouldn't talk about it. All she would say was that it was her business, not mine. I confess I was so relieved that the relationship had come to an end that I didn't press her further."

"And you had no idea it had started up again?"

"None."

"Tell me about Steven Boudreaux's family."

"His grandmother is Desiree Boudreaux. His mother is Flora Boudreaux. Flora's other son, Jackson, is a detective who works for Trahan. They've lived in Bayou Beltane all their lives."

"You're well acquainted with them?"

"I hardly know them."

"Why is that?"

"My father and mother divorced when I was about Nikki's age. I moved to California with my mother when she remarried. My brother and sister stayed here. I remained in California until two years ago."

"Why did you come back then?"

"My husband had just died. I wanted to bring Nikki home."

Logan imagined that Joanna had probably meant the relocation as a fresh start for both her and Nikki. She struck him as a strong woman who faced tragedy squarely, picked up the pieces and moved on with her life.

There was much to admire about Joanna Gideon. Logan

recognized where his wandering thoughts were taking him and quickly refocused his attention.

"What contact have you had with Steven's relatives?"

"I called on Flora Boudreaux when Nikki and Steven first became an item. I talked to her as one mother does to another about the dangers inherent in our children's disparate ages. Flora did not share my concern."

"She did nothing to discourage her son's pursuit of Nikki?"

"On the contrary. She told me she fully intended to encourage Steven in his pursuit. She seemed to take a perverse pleasure in assuring me of that."

Logan marveled at Joanna's calm voice and manner in relating the woman's offensive remark. "Why do you think Flora Boudreaux responded to you that way?"

"She seemed to think I was upset with the liaison because of her son's lack of money and social position. My attempt to convince her otherwise was unsuccessful. She told me it was time I learned the Boudreaux were 'just as good as the Delacroix.' Her exact words."

"Did you object to Steven Boudreaux in any part because of his lack of money and position?" Logan asked.

"Mr. Weston, the man could have been the son of a European prince and it would have made no difference to me. I did not want my sixteen-year-old daughter dating a nineteen-year-old who encouraged her to smoke and drink and who knows what else when she sneaked out of her home to meet him in the dead of night."

"Was Jackson Boudreaux aware his brother was dating Nikki?"

"He had to be. Everyone in town seemed to know."

"As a policeman, Jackson should have cautioned his brother against dating an underage girl."

"If Jackson cautioned Steven, Steven didn't listen."

"Did your father hear about Nikki and Steven?"

"Right around the same time I did. I've never seen him so upset."

"Because of the difference in their ages?"

"It was more than that. When Nikki and I came to Bayou Beltane two years ago, we lived at the family estate during the first year. Nikki became infatuated with my father's chauffeur, a young man fully five years older than she. My father was quite calm about it. He told me he'd get rid of the man if I was uneasy."

"Did you ask your father to do that?"

"No. It wasn't the chauffeur's fault that Nikki had a crush on him. Besides, when I watched them together, I could see that the young man joked and teased with Nikki—obviously aware of her interest—but made no moves to take advantage of her inexperience. Both my father and I decided to just let the situation run its course."

"Did it run its course?"

"Yes. The young man moved on after a few months. And Nikki's attention wandered to others."

"Until it wandered to Steven Boudreaux. You said earlier your father was quite upset. Who was he upset at?"

"He yelled and screamed at Nikki, said Steven was a worthless bastard and ordered her to break it off with him."

"Which made her all the more determined to be with the guy, of course."

"Of course," Joanna admitted.

"Was this 'bastard' comment your father made a description of Steven's behavior or lineage?"

"Both, I suspect. Flora Boudreaux has never been married."

"What about Desiree Boudreaux, Steven's grandmother? How did she feel about this relationship between her grandson and your daughter?"

"I never spoke to her about it. The talk around town is that both Flora and Desiree Boudreaux practice voodoo. And although my cousin Remy says Desiree uses it only for good, I tend to want to keep my distance from such…things."

The door to the jail opened suddenly. Logan and Joanna turned toward it as Nikki came through, Chief Jake Trahan by her side.

"She's all yours, Joanna," Jake said.

From the expression on Trahan's face, Logan had the distinct impression that the man was doing his job but took no satisfaction in it.

Logan watched as Joanna moved toward her daughter slowly, hesitatingly, almost as though she were approaching a wild bird that might take wing at any second.

Nikki was five-eight, an inch shorter than her mother. Her long, wavy brown hair was several shades lighter. Nikki's face was round, her nose a small button, her large eyes the same walnut brown as her hair.

She did not have Joanna's classic beauty, but she was a very pretty young woman. And if Logan didn't miss his guess, behind that hard shell she was projecting to the world, a very scared one.

"Let's go home," Joanna said gently.

"Your father has left his limousine here for our transportation," Logan said. "We have much to discuss."

Joanna turned to him, surprise in both her eyes and the cool tones of her voice.

"Nikki just spent the night in jail, Mr. Weston. She needs a bath, a hot meal, time to recuperate, a good night's rest. Surely your questions can wait until tomorrow?"

"No, they can't."

"Excuse me?"

"Your concerns as a mother are understandable. But you must understand my concerns as Nikki's attorney. I need to know the facts from her, and I need to know them now."

Logan drew open the door and held it for them. "After you."

Joanna's eyes never left his face. She was measuring him with a hard, focused scrutiny that held nothing back.

She didn't like his insistence on talking to Nikki now. If Nikki had been his daughter, he wouldn't have liked it, either. But Nikki wasn't his daughter. She was his client.

Logan didn't want Nikki rested, recuperated. He wanted her scared. He wanted the smell of the jail and the memory of being behind bars still fresh in her mind. Because if they were, he reasoned, she'd be much more likely to cooperate with him.

Joanna knew what he was doing and why. Logan could read the raw pain of it in those deep blue eyes that stared so straight into his. She had the right to refuse him. Indeed, if it had been his daughter and Joanna had been the attorney making this demand, he might have refused her.

But Joanna didn't refuse. She nodded. Then, with a quiet dignity, she led her daughter through the open door of the jail to the parking lot and Philip Delacroix's waiting limousine.

Not for the first time that morning, Logan fervently wished he had met Joanna Delacroix Gideon under different circumstances.

AT THE BACK OF THE DUSTY attic, Gator Guzman plopped his sturdy square body on the floor beside the old wooden file cabinet. He pulled on the handle, but the drawer was warped and refused to budge. Gator anchored one foot against the wall and the other against the cabinet and gave the handle a healthy yank. The drawer reluctantly screeched open.

Gator's granddaddy had made a lot of mistakes in his time. He'd smoked cigars, guzzled a quart of bourbon a day and run around with a lot of loose women. But there was one mistake he'd never made—he had never thrown out anything important.

Gator had inherited his nose for news from his granddaddy. Some of Gator's earliest and fondest memories of growing up were sitting at his granddaddy's knee, listening to him tell of the juicy scandals and secrets that he'd run in his old newspaper, the *Beltane Bugle*.

Gator could still see the gleam in his granddaddy's eyes when he'd spoken about how shocked readers had been by his revelations. And how eager they'd been to get the next biweekly edition of the *Bugle*.

It always bothered Gator that hard times had caused the *Bugle* to fold during World War II. His granddaddy had been forced to seek employment as a mere reporter at the comparatively staid *Slidell Sentinel*. Gator always knew that just as soon as he could, he'd start up another newspaper—one just like his granddaddy's had been.

Gator was twenty-four when he began printing the *Bayou Bulletin* on an ancient printing press on the back porch of the old house his granddaddy had left him. And now he was forty-seven and his newspaper office was in the center of town and the center of every controversy. For Gator had followed in his granddaddy's tradition and gave his readers exactly what they wanted—scandal.

Most everybody was right pleased he was doing it, too. For as protective as they were of their own secrets, they sure did love reading about everybody else's.

Especially when those secrets involved the local folks with money and power. And in this neck of the woods, that meant the Delacroix family.

Every single paper he had printed about Nikki Gideon being questioned and then charged with Steven Boudreaux's death had all but flown off the newsstands into the eager, waiting hands of the nosy good folks of the parish. Yep, nothing better than a big ol' local scandal.

Gator intended to go right on titillating his readers' appetites with it, too. The fact that Senator Philip Delacroix had brought in a fancy New Orleans lawyer to defend his granddaughter was yet another juicy tidbit for tomorrow's story.

Still, Gator had a feeling there could be more. A lot more.

Since he'd first heard of it, the death of Steven Boudreaux at Moon Lake on Delacroix property had struck a memory chord. Gator was sure it had something to do with one of the stories his granddaddy had recounted many years before. Unfortunately, he couldn't check the old copies of the *Bugle;* a warehouse fire had destroyed them.

Which was why Gator was up in the attic, looking through his granddaddy's old notes. His granddaddy had written out all his stories longhand before setting the type. Gator carefully turned the brittle, yellowed sheets, beginning with the handwritten stories for the very first *Beltane Bugle*, published nearly seventy years before. Scandals and dirty little secrets unfolded before his eyes as the months and years flew by.

And then suddenly there it was in the notes for a story sixty years old—Local Woman Drowns in Moon Lake.

Gator began to salivate as he continued to read and discovered that the drowning had turned out to be a murder. Yep, this was what he'd been looking for, all right.

He ate up his granddaddy's account of the events page by page as he followed the arrest of a local man and his subsequent trial. Gator digested every word until he was sated.

When he finally leaned back, he was licking his lips and grinning from ear to ear.

Just wait until the good folks of Bayou Beltane saw tomorrow's headlines!

CHAPTER THREE

LOGAN TOOK AN IMMEDIATE liking to the simple, tropical look of Joanna's eighteenth-century, West Indian bungalow-style home.

It sat on a secluded tributary of the bayou, sequestered within five acres of thick, untamed vegetation. Its skinny, second-story colonnettes rose high enough to join the trees. The wood of its virtually indestructible cypress beams had been naturally weathered, giving it the gentle touch of time.

Logan understood that leaving the cypress in its natural, unvarnished state was a practical decision, considering that paint mildewed so quickly in the moisture-laden air.

Joanna led the way beneath the sturdy, Doric columns that lined the porch leading to the entry of her home. It was comfortably cool indoors. The louvered window shutters allowed the breeze to freely circulate while still filtering the sunlight. A Tiffany lamp graced an antique entry table of polished walnut.

There was no doubt in Logan's mind that Joanna, like her father, had money. This piece of prime real estate and the tasteful furnishings he saw around him proved it.

So, too, did the deceptively simple hand-tailored business suit she wore. Logan's practiced eye had identified it as coming from one of the more exclusive clothiers in New Orleans.

What he didn't know was whether she had inherited her money or had earned it. If he had to guess, he would say the latter. Joanna struck Logan as a woman who would demand that kind of self-sufficiency from herself. People who earned their own way answered only to themselves.

"Has your home been in the family long?" Logan asked,

looking around at the elegant simplicity of the one-of-a-kind furnishings fashioned mostly out of wild cherry and pine.

"I bought it a year ago," Joanna answered.

"Does your father live close by?"

"Yes, at Belle Terre, an old sugar plantation just a few miles down the bayou on the west side of Moon Lake. It's one of those lovely old homes built before the Civil War. Been in the family since my grandfather's time. As I said before, Nikki and I lived there the first year we returned to Louisiana."

Logan wondered if Joanna's move out of her father's home had anything to do with the strained relationship that existed between them. He decided this was as good a time as any to satisfy his curiosity.

"So what happened between you and your father that caused you to move out of the old homestead?"

From the sudden stiffening of Joanna's shoulders, Logan realized that he had struck an extremely sore spot. Still, her voice remained even.

"I worked for my father's law firm the first I came back to Bayou Beltane. When I made the decision to switch to my uncle's firm last year, my father was...displeased. I decided the time had come for Nikki and me to have a place of our own."

"Why did you decide to go to work for your uncle?"

"I discovered that my father and I do not have... compatible lawyering styles. Besides, his firm is mostly concerned with corporate law and my expertise is on the criminal side. My uncle's law firm handles far more criminal cases."

Logan was certain there was quite a bit more to it than what Joanna was admitting. But he was also certain that she was not one to speak of sensitive family matters to a stranger.

She gestured for Logan to enter a small reception room. "Dinner will not be long."

Joanna was good to her word. She had the dining table set and the food on it in less than ten minutes. A fresh green salad was followed by hot crab cakes on a bed of lightly seasoned mixed vegetables. The rolls she served with it had been warmed to crispy flakiness in the oven. The tea was tall and iced.

Logan thoroughly enjoyed his meal in the small exquisite dining room, reminiscent of another age. The solid mahogany table glowed from a century of hand polishing. A cypress punkah hung from the ceiling, a fan that would have been set in motion by a servant many generations ago.

When the meal was over, he rose and turned toward Joanna. "It's time that Nikki and I had our first attorney and client conversation. Will you excuse us?"

Joanna remained seated as she looked over at her daughter. "Nikki, I want to stay involved in your defense. I need to know if you are comfortable with that."

Nikki shrugged. "Whatever."

Joanna's eyes returned to Logan. "I'm staying." Her look was determined. He knew a moment of acute unease. He rested his hands on the back of the dining room chair and concentrated on making his tone as understanding and gentle as he could.

"You are far too closely involved to represent Nikki."

"Yes, I am," she said, in that slightly husky, raw-silk voice of hers that asked for no quarter and gave none. "I stepped aside for you this morning because that was the best thing for Nikki. I will continue to stay in the background because that is also the best thing for her. However, I will *not* fade away. I intend to have input into my daughter's defense."

Logan had once tried working with another attorney on a case. It had proved a disaster because of basic and continuing disagreements in defense strategy. The client had ultimately fired them both in disgust. Logan swore he would never make that mistake again.

"I work alone," he said gently, but emphatically.

"Not on this case," Joanna said, just as emphatically.

"Ms. Gideon—" he began.

"Mr. Weston," she quickly interrupted. "If this is not acceptable to you, then you can consider yourself fired."

"*You* didn't hire me."

"But I can fire you. My father is not Nikki's lawful guardian. I am. I know your reputation, Mr. Weston. It is excellent. Your performance in court this morning was also most impressive. However, if you do not agree to my being in the second chair on my daughter's defense team, then I will get an attorney who will."

And she would, too. He could see it in her eyes and in the firm set to her lips. Joanna Gideon wasn't issuing a threat. No, threats were not part of this woman's cool, sophisticated style. She was simply stating her position.

Logan thought about thanking her for dinner, wishing her good luck in getting the right attorney for Nikki, and then leaving. He seriously thought about it.

What stopped him was the thought of how he would respond if another attorney had told him he was to have no role in his own daughter's defense.

Representing a loved one in a legal action was *always* wrong. But if the roles were reversed and it was his daughter being accused, would he totally step aside and give up any input for her defense?

He knew the answer was no. He wouldn't allow another attorney to push him totally out of the picture. He would insist on being a part of the team, just as Joanna was insisting.

Logan prided himself on never acting hastily or inconsiderately. He had no intention of doing so now. He took a moment to review the possibilities of Joanna's proposal.

His legal assistant was on leave, so there was no question that he would need someone to help with the work.

· He knew nothing of Joanna's legal background. However, he doubted Philip Delacroix would have said she possessed both the expertise and track record for this criminal defense unless she did.

She had firsthand knowledge of her daughter and the people of Bayou Beltane. That, too, would be helpful. The fact that she had accepted his need to interview her daughter right away was yet another factor weighing in her favor.

But she was obviously exceptionally strong-willed and opinionated. And her close association with the accused was bound to cloud her better judgment.

That would be the chief stumbling block to their working together. If she interfered with what he was attempting to do, she could jeopardize everything. He was not going to set himself up for a repeat of his last teaming disaster.

"Ms. Gideon, I will remain as Nikki's lawyer and allow you to second-seat me on her defense provided you agree to a couple of ground rules."

Joanna stared directly into his eyes. "What are they?"

"One, my legal judgment must prevail. You may freely offer your thoughts and recommendations on legal interpretation and strategy, but *never* in front of our client. And when it comes time to make a decision on what course to take, that decision will *always* be mine. All disagreement must immediately cease."

He could see her thinking over his words very carefully before answering. When her answer finally came, he knew she did not give it easily. "Accepted."

"And lastly, and this is equally important, we don't split your father's retainer."

A look of momentary surprise stole over her face. And then he saw her eyes drop down to the teasing smile on his lips.

The deep, sweet, husky laugh that broke from her throat seemed to catch her as much by surprise as it did him. The warmth of it flushed her cheeks and turned her cobalt eyes into pure crystalline gemstones.

Logan had thought Joanna beautiful before. But now, hearing the music of her laugh, seeing her radiate with its glow, he found her so astonishingly stunning that she took his breath away.

The muscles in his stomach knotted, hard.

It was at that precise moment that he knew he had been wrong. Her strong will and emotional tie to Nikki had never been the chief roadblocks to his working with Joanna.

His far-too-strong desire for her was.

"NIKKI, I AM YOUR LAWYER," Logan said, his deep voice resonant with authority. "That means I give you legal advice and you take it as though it were gospel."

Joanna had quickly put the dishes in the dishwasher and now sat at the dining table with Logan and Nikki. She knew exactly what Logan was doing. She had done it herself many times before.

The first official interview with a new client was the time to set the stage for the relationship as well as to define terms and come to a basic understanding of roles.

It was not going to be easy remaining quiet while Logan went through this process.

But Joanna knew that was to be her place from now on. She had given Logan her word that she would not question anything he did in front of their client.

She wouldn't.

But she couldn't keep from questioning the unprecedented sensual upheaval that this man's presence had so suddenly unleashed into her life.

He had issued nothing less than an invitation with his slow smile and suggestive tone when he had called her by her first name. A sweet answering ache had immediately risen inside her.

Shocked, appalled, she had squelched her response.

But the memories of that surprising invitation and her immediate physical acceptance of it continued to lick hotly in her mind and body, keeping her intensely aware of Logan—in a way she hadn't been aware of any man in a long time.

A *very* long time.

Sixteen years.

The day she'd learned that her beloved Richard had been in an accident that left him paralyzed from the waist down. The day Joanna had simply put all thoughts of physical desire right out of her very disciplined mind.

And they had never returned. Until now.

The realization that she was once again responding to a man was jolting. Disturbing. Exciting. Enticing.

And thoroughly inappropriate. Logan was her daughter's attorney. Joanna didn't know what had brought on this insanity. Perhaps the emotional shock of Nikki's arrest and indictment?

Or was it the fact that Logan had appeared like a legal Sir Lancelot at the exact moment she needed one? She had never been rescued before. It was a heady and rather thrilling experience.

"Nikki," Logan said, "from the moment you were indicted for second-degree murder, the juvenile court lost its jurisdiction over you. You were detained in an adult jail and will be tried as an adult. Do you know what the sentence is for someone convicted of second-degree murder in the state of Louisiana?"

"No."

"It's life in prison. No parole. Your very life is at stake here. You have some hard decisions to make and some even harder experiences to get through. They are going to take all your strength and maturity. Your mother and I are going to be with you all the way. But you need to understand exactly what we can and can't do for you. Are you ready to hear it?"

Nikki swallowed and nodded. Joanna could tell she was listening intently. It wasn't just because of Logan's words. It was because of him. Power emanated through his well-modulated baritone. Logan was a man who commanded attention.

"Nikki, as your attorneys, your mother and I can never divulge anything you tell us, unless you give us permission to do so. If we were to divulge something you told us and we did not have your permission to do so, we would be disbarred, disgraced. What's more, whatever we revealed could not be used in a court of law against you. Do you understand what I've said to you so far?"

Nikki nodded.

"Because of this, Nikki, many defendants believe they can bare their souls to their attorney. But even though your mother and I can never repeat anything you tell us, there is something you must understand. If you tell us you are guilty, we are then prevented from taking certain actions in your defense.''

''What actions?'' Nikki asked.

Joanna didn't miss the false bravado in her daughter's tone. She wondered if Logan understood how tender her daughter was beneath that hard shell she projected to the world. Or did only a mother see those things?

''I cannot put you on the stand in a court of law and let you tell that court that you are not guilty,'' Logan answered. ''Because if I know you are going to lie under oath, I am ethically restrained from letting you do so. Do you understand?''

''Yeah.''

''Nikki, this is really important to us and to you. Please repeat back to me in your own words what I just told you.''

''If I tell you I committed a crime, you cannot tell anyone else,'' Nikki said. ''But if you know I committed a crime, you cannot let me swear in court that I'm innocent.''

''That's it, Nikki. Now, because of this ethical rule that attorneys must live by, most will not even ask their clients if they have committed the crime for which they are accused. Attorneys are afraid of what their client might tell them. In your own words, can you tell me why?''

''Attorneys don't want to hear that their clients are guilty.''

''Why not, Nikki?''

''Because then the attorney can't let the client take the stand and say they're innocent in court.''

''Okay, Nikki. I've just told you about most lawyers. Now I'm going to tell you about myself. I want to hear the truth. I believe that knowing if my clients have committed a crime helps me to mount the best defense possible for them. It also keeps me from mounting the wrong defense and making costly mistakes. That can happen if the prosecution surprises me by presenting contradictory evidence pointing to my client's guilt.''

Logan paused to smile. Joanna felt certain he was trying to lessen the tenseness of the moment.

"I also believe it's easier for a client to just tell the truth to me because then they don't have to keep remembering what they can say and what they can't say. Do you understand?"

Nikki nodded.

"But just because I think telling the truth is best, that does not mean it is. You must consider carefully everything you choose to tell me. You have to make the decision as to what is best for you. Repeat back to me what I just told you."

"You want to hear the truth from me, but I don't have to tell you because it may not be in my best interest to do so."

Logan smiled. "Your mother said you are very intelligent. She did not exaggerate. I'm going to ask you questions about the night that Steven Boudreaux died. You do not have to say a word. Indeed, it may be better for you if you didn't. Do you want to talk about it?"

"Yeah."

"Be certain of this, Nikki. I'm asking you these questions so that I can mount the best defense for you. If you are *not* responsible for Steven's death, the information you give me will help me to fight the charges against you. If you *are* responsible for Steven's death and you tell me, I will still fight for you with every ounce of my ability. Do you understand?"

"Yeah."

"Okay, Nikki. Tell me what you want to tell me."

"I did it. I killed him."

Joanna's heart constricted in her chest at her daughter's bold and blatant admission of guilt. She had been hoping against hope that there had been some mistake, that Nikki's earlier confession had been caused by the shock of hearing about Steven's death.

But now Joanna knew there had been no mistake.

And there was no hope.

CHAPTER FOUR

"YOU ARE STEVEN Boudreaux's grandmother?" the funeral director asked, his face a mask of solemnity despite his obvious youth.

"He was christened Etienne," Desiree Boudreaux said. "Steven was the name he used in town."

"Forgive me, Ms. Boudreaux," the man said. "The medical examiner's office hasn't sent over the paperwork yet. They are often tardy when an autopsy is involved. You have my deepest sympathies on the passing of your grandson."

Desiree could tell the funeral director was not really sympathetic. He was just mouthing a platitude he had mouthed hundreds of times before. Still, she was grateful for his offered arm as she entered his establishment. It was neither age nor physical infirmary that caused her step to falter. It was the sorrow that blurred her eyes and burned a hole in her soul.

Desiree understood and accepted death's part in the struggle for life. One spent one's time upon the earth as well as one knew how, and then one left to make way for the children.

It was the natural order.

But there was no natural order to Etienne's death! Parents were supposed to go before their children and their children's children.

Her grandson had just begun to live. He was the future. And here she was, having to bury that future.

This was too cruel. Too terribly, terribly cruel!

"Are you ready to view the caskets now, Ms. Boudreaux?'' the funeral director asked. ''We have a splendid assortment.''

He had said that with such pride. How could one call a casket splendid? ''My daughter is parking the car,'' Desiree said. ''I will wait until she is with me.''

The funeral director bowed his head with somber respect, but Desiree could see his eyes surreptitiously darting to his wristwatch as he led her to a chair.

''I will attend to a few matters in the meantime. I'm sure you will be comfortable waiting here.''

Comfortable? In this box of a room where sorrow was etched into the very walls from the hundreds of poor souls who had sat here before her?

Desiree took the offered chair with a weary sigh. She wanted to scream at this man for his robotic inanities.

''Just press this bell here when you and your daughter are ready, ma'am. It will ring me up in the back.''

The funeral director disappeared behind a solid door, leaving Desiree alone with the ticking of the old wall clock and the cold grief curling deep inside her.

It seemed like only yesterday that she was hugging Etienne to her breast to soothe his baby cries. And then gathering him into her arms to wipe away his tears when, as a young boy, he had skinned his knee.

Such a handsome young man he had become! So full of bold talk and his mama's engaging smile.

Except Flora smiled so rarely now. This last year she'd changed so much, Desiree barely recognized her daughter.

It wasn't the years catching up to Flora. It was the icy hatred that seethed inside her, blocking out the life-giving joy, turning down the corners of her mouth and sagging the skin beneath her eyes and cheeks.

Desiree knew she had to accept partial blame for the change. She had made many mistakes in her life. But the biggest mistake of all had been telling Flora about them.

She had meant to help her daughter. But she had done harm, not good. All Desiree's good intentions were meaningless now, worthless. She was paying for the harm she had done, just as everyone must pay.

She had tried to talk Flora out of this madness that was possessing her more and more every day. But it was no use. She had begun to fear for both her daughter's sanity and her soul.

Desiree looked up at the wooden clock on the wall and saw that a full ten minutes had passed. Where was Flora?

Desiree rose and looked out the window, squinting into the brilliant April day. Her eyes swept over the parking lot, looking for Flora and the rented car. She located it finally, but Flora was nowhere to be seen.

And then Desiree caught a flash of her daughter's gray-streaked black hair. Flora was standing at the curb, leaning into a green minivan, talking to the driver.

It was Gator Guzman's minivan.

Desiree stepped back from the window as uneasiness lanced through her. What was Gator Guzman saying to Flora? And she to him?

A moment later the front door of the funeral parlor banged open. Flora came flying in, her eyes darting around the room. She swept over to her mother, the sleeves and hem of her black dress streaming behind her in her haste.

"Where's the funeral director?" she demanded, as though he had been the one keeping her waiting.

Desiree stared at her daughter, noting with growing dread the quickness of her movements and the predatory light glinting in her dark eyes.

Flora had displayed nothing but an empty, grief-stricken silence on the trip into town. Now she was suddenly brimming with purpose and impatience. Something had happened to change Flora's mood. And whatever it was, Desiree felt certain that it did not bode well.

"Flora, you be careful of Gator Guzman. He feeds on the weaknesses and failures of others. He's only friendly when he wants something."

"You think I don't know that, Mama? I'm no fool! Gator thinks he's gonna use me. But I'm using him!"

"What are you doing, child?"

Flora avoided her mother's eyes. "You'll know soon enough. Everyone will."

Desiree's breath stuck in her chest. "You gave me your word you would say nothing about what I told you. You swore it on your blood!"

"You think everything is about you and your precious secrets, Mama? Well, it's not! I have secrets, too! And wounds that go deeper than you've ever known!"

Desiree grasped her daughter's shoulders firmly, her old hands shaking but still strong. She sought Flora's eyes until she held them.

"I know you are grieving for our Etienne, child. I, too, am in pain. But do not strike out in your pain. Remember, the evil that one does always comes back."

Flora's dark eyes blazed. "What of the evil that has been done to me? My child is dead!"

"Flora," Desiree said softly, her voice a sad sigh, "it's your own guilt that torments you."

Flora tried to tear herself away from her mother's grasp, but Desiree held on tightly to her shoulders. She had to say this. Flora had to hear it.

"You told Etienne to go after Nikki Gideon," Desiree said. "You filled his head with all those wild ideas of getting his hand on Delacroix money by marrying into the family. You were using Etienne to get back at Philip."

"So what if I was?" Flora shouted. "How can you of all people blame me?"

"Blame you for your anger at Philip? No, I do not blame you for that. But I do blame you for using your own child as an instrument of revenge against him. You've lost your boy, Flora. You've lost your Etienne."

A sob tore through Flora's throat. Desiree felt her daughter's shoulders shake.

"They murdered him!" Flora sobbed. "Don't you understand, Mama? They murdered my baby!"

Desiree gathered her daughter into her arms and held her. Were it within her power, Desiree knew she would take the pain away from Flora. It would be wrong; Flora had to feel the consequences of her actions. But still the mother in Desiree would do it.

"Don't let the anger blind you, my child," the old woman said. "Forgive yourself for what you set in motion. And forgive the girl. Forgiveness is the only light that will lead you out of the darkness of this tragedy."

"No!" Flora sobbed to the sorrow-filled walls. "I will not forgive! I will have my revenge on that girl and all the cursed Delacroix! I swear it!"

Desiree leaned back. The raw hatred rasping in her daughter's voice was bad enough. But what Desiree saw in Flora's eyes sent an icy shiver down her spine.

"ALL RIGHT, NIKKI," Logan said, keeping his voice deep and even as he leaned back in his chair. "You've told me you killed Steven Boudreaux. Now we'll talk about why."

Logan was careful to keep his expression and voice non-judgmental. He was not going to overtly react to Nikki's shocking admission and the lack of emotion in its delivery.

She leaned her elbows on the table and stared at him with focused, unblinking eyes. Logan could see the tension in her body hadn't lessened at her admission of guilt.

He had seen this kind of cool, defiant mask before. Normally the youngsters wearing it had put it on so that they wouldn't be hurt. Because they had been.

He'd lay odds that beneath Nikki's seemingly impervious exterior beat a heart that was badly bruised and damn scared.

"Let's start at the beginning," he said evenly. "Tell me how you met Steven."

Logan had promised Nikki he'd still represent her and do his best for her even if she was guilty. He meant it.

But the surprise that now appeared on Nikki's face told him that she hadn't really believed him. Sometime in this young woman's life she had lost her trust in promises.

Nikki took a sip of her tea. "I'd seen him at Rick's," she began, her voice calm, composed. "He was a cook there."

"When did you first notice him?"

"Last year. Sometimes, when it was slow, he came out and waited the counter. He took my order a couple of times. Then this one Saturday when his shift was over, he came and sat with me. We got to talking. He asked me out."

"How long ago was this?"

"Last November."

"What was there about Steven that made you want to go out with him?"

Nikki shrugged. "He liked me and he was so cool."

"So where did you go on your date?"

"A movie in town. It was a mistake. My cousins saw us there. My mother and grandfather found out about my being with him and they both freaked."

"You didn't tell your mother you were going to this movie with Steven Boudreaux?"

"I would have only gotten a lecture."

"So what did you tell her?"

"Just that I was going to the movie and I wouldn't be home too late. I wasn't."

"Did you go out with Steven again?"

"Yeah."

"Where?"

"I told him I didn't want to freak out my mother and grandfather anymore so we had to keep out of real public places. He said that was cool with him 'cause he didn't have much money to spend. Mostly we just hung out."

"Where?"

"We sat in his truck and had a few smokes and listened to music and made out and...stuff."

Logan could guess what that stuff was.

"Were you in love with Steven, Nikki?" he asked as gently as he knew how.

"Yeah."

"Did he love you?"

"He said he did. I think most of the time he did. But sometimes..."

Logan watched as the tension built in Nikki's shoulders.

"What did you think sometimes, Nikki?"

"Sometimes he'd do stuff and I...I didn't believe he could do it and still love me."

"What kind of stuff?" Logan asked, putting only a gentle inquiry in his tone.

"He'd...slap me around."

Out of the corner of his eye, Logan saw Joanna's involuntary start. He understood she was shocked by her daughter's words. His own stomach had just gone cold and hard as a rock.

"When did he begin to do that, Nikki?" Logan asked, careful to keep his voice perfectly even and free of his reactions.

"The first few weeks everything was cool. We'd park. Talk. Sometimes we'd drink a beer or two, but neither of us had too much. Then..."

"When did it start to get to be too much?" Logan asked.

"One night when I sneaked out of the house and met him down the lane, he came staggering toward me drunk. He'd come down the bayou by pirogue—you know those things that look like part flatboat, part canoe?"

"I'm familiar with a pirogue, yes," Logan said.

"He'd tied it up to the old dock at the end of the property here. He had this idea we'd use it to get to Moon Lake on my grandfather's place. We'd parked there in his pickup on clear nights. The moon's reflection is real pretty on the water."

"What happened that night?"

"He was so drunk he was falling all over the place. I told him I didn't think he could see straight, much less steer a boat. He got really mad at me. Started swearing. Told me I wasn't his mama. Then he slapped me really hard."

"What did you do, Nikki?"

"I ran away from him into the house. The next day Steven was waiting for me when the van from my private school left me off down the lane. He said he was really sorry for hitting me. He said it was the beers he'd had. He asked me to forgive him."

"Did you?"

"He sounded really sorry."

"So you forgave him."

Nikki shrugged.

"And it happened again."

Nikki's fingers spread around her glass of iced tea. She clasped it tightly.

"Everything was cool for a couple of weeks. Then one night we went to a party at Eddie's."

"Eddie who?" Logan asked.

"Just Eddie. He was Steven's friend."

"Where does Eddie live?"

"In Slidell somewhere. I didn't pay any attention to the address. The music was hot. Everybody was getting tattoos. We were drinking so we wouldn't feel the needle. Only Steven was really chugging down the beers. Then he started coming on to this girl, right in front of me."

"What girl?"

"Some redhead who was getting a tattoo above her right boob. Steven kept telling her to pull her blouse down a little more."

Logan didn't respond to the disgust in Nikki's voice. "What happened then?" he asked.

"The redhead laughed and said he'd have to come to a private showing. I told Steven I was splitting. He grabbed my arm and dragged me out to his pickup. He shoved me inside. When I tried to get out, he yanked me back in and started slapping and punching me. I couldn't...defend myself."

"What happened then?" Logan said, holding back his emotions with a determined effort.

"He drove me home, cursing like crazy. I thought he was going to smash up the pickup and us for sure. But we made it okay. The next morning my arm and shoulder really hurt from his yanking me back into the car. Mom saw me wincing. I told her I'd wrenched it. She took me to the emergency room. I had a sprained shoulder."

"Did Steven come by the next day to apologize again?"

"It was a couple of days later. He told me he would go

back to the tattoo artist and have my name tattooed on his chest."

"And you forgave him again."

"I told him that if he ever got wasted or scoped another girl in front of me again, he was toast," Nikki replied in a pseudo-defiant voice. "He said the only reason he drank and came on to other girls was because…"

"Yes, Nikki?" Logan prompted when her voice trailed away.

"Because I still refused to go all the way."

"You're speaking of sexually?" Logan asked gently.

"He told me he'd been patient a long time but that he was a man with needs. He said I had to stop acting like a child and grow up. He said if I loved him I'd do it."

Logan silently seethed at the manipulation that Steven had used on Nikki. Men who told women to "grow up" only did so to get them to deny their feelings and do what the selfish bastards wanted. For a nineteen-year-old to have laid that line on a sixteen-year-old was as emotionally abusive as the bastard's fists had been physically abusive.

Once again Logan fought to keep his tone neutral, his reactions to himself.

"What did you say to Steven in response to these things he said to you?"

Nikki shrugged. "I told him I did love him, but I just needed a little more time. He said he'd try to be patient a while longer because he was so crazy about me."

"How did things go after that?" Logan asked.

"Okay. We talked a lot about getting married. Except he told me he'd have to get me pregnant first so my mom would be forced to let us."

"What did you think about this plan?"

"I wanted to graduate from high school first. My dad taught college. It would have disappointed him a lot if I never even made it through high school. I know he's dead, but…"

But she still cared what her dad would have thought of her, Logan realized. "So you put Steven off?" he asked.

"He kept saying that I could get my high school diploma and even go to college if I wanted after we were married. He said as soon as I got pregnant, we would have lots of money and could do anything we wanted. He said he couldn't wait for me anymore."

"When did it happen?" Logan asked, hoping like hell it hadn't, but phrasing his question to make it easy for Nikki to tell him if it had.

Nikki's fingers whitened as she clasped the glass of iced tea with both hands.

"Valentine's Day."

"Tell me about it."

"Steven took me to a real nice motel room off the highway beyond Covington so we didn't have to do it in the pickup."

Logan knew this was hard for her. He put a note of encouragement in his voice. "Please go on."

"He bought me flowers and this magnum of champagne. At first it was kinda romantic."

"When did it stop being...romantic?"

"Afterward, when he started drinking out of the bottle."

Nikki paused. Her tone was still tough, but she tightened her clasp on the glass. Logan waited until she was ready to continue.

"I told Steven I had to get home. He kept pulling me back into bed. He said I was his woman now, and he'd say when I could leave. He said it kind of kidding at first, playful like. But the more he drank, the less playful he became."

"Did he become physically abusive?"

"When I tried to leave."

"He hit you?"

"Yeah. Really hard. And he kept hitting me. I begged him to stop. I told him I was just kidding about leaving. I told him I'd stay with him as long as he liked."

"Did he stop hitting you then?"

"Yeah. Cussed me out instead. He told me I deserved my bruises for 'playing my little-girl games' with him. When he passed out about an hour later, I grabbed my clothes and stuff and got out as fast as I could. I finished dressing in a gas station rest room next to the motel. I called a taxi from there.''

"When did he next come by for forgiveness?"

"A day or so later. I told him no way, it was over."

"Until?" Logan said.

"Until last Sunday afternoon."

"Did you go out with Steven anytime between Valentine's Day and last Sunday?"

"No. The only reason I went into Rick's last Sunday was because I knew it was his day off."

"Still, you saw him there?"

"Having a Coke at the counter. Soon as he saw me, he came over. He tried to put his arm around me. I pushed him away. When I started to leave, he asked me if I was pregnant.''

"Are you, Nikki?" Logan asked, very gently.

"No. I told him I was glad I didn't get stuck with a brat of his that would have tied me to him forever."

"What happened next?"

"He kept telling me how crazy he was for me. He swore he was never going to drink again."

"So, you forgave him once more?" Logan said, once again making sure that all his tone contained was polite inquiry.

"Nah. He'd no sooner gotten that little speech off his chest when that redhead from Eddie's party came swinging her hips into Rick's. She walked right up to him and put her hand on his shoulder. She was there to meet him!"

"What happened?" Logan asked.

"I told him to go to hell."

"What did he do?"

"He blocked the door when I tried to leave. Swore he wasn't moving in on the redhead. He said he had just agreed to drive her to Eddie's."

"Did you believe him?"

"She said that was the way it was. Steven told the redhead she'd have to get a ride with someone else. She left."

"Was that when you forgave him?"

"I didn't forgive him. Exactly. I agreed to meet him at Moon Lake around ten that night to talk."

"Why did you agree to meet him, Nikki?"

"He told me he had given up booze for me. He told me he'd give up anything for me. He said I was going to be his wife. He said he wasn't going to screw up again."

"And you believed him?"

"Steven was...so cool when he wasn't drinking. I thought that if he had stopped drinking... I guess I wanted to believe it would work."

"But you found out differently?" Logan asked.

Nikki swallowed hard and nodded.

Logan knew that despite her cool, almost defiant demeanor and tone, telling him these things was damn rough on her. In fact, her tough act was probably all that was holding her together.

"What happened when you met Steven Sunday night at Moon Lake?" Logan asked.

"I got there late 'cause I'd had a flat on the way. I pulled into the spot just over the bridge where we always parked. His pickup was nowhere in sight. I figured he'd come and gone. I'd left the tire iron on the passenger seat. I could see it was leaving a grease mark, so I got out of the car to put it back in the trunk. Before I could open the trunk, Steven stepped out of the trees and grabbed me from behind."

Nikki paused and Logan got his first glimpse of what lay behind her tight mask of control. Her face was white as a seagull's wings, her pupils black pinpoints of fear.

"I could smell the liquor on him right off. I told him to let go of me. He wouldn't. He was so drunk his words were slurred and made no sense. I tried to pull away. His fingers were entwined in the chain around my neck, the one that held the crystal heart my dad had given me. It was cutting into my skin. I told him he was hurting me. His breath wheezed in my ear like he was laughing. I lifted the tire iron and struck him with it."

Nikki paused to swallow hard. Logan realized that in recounting this part, she was reliving some of what she had felt that night when she had faced a drunk, abusive Steven.

"What happened then?" Logan prodded gently.

"He let me go, staggered back. I ran for the cover of the trees, still clutching the tire iron. I knew I was going to hit him again if he came after me. But he didn't come after me. I watched from behind a tree as he staggered away from the car, toward the lake. I dropped the tire iron, ran back to the car and drove away as fast as I could. I almost hit another car coming the other way on the bridge."

"Did you see who it was?"

"No. It all happened too fast."

"Did you see Steven fall into the lake?"

Nikki shook her head as she finally unclasped her hands from around the glass of iced tea and stared down at them. "I knew he was hurt, but I thought he was all right. I mean, he was walking and everything. I never thought…"

Nikki stopped, swallowed hard. She straightened her shoulders and looked directly at Logan, her eyes bright, her tone tough, pulling no punches.

"I hit him," she said. "I killed him."

Logan leaned over and cupped her cold hands with his warm ones. For the first time since she had begun her story, he allowed his expression and voice to show all the concern and compassion he felt for her.

"You didn't kill him, Nikki. You simply defended yourself. It's what anyone would have done in your place. Steven Boudreaux did not die at your hand, but at his own. You must never, ever again say that you killed him. It isn't true."

Logan watched as the cool, protective shield on Nikki's face crumbled beneath the compassion in his tone and touch.

She dropped her head with a heart-wrenching sob. The thick walnut curtain of her hair closed over her face, at long last marking an end to her act of false bravado.

Joanna was kneeling by her daughter's side in a second, her arm around her, holding her steady, holding her close.

"It's all right, Nikki," she said evenly, calmly, quietly, in a voice as deeply soothing as a warm gentle rain. "I'm here. Everything's going to be all right."

Despite the absolute command she had over her voice, Joanna's eyes were teeming with tears.

Logan slowly released his hold on Nikki's hands, rose and left the house.

For the better part of the next hour, he walked up and down the bayou, letting the warm spring breeze brush his face and fill his senses with something other than cold, hard fury for a dead man.

He had absolutely no idea how Joanna had sat without saying a word through her daughter's story of abuse at Steven Boudreaux's hands. Had it been his daughter, he doubted he could have sat still for five seconds.

Joanna had to be forged from pure steel. It was easy to see where Nikki got her strength.

But it made it all the more difficult for Logan to understand why the girl had put up with the kind of abuse Steven Boudreaux had dished out.

Logan already knew what he had to do for Nikki legally. He wondered if Joanna knew how much more had to be done for her emotionally.

Both mother and daughter had been through a lot. Before this was over, he knew they were going to have to go through a lot more.

He reminded himself that the only thing that should concern him was the legal part. The only thing that *must* concern him was the legal part. He had to stay emotionally detached in order to remain alert and effective.

But he wasn't feeling emotionally detached.

He was still aching to take Joanna in his arms and kiss away those sad, sweet tears that she had so bravely refused to shed.

CHAPTER FIVE

SHELBY DELACROIX WAS so caught up in her telephone conversation with her cousin that she didn't at first notice the headline on the Thursday morning edition of the *Bayou Bulletin,* which sat on the kitchen counter.

"Don't worry, Joanna," Shelby said. "I'll make sure we get those depositions you had scheduled for today. All of your pending cases have been reassigned."

"You're a wonder, Shelby," Joanna's calm, even voice said through the receiver.

"Takes one to know one, cuz. So, how's Nikki doing?"

"She has to be scared to death, but she's not showing it."

"Joanna, I'm here for you both. If either of you needs anything—and I mean anything—you call me now, you hear?"

"Thanks so much, Shelby. For everything."

Shelby exchanged goodbyes with Joanna and hung up the phone. She let out a sigh as she wandered back over to the coffeepot. She poured herself a second cupful and took a big gulp. This was definitely a two-jolts-of-caffeine morning.

Her late nights at the office were taking their toll. It had been a hectic week trying to fill in for Joanna. The whole Delacroix family had felt the emotional shock waves of Nikki's arrest and indictment for Steven Boudreaux's murder.

Shelby was proud to know that the family had all been on the phone to Joanna, offering her their help. The Delacroix could certainly feud up a storm, but when it came to standing by a member in trouble, they could always be counted on.

The second cup of coffee hit her empty stomach hard.

Shelby was starting toward a dish laden with beignets when she brushed by the paper and finally saw the headline: Delacroix Linked to Both Old and New Murders at Moon Lake.

Shelby set her coffee cup on the counter and grasped the edges of the newspaper with both hands as she read further.

"The recent murder of Steven Boudreaux bears an uncanny resemblance in many respects to the murder of Camille Gravier, a local woman killed here sixty years ago."

Shelby could barely keep her pulse rate under control. The Camille Gravier murder trial was what her aunt Toni had been telling her about at her great-aunt Mary's eightieth birthday party last year. A drifter, Rafael Perdido, had been convicted of the crime and later died in prison. The case had been Shelby's great-grandfather's last case—the only murder case that the famous defense attorney, Hamilton Delacroix, had ever lost. Toni had somehow gotten hold of Hamilton's notes on the case.

Before Toni could tell Shelby much more about the case, Aunt Mary had collapsed from a sudden heart attack. It was later, as Shelby and Toni sat around Mary's hospital bed, that their weak and emotionally distraught elderly relative had spoken of things better left buried. Aunt Mary had pressured Shelby into promising she would destroy Hamilton's notes.

Shelby would have kept her promise. She was a woman of her word. Which was why Toni decided not to hand Hamilton Delacroix's notes over to her.

Toni couldn't condone destroying Delacroix family history. She had locked the files away where they would be safe. But after Shelby found out about her fiancé's connection to the Gravier family, she'd decided to ask Toni to let her have a look at the notes.

Now, here in her hands, she had a blow-by-blow account of the events that had happened those many years before. Shelby ignored the beignets for the far-more-tempting pages before her.

She scanned to where the *Bulletin*'s editor, Gator Guzman, had listed the similarities between the two crimes.

Murders of Camille Gravier and Steven Boudreaux
- Occurred at Moon Lake on Delacroix property
- Victims both drowned after struggle
- Both Delacroix known to have had a relationship with their victims
- Both Delacroix known to have been at scenes of deaths

She began to read the story. The writing was awkward, wordy, outdated, part detective novel, part news report. She could tell that Gator hadn't written it. She figured he had probably dug up and reprinted an account that had run sixty years before.

Apparently, late one hot and sultry June night, the body of Camille Gravier—beautiful red-haired, green-eyed, nineteen-year-old daughter of a local fisherman—had been pulled out of Moon Lake by the sheriff and his deputies. The doctor, roused out of bed to look at the deceased, had immediately taken note of the young woman's torn clothing and the bruises she had sustained. His opinion was that Camille Gravier had struggled with an attacker before she drowned.

Two men were considered suspects by the sheriff's office: Rafael Perdido, a drifter, and Charles Delacroix, son of a prominent local attorney, Hamilton Delacroix.

Shelby's pulse raced even faster. No, this couldn't be possible. *Charles Delacroix?* Her grandfather had been a *suspect* in the murder?

She quickly read on. Charles Delacroix and Rafael Perdido had both been detained because their clothes were wet and both men admitted to being in the lake that night. Delacroix was later released when his sister, Mary, told the sheriff that he had gone into the lake to try to save her friend, Camille, after seeing Perdido waist-deep in the water holding Camille's body.

The surprise of those words hit Shelby hard. Aunt Mary

had been there? Camille had been her friend? Was this the reason that the subject had proved so painful for Mary?

As Shelby read on she learned that Perdido had been charged with the murder and Hamilton Delacroix had taken on his defense. Charles Delacroix became the star witness against him. He testified that he and Camille had been dating for several weeks. He was supposed to meet Camille by the lake that night when he came upon Perdido.

Shelby's heart was thudding as she put down the newspaper. This was too much to take in all at once. Her own grandfather had been romantically involved with Camille Gravier?

Why had he never spoken of this case? His father had been the defense attorney! Charles had been the star witness for the prosecution! What was he hiding?

Shelby did not like the thoughts that had begun to run through her head. She told herself there was a perfectly logical explanation. Charles Delacroix wasn't just her grandfather, he was the gentlest, kindest man alive. He couldn't be involved in anything shady. Could he?

Oh, dear Lord, what was going on? Something was wrong here. Very, very wrong.

The doorbell rang. Shelby dropped the paper on the counter and moved to answer the summons in a kind of daze. When she saw the face looking back at her through the peephole, her mind snapped back to the present and her pulse went wild as she swung open the door.

"Oh, Travis!"

"Hey there, darl—"

Shelby rushed into his open arms before he could finish his greeting. Travis's rangy, hard-muscled frame closed around her instantly.

He kissed her hungrily. Shelby returned that hunger, clasping the wonderful reality of him to her tightly.

"Whoa," Travis said, laughing as they finally came up for air.

He picked her up and carried her into the house, kicking the door closed behind them as he set her back on her feet.

"Darlin', that's just about the best hello I've ever had."

"Oh, Travis," she whispered, clinging to him. She couldn't believe that just at the very moment she had needed the warmth and security of him, he had appeared.

"I'm so glad you've come! You don't know how much I've missed you. I hate our being apart!"

"Then come back to Texas with me, darlin'."

The unexpectedness of the request caught Shelby off guard. She leaned back, out of his arms. "But Travis, I—"

"I'm no good at this long-distance loving, Shelby. Truth be told, it's making me as ornery as an old bull. I've come to marry you and take you back to Texas with me. Right now."

Shelby saw the mixture of tenderness and determination on Travis's face, heard it in his voice. It filled her with a warm, sweet yearning.

She sighed from deep in her heart. "Oh, Travis, I do love you so! But I can't just take off with you now and go to Texas. So many things are happening. Why, just before you knocked on the door, I discovered that my grandfather..."

She stopped, suddenly aware of the import of the words she had been about to say.

Camille Gravier was Travis's great-aunt. He'd come to Louisiana last fall looking for a link between the Delacroix and Camille's death. It had taken Travis a long time to let go of his suspicions and accept his great-aunt's death as a tragic event not tied to her family.

How was he going to respond when she told him about what she had just read in the newspaper?

"What did you discover about your grandfather?" Travis asked.

It was not in Shelby to lie. Or to withhold the truth. No matter what the consequences. She looked at Travis squarely. "My grandfather was considered a suspect when Camille Gravier was killed. He admitted to having a relationship with her."

"And your point, darlin'?" Travis asked, not a drop of surprise in his voice.

"Travis, you *knew?*"

"That Camille played it fast and loose with your grandfather? Well, sure. Like I told you last year, it was her favorite recreational sport with a lot of the young men around that time. And one of them got her pregnant."

Shelby stepped out of Travis's arms as the shock of his words hit her. "Camille was pregnant? You never said a word about that! Or about the fact that my grandfather was one of the men who dated her!"

"Shelby, he's your grandfather, and she was pregnant out of wedlock. Where I come from, it's considered a mite impolite to be bad-mouthing your relatives or those folks who you're figuring on making your relatives. Darlin', come on. It's time we tied the knot."

The determination in Travis's eyes told Shelby that she was facing a man who knew exactly what he wanted. Her.

Something like panic began to surge through Shelby.

"You don't know what's happened. My cousin Nikki has just been indicted for murder! Joanna has had to give up all her cases while she fights for her daughter. She needs my support. And my grandfather needs me to handle the extra work at the firm. Travis, I need to be here for them now."

Travis's hands came to rest on her shoulders. "I need for you to be with me now. I love you, Shelby."

"Travis, that's not fair. You make it sound like I have to choose between you and my family."

He dropped his hands and his beautiful, gray-green eyes suddenly seemed lusterless, colorless. "Looks to me like you already have."

"Travis, please don't say that."

"Shelby, I can't move the ranch to Louisiana."

"I...know."

He captured her hands and held them, searching her eyes. "This isn't the first time we've talked about marriage. How did you think it was going to work?"

"I—I guess I just fell in love with you so fast, I didn't give myself time to think."

Travis's jaw was tight, his mouth strained at the corners

as he released her hands. "I'm going back to Texas now, Shelby."

"But what about the wedding?"

He turned and headed toward the door.

"Travis?"

He didn't stop at her call. Or even look back. He was out the door and had closed it behind him before she had time to take another breath.

Shelby stood staring at that closed door for a very long time, her throat constricted, her heart nothing but an aching lump inside her chest.

Oh, Lord, what had she just done?

"WHAT DO YOU HOPE to accomplish by appearing before the grand jury today, Weston?" Philip Delacroix demanded as he cornered Logan outside the courtroom.

Logan tried to ignore the arrogant tone of Philip's voice and concentrate on what he knew lay behind the man's words—his concern for his granddaughter.

"I'm filing a motion that asks them to reconsider their decision, Senator," Logan explained.

"On what basis?"

"That the grand jury did not have the benefit of all the available evidence when the case was presented to it. I want them to hear Nikki's explanation of how she was forced to fight off a drunk and abusive Steven Boudreaux when he attacked her on the night of his death. This way we have a chance to get the charges dropped now and spare Nikki the painful ordeal of a trial."

"Will the grand jury listen?"

"You're closer to them than I, Senator. You tell me."

"You think they selected anyone who was my friend to sit on this grand jury?"

"I know they're not your personal friends, Senator. But they come from your district and are therefore your constituents. I'm assuming you must know something about their concerns and attitudes."

"They're storekeepers, librarians, firemen, housewives,"

Philip said with a dismissive wave of his hand. "What do I know of such people?"

Logan was well aware that Philip Delacroix could glad-hand with the best of them in public. He wondered what his constituents would think if they heard their state senator talking about them with such an obvious air of superiority in private.

Logan was saved a response to Delacroix by the appearance of Joanna and Nikki in the doorway of the courthouse.

Joanna's step was sure and firm as she approached. As always, her business suit was simply tailored and understated, revealing only the grace and natural elegance of the woman who wore it. The expression on her face was a portrait of pure strength of character, putting Philip Delacroix's particular brand of arrogant self-importance to shame.

With the exception of her tall, slim frame, she resembled her father not in the least. Logan wasn't disappointed.

"Keep me informed," Philip Delacroix said as he turned away. He left the courthouse without so much as a word to his daughter or granddaughter.

Logan looked over at Nikki. She was withdrawn and quiet, but at least the unnatural tenseness that had gripped her body was gone. She still had a lot of hurdles to overcome. He hoped to get her over a major one today.

An officer of the court came out to tell Logan that the grand jury was ready to hear his motion. Logan knew he was the only one to be let inside during this pleading. He gestured for Joanna and Nikki to take a seat on the hallway bench, then followed the officer into the courtroom.

Logan stood at one end of a long table. The foreman of the grand jury was at the other end, around him the men and women who had been gathered to sit in judgment on the actions of a fellow citizen. They were as Philip Delacroix had described them—simple, everyday folks, of various shapes, sizes, ages and colors, chosen from all walks of life.

Logan talked to them about Nikki just as he would have talked about his own daughter, Shari—with intimate understanding of the difficulties facing a girl growing into womanhood. And with compassion for her disastrous choice of a first love.

When he asked them to let Nikki tell them her story in her own words, Logan liked the expressions he was seeing on their faces.

"We will have a short conference to discuss your motion, Mr. Weston," the foreman said. He was a hefty, middle-aged black man wearing a gold wedding band and the look of an understanding father.

Logan sent him a smile of genuine gratitude. "Thank you."

He turned and followed the uniformed officer of the court into the hallway where Joanna and Nikki waited.

"We'll know in a few minutes," Logan said to them, careful not to let his excitement show, despite the fact that he knew the grand jury was going to vote to hear Nikki. He just *knew* it.

"Murderer! Murderer!"

Logan swung around, startled at the sudden, strident sound shattering the previous quiet of the courthouse hallway.

The face of the woman spewing out that accusation was contorted in anger. She was wearing all black, the sleeves and hem of her dress cut in strips like jagged knives. Her long, gray-streaked hair flared behind her like dirty smoke.

And she was plummeting down the courthouse hallway right toward Nikki.

"You killed him, you murderer! You won't get away with it! I won't let you get away with it!"

Logan quickly stepped in front of Nikki to prevent the woman from reaching her. A second later the courtroom door swung open.

The woman moaned and dropped to the floor in front of him. A camera flashed from Logan's left and another immediately on his right. Half a dozen photographers had suddenly materialized.

"What's going on here?" the foreman demanded.

Logan realized that the loud commotion had brought the entire grand jury to the door.

"She killed my baby!" the woman wailed, writhing on the floor. "And now her big-city lawyer is trying to get her off!"

Her baby? So this was Flora Boudreaux.

"All I want is to be heard," she wailed. "Do I ask so much?"

Logan read the conflict on the jurors' faces. It was clear they didn't know what to think of this scene. And all the while cameras were catching every angle, including their expressions as they gazed in confusion at the prostrate woman at their feet.

"What is it you want to say?" the chairman finally asked after a very long, uncomfortable moment.

Flora Boudreaux swung to her knees and clasped her hands against her breast. More camera lights flashed.

Logan could clearly see the orchestration in these movements, the careful timing as she played the wronged mother to her intended audience.

Flora Boudreaux had obviously come to give a performance. And she was holding nothing back.

"I appeal to you," she said in a voice so pitiful it made Logan's stomach turn. "Do not listen to the lies of this girl's high-priced, big-city mouthpiece. Listen to this poor mama's pleas. Do not let my boy's death go unpunished! I beg of you. On my hands and knees, I beg this of you!"

And all the while the cameras flashed like a swarm of fireflies.

JOANNA WAITED UNTIL she had drunk two strong-as-sin cups of black coffee before she retrieved the morning edition of the *Bayou Bulletin* from her door.

The front page consisted of an enormous picture of Flora Boudreaux on her knees in front of the grand jury foreman, with Logan, Joanna and Nikki in the background. The headline took up the other half of the page.

Grieving Mother Begs for Justice
Grand Jury Is Swayed
Indictment against Senator's Granddaughter Stands

Joanna dropped the paper on the patio table and sank into one of the green garden chairs with a deep sigh.

She wasn't surprised the grand jury had refused to listen to Nikki after Flora Boudreaux's well-rehearsed performance in front of them. If they had tried to give Nikki a break after that, they would have been open to charges of preferential treatment for a senator's granddaughter.

So now, on top of everything else she had endured, Nikki would be forced to face the hell of a trial.

Joanna rested her head in her hands and let out a heavy sigh. She hadn't thought there could be any pain to match what she'd felt when the doctor had told her that Richard was going to be paralyzed for the rest of his life. Then she had listened to her daughter describe the abuse she had endured at the hands of Steven Boudreaux, and Joanna's heart had broken open and bled.

How could she have been so blind as to not know what was going on? She should have known. She should have protected her child!

A silent sob caught deep in Joanna's throat as unshed tears burned in her eyes. Nikki hadn't said a word in all that time, through all that pain! Why had she endured it? Where had Joanna gone wrong? How had she ended up failing Nikki so badly?

Yes, she'd been carrying a heavy caseload at the firm. But she'd made it a point to be home with Nikki in time for supper every night. And when she'd been forced to work a weekend, Uncle Charles always understood when she insisted on taking the work home.

She had been there for Nikki. She had made sure she was.

Joanna exhaled heavily as she leaned back in her chair.

No, that was a lie. No matter what she wanted to believe, she hadn't been there for Nikki. Her physical presence meant nothing. Nikki and she could have been in separate countries for all the communicating they did.

Joanna had lost a vital connection to her daughter. She

didn't know how. She didn't know why. She didn't know if she could ever get it back.

She only knew she had to try. With everything in her, she had to try to reach Nikki.

Joanna caught a movement from the corner of her eye. She looked up to see Logan coming down the path.

Her pulse took an unsteady leap.

She knew he'd be here, of course. They had agreed to meet this morning to discuss their next legal move on Nikki's behalf. Still, the sight of him warmed her blood as thoroughly now as it had the first time she'd seen him in the courtroom.

The early morning light ran over his powerful shoulders, turning his thick, short hair the same pale yellow as the spring blossoms in her forsythia shrubs. His measured stride spoke of unwavering purpose, direction, endurance.

It was easy to be a winner. Logan had shown Joanna he knew how to lose. The unconcerned ease with which he had accepted the grand jury's decision had been very revealing.

His refusal to let it break his stride had done more for her morale than any words of compassion he could have offered. He put his energy into what he could do and did not lament over what he couldn't.

He was a man who was prepared for whatever faced him.

But she was still totally unprepared for the streak of pleasure that shot through her as she rose to greet him.

"Good morning, Ms. Gideon."

His words were spoken slowly, deeply, in his rich Southern accent. They rubbed gently at her ears and poured warmth down the vertebrae at her neck and back. Feminine quivers she had thought deeply buried and forgotten suddenly surfaced.

She was putting her daughter's life squarely into Logan's hands. But she knew she did not dare put her own hand in his at their greeting.

"The morning air is pleasant," Logan said. "Shall we talk out here?"

Joanna nodded as she gestured to the patio chairs. He immediately held hers out for her.

He reminded Joanna of an old-fashioned Southern gentleman—that special breed of man to whom courtesy seemed a second skin. Joanna hadn't thought they made men like Logan Weston anymore. Despite all her independence and self-sufficiency—or maybe because of them—she found Logan's courtesy both charming and disarming.

"Is Nikki up?" Logan asked as he sat across from her.

"She's getting ready for Steven's funeral."

"She mustn't go to his funeral," Logan said.

"I agree I would prefer she did not," Joanna said. "But it seems important to her. She's been so quiet since she told us about the night of Steven's death. In insisting on going to his funeral she shared the first real animation I've seen in days. I didn't want to squelch it."

"As her attorney, I am telling you Nikki must not attend Steven Boudreaux's funeral."

Joanna leaned forward, hearing the deadly serious tone beneath Logan's words. "What is it? What's happened?"

"Your father has learned that Flora Boudreaux and the editor of the local newspaper are arranging to shoot another scene between Flora and Nikki at the funeral today. The Boudreaux woman is determined to smear Nikki in the press. Her appearance before the grand jury was only the beginning."

"How did my father find out?"

"He said his source was confidential."

"His sources generally are," Joanna said. She rose, unable to sit still another second while all the alarming ramifications mounted in her brain. Logan immediately stood as well.

"We can't let this case be tried in the press," Joanna said, walking to the edge of the porch and looking out at the calm waters of the bayou drifting by, willing them to calm her. "Flora Boudreaux will turn every prospective juror in Bayou Beltane against Nikki before her case even comes before the court."

"I'm convinced that's exactly what she's set out to do," Logan said, stepping beside Joanna.

"How can we stop her?" Joanna asked.

"Any action we take against Flora Boudreaux would only result in generating more publicity for her cause. We'd look like the big-time, big-money bullies picking on the poor grieving mother. That would play right into her hands."

"You're right," Joanna said. "You know what this means, of course. We can't let Nikki be tried in Bayou Beltane."

"Which is why I've filed a motion for a change of venue to New Orleans."

"Flora will try to stop it when she hears," Joanna said.

"The judge will be handing down his decision late this morning, at precisely the same time that Steven Boudreaux will be laid to rest."

Joanna turned to face Logan. "You deliberately set it up so that Flora Boudreaux would be unable to be present to try to thwart the change of venue."

He smiled, slow and easy and with consummate charm.

"And for when Gator Guzman will be too busy setting up his photographers to shoot the expected funeral confrontation between Flora and Nikki to think of checking the courthouse calendar."

Joanna's lips drew back in a smile, both for the lawyer she was seeing and the man. She fought a very strong urge to throw her arms around Logan and hug him.

Something of her feelings must have shown on her face, because suddenly Logan's eyes were on her hair, caressing its long, thick strands as they fell to her shoulders. Joanna swallowed hard, finding it difficult to breathe. Her hands were suddenly perspiring despite the pleasant coolness of the morning.

Slowly, his gaze made its way across her neck to the edge of her chin and then up to her bottom lip. He paused there, taking in the curves and contours of her mouth so intently, so firmly, that Joanna could almost feel the pressure on them.

Her lips parted with a soft, beckoning sigh.

Logan's eyes immediately rose to lock with hers. He took a step closer, then another.

Joanna could feel the power of him, smell the enticing mixture of male scent and rich sandalwood soap as he towered over her. The sunlight shone on his hair, turning it into liquid gold.

She had plenty of time to move away, turn her head, make any kind of small gesture that would have stopped him.

She didn't.

She felt his breath against her forehead like a hot wind as his arms circled around her shoulders. A sharp tremor skittered across her muscles as they registered the warmth and claiming strength of his touch.

He bent his head to brush his lips over hers, gently asking a question. Joanna answered with a soft cry from deep in her throat, as welcoming as the sudden frantic beating of her heart.

Logan drew in a ragged breath before his mouth came down on hers to claim it in earnest. Desire jolted through Joanna, too hot, too fast for her to fully comprehend. But her body understood. It was already softening, melting against him.

Logan's hold tightened, bringing her breasts full against his chest. Her nipples peaked hard against his ribs. He pressed his mouth against hers with a hungry, insistent pressure.

Her lips parted, a breathless moan escaping at the bold, sweeping caress of his tongue. Fire, hot and sweet, exploded inside Joanna.

"Mom, where are you? I can't find my black stockings."

Sanity returned like a shock wave with her daughter's voice. Nikki was calling from somewhere inside the house! She could be stepping outside any second!

Joanna immediately broke off the kiss, stepped back out of Logan's arms, turned toward the front door. Her face felt like a radiator, her heart like a jackhammer.

A second later the front door whooshed open and Nikki

stepped out on the porch, blinking in the blinding morning sunlight.

"Oh, Mr. Weston. I didn't know you were here. Mom, I need my black stockings for the funeral."

Joanna's mind was spinning faster than a top. Her daughter's question registered not at all on her brain. All she could think about was the relief of knowing that the bright sunlight was preventing Nikki from seeing her face too clearly.

It was Logan who stepped forward to answer Nikki. "You're not going to the funeral," he said in a polite but emphatic voice. "Come. I'll explain why."

Joanna did not follow them inside the house. She could not. It took a full five minutes before her mind returned to even a semblance of order and her body stopped shaking.

She couldn't believe what she had just done. The reality of it ripped through her. What could she have she been thinking?

She hadn't been thinking.

She had been *feeling*. And what she had been feeling was the astonishing reawakening of her own sexuality. Her knees were shaking. Her breasts and belly aching. It felt as though every nerve cell in her body had suddenly come alive. She was appalled and astounded and thoroughly aroused.

She assured herself that even if Nikki hadn't interrupted, nothing further would have happened.

It couldn't have. She and Logan were both professionals. Neither of them were people who let their emotions rule them. And as attorneys, they both knew how important it was to keep a line drawn between their business and personal lives.

But they had both erased that line. They had kissed.

And what a kiss. She was still trembling from it. And she knew exactly what it meant. A total disregard for ethical conduct. On her part. And his.

An attorney did not get personally involved with his client. And a client sure as hell did not get personally involved with an attorney representing her daughter.

So now what? Fire him?

She had to. There was no choice. The situation was too fraught with emotional disaster to do anything else.

But if she fired him, she'd lose the best attorney Nikki could have. She'd seen enough of Logan to be sure of that. Her daughter's life was at stake.

Dear Lord, what was she going to do?

CHAPTER SIX

PHILIP DELACROIX'S ANGER seethed as his chauffeur drove him to his law offices in Bayou Beltane. That scandal rag of Guzman's was getting to be a real irritation. It was bad enough that Gator was working with Flora to smear Nikki's reputation and further implicate her in the Steven Boudreaux murder case. Now the gossipmonger was dead set on re-hashing everything about the Camille Gravier murder, too!

One of these days Philip was going to have to do something about that nosy reporter. But at the moment, he had his hands full doing what he could for Nikki.

Everyone said Weston was the best. He'd better be. It was going to take the best to get Nikki off.

Damn fool girl. If only she had listened to him about Steven Boudreaux! Of all the young men she could have picked, why did she have to pick him?

What was wrong with the girl?

What was wrong with all girls that age, he supposed. They believed everything a boy told them. The fools! Didn't they know that young men Steven's age were after only one thing—and would say and do anything to get it?

Hell, it was what he had done. Philip wasn't so old that he'd forgotten what being nineteen was all about.

A youthful smile drew back his lips as the memories filtered through his mind. The lazy, sultry summer days—and lusty nights. Long, flowing auburn hair, white thighs and sparkling emerald eyes. Philip was still smiling as his chauffeur pulled into his reserved parking space at his law office.

He dismissed the man and walked through the enclosed courtyard at the back to his private entrance. He halted abruptly when he saw the fresh gris-gris of wet salt in the shape of a cross on the concrete path leading to the door.

Voodoo! His body went stiff as the bitter taste of anger mixed with fear in his mouth. The combination coated his tongue and leaked down his throat in a choking bile.

Philip knew perfectly well that this cross meant trouble for him. He also knew it had to be from those damn witches!

He'd been far too lenient for far too long. It was time to get tough.

He gave the cross a wide, cautious berth. His fingers shook as he stuck his key into the lock. He pushed open his office door, slamming and locking it behind him the moment he was inside. He circled his enormous walnut desk and snatched up the phone. He punched in the number for the police station.

"This is Senator Philip Delacroix. I want to speak to Detective Jackson Boudreaux," Philip said without preliminaries.

A click later and Jackson was on the line. "Aren't you taking a chance calling me here?"

"I'm reporting a threat against my life!"

Philip told Jackson about the voodoo cross he'd just found on the threshold leading into his office.

"You don't really want me to make an official report on this, do you?" Jackson asked.

Philip should have known Jackson wouldn't take it seriously. He hadn't taken it seriously all those other times Philip had told him about the voodoo dolls and mojoes cast on him, either.

Jackson never understood. How could he? He'd never been hexed by those voodoo hags!

"Take down the report," Philip ordered through clenched teeth. "I want someone over here photographing the evidence. And then I want you to arrest them."

"Philip, I can't arrest someone for making a cross of wet salt. At the outside, it's defacing private property—a misdemeanor. And that's only if I could prove they did it."

"You know they did it! Get rid of *them!*"

"It's a stupid superstition. It can't hurt you."

"It's not just the voodoo! Since when do you need me to give you chapter and verse on what Flora and Desiree have been doing?"

"Flora's the only one making trouble," Jackson said.

"They're two of a kind," Philip said. Jackson had no idea how much more he feared Desiree than Flora. That old woman knew too much, way too much.

"They're just a couple of old women, Philip. Smart thing to do is let Weston handle the legal end for Nikki and be prepared to thwart any real mischief they try to make for you."

"I didn't ask you what would be smart!" Philip snapped. "I told you to get rid of them!"

There was a long, silent pause on the other end of the line. "You gonna have to be more specific," Jackson said finally. "What exactly do you mean by 'get rid of them'?"

Philip heard the tightness in Jackson's voice. Still, he was confident Jackson would do what he was told. He always did. Philip was Jackson's ticket to the good life. They both knew he wasn't going to blow it.

Not even now when Philip demanded he take action against his own mother and grandmother.

"Make them leave Bayou Beltane," Philip said. "I don't care how. Just do it. And do it *today!*"

Philip slammed down the phone.

LOGAN DROVE HOME on autopilot. The day had had its positive accomplishments and he was doing his best to dwell on them.

Nikki had been prevented from going to Steven's funeral, thereby foiling Flora Boudreaux's attempt to cause yet another confrontation to be photographically reenacted in the next day's *Bayou Bulletin*. The transfer of Nikki's case to New Orleans had gone without a ripple.

Important accomplishments, yes. But he still couldn't believe what had almost happened between himself and Joanna that morning on her porch.

What he had almost let happen.

The way that beautiful smile had lit her face when she realized that he had Nikki's legal concerns well in hand was tempting enough. But the frank personal approval of a woman for a man that had glowed in her lovely eyes had undone him. Her attraction to him was filled with honesty and not a hint of artifice. For a second there he'd been certain that Joanna was going to follow up on that personal approval with some personal action.

Logan had held his breath in hopes she would, in eager anticipation that she would.

But she had controlled whatever impulse momentarily possessed her and had dropped right back into that cool, seemingly effortless composure at her command.

And Logan had wanted to strangle her. Instead he'd done something far more dangerous. He'd kissed her. And she had responded to him. He'd tasted hunger and desire on her lips. He'd felt her body burn where it touched his. If Nikki hadn't interrupted, he would have taken Joanna right there and then on her own porch.

The stark reality of that thought shook him. For the first time in his life he had lost it. Joanna had absolutely no idea what she was doing to him. She couldn't.

For a thirty-eight-year-old lawyer who had been married for most of her adult life and who had a daughter nearly grown, she was an enigma. There was an artless and mind-boggling openness about her personal attraction to him that Logan had from the first found absolutely astounding and impossibly irresistible.

And thoroughly maddening.

There had to be something that had made her this way. What kind of a marriage had Joanna had that left her without any of the normal studied feminine ploys and pretenses that women used to camouflage their interest in a man?

Logan forced himself to take a deep breath and face reality. If Joanna didn't fire him, he was going to have to resign.

Or learn to respond to her reactions to him—and his to

her——with complete control from now on. He could not repeat his behavior of that morning.

A lawyer did not get personally involved with his clients.

As Logan parked in front of his home facing Coliseum Square in the lower Garden District of New Orleans, he looked up in surprise to see his daughter, Shari, waiting on the doorstep.

"Why didn't you let yourself in?" Logan asked after he got out of the car and gave her a quick hug.

"Forgot my key."

"Shari, we have more than our share of crime here," Logan said as he unlocked the door. "You should be more careful. I might not have gotten home before dark. Why didn't you wait in your car? Where *is* your car?"

"Mama gave me a ride."

"Your mama knew that you didn't have your key, and she still drove away and left you here alone?"

"Get real, Daddy. You know she still treats me like I'm twelve. I told her I had my key. If I hadn't, she would have insisted on staying around until you got home."

"What would have been so bad about that?"

"She had the brats in the back seat. All my brothers do is whine and fight. I couldn't stand it anymore. If I hadn't gotten out of the car right there and then, I swear I would have had to kill them both. Self-defense."

"Self-defense, huh?" Logan said, amusement running through his tone as he closed the door behind them.

"They were violently attacking my emotional health."

"Novel argument," Logan said, smiling as he led the way upstairs to his apartment. "Doubt a jury would go for it, though."

"They would if you stocked it with older sisters who knew what it was like to have to put up with bratty younger brothers. You have no idea how lucky you are you just had me, Daddy."

Shari leaned up to plant a kiss on his cheek.

"And now I'm going to the kitchen to make us the best roast beef po-boys you ever had and you can tell me all about this case that was so interesting you even agreed to cancel your vacation to take it."

"Uh-oh. Why do I suddenly get the feeling I'm being fattened for the slaughter?"

Shari tried to look innocent. "I don't know what you mean."

"The last time you offered to fix me supper and listen to me talk about work, you wanted a CD system for your car."

The guilty look on Shari's face said it all.

"What is it this time?" Logan asked.

"It's just a little fender bender."

Logan's tone automatically stiffened with concern.

"You were in an accident? What happened?"

"I was backing out of this parking space and I sorta ran up the curb into a post. But the post is okay."

"Delighted to hear it," Logan said, trying not to smile. "Now, how about my daughter?"

"Daddy, I'm fine. But the damage estimate has come in at fifteen hundred."

"Fifteen hundred dollars? Where did you bend this fender, across the hood?"

Shari made a face. "It's bent into the back tire, which is why I can't drive it. I know I should have been paying more attention. Mama's already read me the riot act, so please don't. Sometimes I think the worst thing about having divorced parents is everything you do wrong gets a lecture rerun."

Logan dropped his briefcase on a living room chair and loosened his tie. "Fifteen hundred is a lot of money."

"Just what I said to that garage," Shari said, as though vindicated. "Ridiculously expensive!"

"What did your mother say?"

"That I should report it to the insurance company. But a claim will ruin my record and up my rate through the roof! Since you agreed to pay for my insurance until I get through college, I'm really only thinking of you."

Oh, sure.

"I have to have wheels, Daddy. It really bites having to

be driven around like a kid. I have that job lined up this summer. I could pay you back?''

Logan had heard that one before, more times than he could count. Only last week she had "promised to pay him back" for a pair of shoes she just had to have.

But this week Logan had heard the spine-chilling tale of a girl his Shari's age. A girl who had been emotionally and physically beaten by her boyfriend. A girl who had finally defended herself, only to find that she was now facing a charge of murdering him.

Logan knew he should be counting his blessings that his daughter's biggest worry was finding the money to fix a fender bender. And he was.

"All right, Shari," he said, wrapping his arm around her shoulders. "I'll *loan* you the fifteen hundred."

"Thanks, Daddy. You're the best. And I'll pay you back."

The warmth from his daughter's smile was all the payment Logan knew he was ever really going to get. But that didn't matter, because it was enough. More than enough.

JACKSON TOOK A SWIG of brandy and grimaced as the fire of it exploded down his throat. He didn't like his liquor sweet, but it was the only thing in the house. And he sure as hell wasn't going to say what he had to say to the two women sitting across from him while he was sober.

Outside, the mosquitoes batted the thick-meshed screens of his grandma's old bayou home. They hid in the heat of the day, but the humid night always brought them out looking for fresh blood. Their damn insistent whine was almost as irritating as his mama's.

"She didn't show!" Flora complained, her voice a combination of anger and angst. "I heard tell everywhere that she was gonna be there. What could've happened?"

Jackson took another swallow. And another. He wondered what his mama would say if he told her why Nikki Gideon hadn't shown up at Steven's funeral.

She'd never know, because he wasn't stupid enough to tell her.

Jackson knew when to keep quiet. He'd been eight when he'd first seen Philip Delacroix sneaking out of his mama's bedroom early one fine morning. It was right about then he'd figured out who his missing daddy was. Flora had gotten all upset when he'd confronted her. She'd made him swear he wouldn't tell.

Jackson hadn't. He supposed Flora had still loved Philip then, and the chunk of money he left with her every time he decided to spend the night.

Jackson rather liked that money himself. And all the things it bought for them. He'd decided at that young and eager age that being quiet and in the good graces of his daddy was just where he wanted to be.

Then Steven had come along. And Philip's marriage had disintegrated into divorce. Flora had been excited and happy about the divorce. She probably had some illusions that Philip might actually marry her now that his wife was out of the picture.

But what happened was that a divorced Philip was now free to bed much younger and more beautiful women than his aging mistress. He stopped coming to see her. And Flora learned that her chief allure had been the fact that she was just up the bayou, a convenient stop for a married man. It took no time at all for whatever feelings she had for Philip to turn to hate.

She had badgered Jackson to get close to his daddy, to become his right hand so he could find out things for her. Jackson had been happy to do it. But not for his mama's reasons. For his own. If Flora was going to cause Philip trouble, Jackson wanted to know and be the one to "warn" his daddy.

And it had worked. Flora thought he was helping her. Philip thought he was helping him.

The truth was, Jackson helped no one but himself.

Sometimes he'd warn Philip. Sometimes he'd feed a little information to Flora to let her cause Philip some trouble so Jackson could step in and be the indispensable—if unacknowledged—son.

He'd let his mother know about Weston's motion before the grand jury that might have set Nikki Gideon free.

And he had been the one to "save" Philip's granddaughter by telling Philip about Flora's intent to cause another scene with Nikki at Steven's funeral.

Philip had been so appreciative. So rewarding. Jackson's smile was smug as he took another swig of the brandy.

Yes, his daddy had come to trust and rely on Jackson for many things, using him for all sorts of "odd jobs." With each favor Jackson had performed, his position with Philip had solidified. He was in good now. And getting very well paid. He didn't even care what Philip asked him to do.

Until tonight. Jackson downed the rest of the liquid in his glass with an angry swallow.

Jackson had been the first to say that Flora had crossed the line when she'd sicced Steven on Nikki. Crazy old fool! He had tried to talk some sense into her. When that failed, he'd tried to talk some sense into his younger brother.

But Steven wouldn't listen. They'd never been close. Jackson's fear that Steven might also try to make a claim on Philip's fortune was the reason he'd never told Steven about Philip bedding their mama all those years before.

All Steven knew was the nonsense Flora had been feeding him—that through Nikki, Steven had a chance at the Delacroix fortune.

Jackson remembered the day he'd had to bring *that* news to Philip.

He shuddered as he went to take another swallow and found his glass empty. His mama had finally grown quiet. Her glass was empty, too. His grandma's was still full.

Jackson looked over at Desiree's face to see silent tears leaking out of her old eyes. He quickly looked away.

He could take Flora's loud, angry grief a thousand times more easily than he could take Desiree's silent sorrow.

Jackson reached for the bottle and filled up both his mama's and his own glass again before leaning back in his chair. He chugged the brandy until the glass was empty. His eyes strayed to the picture of Steven that lay on the elaborate altar the women had so lovingly prepared, full of candles and flowers and mementos of his brother's life.

Jackson closed his eyes, annoyed to realize that he was beginning to succumb to their pitiful, palpable grief. He didn't want to feel this—not any of it.

Flora was a crazy old loon for believing in that voodoo crap. But she was still his mama.

And although Desiree thought she possessed all these secret powers, Jackson knew his grandma was nothing but a harmless old soul who kept mostly to herself, making her silly potions and charms.

How was he going to run these old women out of the only home they had ever known?

Jackson wasn't going to do it. Philip had asked too much of him this time. He didn't care if his daddy cut him loose. He'd find someone else to sell his services to.

Jackson exhaled heavily. He knew he was kidding himself. There was no way he was ever going to find another Philip Delacroix in Bayou Beltane.

Damn. Damn. Damn.

"Child, you listening to me?" Flora demanded.

Jackson looked over at her, unaware she had said a thing. Her face was flushed and fuzzy. "No," he said.

"You're gonna avenge our Etienne! You're gonna get that girl!"

Jackson was damn tired of both Philip and Flora telling him what he was going to do. He wasn't their pawn. They were his! He leaned forward, feeling the liquor, knowing his words were coming out as fuzzy and unfocused as his vision.

"I'm not doing nothin' about nothin'. He never listened to me. Nor you, neither. He made his bed. A coffin! And now he's lying in it!"

"Jackson! How dare you say such a thing!"

"How can you be so stupid to think that Philip would ever let his son marry his granddaughter?"

"What nonsense is this? Etienne wasn't Philip's son!"

Jackson felt the jolt of Flora's words opening his eyes. But the brandy was buzzing so fast in his brain that it took a moment for all the ramifications of what she had said to sink in.

"Not his son? But Philip thinks—"

"I know what Philip thinks!" Flora interrupted. "I made right sure he lived with the torture of thinking it, too! But soon as Etienne got Nikki pregnant, I would of told Philip the truth. Etienne would of married her. Been set for life. We all would of been set for life. Don't you see?"

Jackson was beginning to.

"Who was Etienne's daddy?" he asked.

Flora sat back. Her glass was empty. Her eyes were glassy. Her voice was as slurred as his own.

"Just some drifter who kept me company. Philip's attentions were slipping a mite during those days. He kept saying his wife was getting suspicious. So I took another lover for a while. Philip never knew. He was here just often enough to think Etienne was his. So I let him go right on thinking it. And paying for it. Just like he was paying for you."

"But I'm really Philip's son, right?"

"No doubt there, child. Philip is your daddy, just as sure as the night is black."

Jackson let out a relieved breath. That had been his ace in the hole. For a moment there, he'd thought he'd lost it.

"Philip's always taken to you, child. Now, you get in good with him like I told you to. When he dies, you'll be in his will. I just know it."

Jackson wondered whether Flora had forgotten that just a moment before she had been demanding that he get back at Philip's granddaughter in retaliation for Steven's death. Just how in the hell did she think that would put him in Philip's good graces?

She was probably too drunk to think.

He wasn't.

He'd just learned something damn important—something that might even save his butt.

Giving Philip Delacroix the welcome news that Steven was not his son was going to go a long way toward making up for Jackson not running off Desiree and Flora. A long way. Hell, Philip might just forget he'd ever ordered it.

CHAPTER SEVEN

JOANNA STOOD OUTSIDE the New Orleans courtroom next to Logan, waiting for Nikki to return from the rest room. It was the first time they had been alone since that morning on her porch when he had kissed her.

Joanna knew she had to address the subject of that kiss with him, but she was feeling unsure of how best to begin.

"I hope you will accept my apologies for the other morning," Logan said, taking the initiative from her. His voice was formal. He was intently studying the wood grain on the door.

"I can offer you no satisfactory explanation for my behavior," he continued. "Indeed, no satisfactory explanation exists. My actions were inexcusable. If you would like me to resign after the preliminary hearing today, I will understand."

Joanna was relieved and touched by his words. His taking the full blame spoke of the true gentleman he was. She liked that about him. She liked far too much about him.

That was the problem, of course. But the bigger problem was losing him as Nikki's attorney. Joanna had agonized over that possibility and come to the conclusion that he was too good to lose. There had to be a way to work this out.

"It was inappropriate behavior on both our parts," she said, her honesty not allowing her to pretend otherwise. "But I'm convinced that the insanity was a temporary one. I'd like for you to stay on. For Nikki's sake. Will you?"

He studied the door's wood grain a moment more before his eyes went to hers. The look he gave her was that of one professional to another.

"You have my word there will be no repeat of that very inappropriate behavior," he said.

Joanna sighed in relief. Now she did not have to make do with second best. Nikki would have the most qualified representation possible.

An odd sense of happiness rushed in on the tail of her relief. Joanna told herself it was solely for Nikki's sake and had nothing to do with the fact that now she would be able to continue to see and work with Logan.

Nikki rejoined them and they entered the courtroom to face her preliminary hearing on the charge of second-degree murder.

Joanna and Logan had talked over their strategy and had agreed that it was not the time to cross-examine any witnesses nor to put on a defense. They knew the evidence Chief Jake Trahan had gathered was sufficient to send the case to trial. They also knew the less the prosecution was aware of their defense strategy at this point, the better.

Tallie Arbour was the New Orleans assistant district attorney who presented the bare-bones evidence needed to establish that a crime had been committed and that there was probable cause that Nikki had committed it.

None of the evidence was fresh. Joanna had it memorized. She did not dwell on its presentation, but rather on its presenter.

A.D.A. Tallie Arbour was a petite five-five, with silky black curls that framed a perfect face of enormous dark eyes and the kind of full mouth that fashion models braved silicone injections to acquire.

Tallie's tasteful gold jewelry set off her coffee-hued skin to perfection. Her slim figure was clothed in a crisp, fashionable suit that showed not one crease despite her constant sitting and standing.

But Joanna could tell that Tallie Arbour was no mannequin. This petite black woman carried herself like the future judge she no doubt would one day become. There was no hesitation in her actions. Or voice. No wasted questions. No wasted movements.

Just a focused, unrelenting energy and competence that sent a chill down Joanna's spine. Tallie Arbour was going to be a formidable adversary.

The judge was Timothy Wooten, fairly new to the bench, barely forty, in the process of losing his brown hair and gaining a tummy. Wooten obviously knew he had drawn a media-attracting case. He was trying his best to do everything by the book. Trouble was, he wasn't all that familiar with "the book" yet.

But he could certainly tell when the prosecution had done its job. After Arbour finished her presentation, Wooten ruled probable cause had been established and started shuffling through his papers to check his calendar for an arraignment date.

Logan rose to address the bench for the first time that morning. "If Your Honor pleases, a separate arraignment will not be necessary. Miss Gideon is ready to enter her plea of not guilty at this time. The defense also respectfully requests the court set as early a jury trial date as is possible."

Joanna knew why Logan was doing this. Together they had carefully investigated both the prosecutor's caseload and the judge's calendar, and were pushing forward with a bold plan.

Joanna could see that Judge Wooten had obviously been caught unprepared by Logan's request. He squinted down at the calendar.

"I, uh…well, a case I had scheduled for the third week in June has been settled, so I suppose—"

"Your Honor," Tallie Arbour called out quickly as she rose. "The prosecution would find it a great hardship to go to trial on this case with such a short preparation time. I would need at least a year before—"

"A *year?*" Logan interrupted, looking at Arbour as though she had made an outlandish suggestion. In reality, crowded courts and caseloads often led to a year between preliminary hearing and trial.

"Your Honor," Logan continued, turning to face him. "A year is far too long a time for this young woman to have to carry the stigma of this serious charge made against her. Nikki Gideon's right to a speedy trial is guaranteed by nothing less than the Constitution of the United States. Is her right to be denied simply because this prosecutor cannot schedule it in?''

Judge Wooten's eyes went to the row of reporters sitting in the back of his courtroom. Joanna had a feeling that at that moment he really wished he had forbidden them entry.

But Joanna and Logan had counted on their being there.

A more experienced judge would have sensed the difficult position he'd been placed in and would have advised both parties that he would take the matter under advisement. Then he would have adjourned court and retreated to the quiet of his chambers to contemplate working out a compromise.

But like many new judges, Wooten felt himself under the gun to prove himself. Instead of a strategic retreat, Logan and Joanna were hoping that he would charge right in. He didn't let them down.

''The defendant's constitutional right to a speedy trial must take precedence,'' Wooten said after only a slight pause. ''I'm setting Miss Gideon's trial to begin June 22. The state may choose to prosecute her at that time or drop the charges. What's your pleasure, Ms. Arbour?''

Tallie Arbour's face was an unholy matrimony of beauty and barely suppressed anger at being outmaneuvered. The fact that her voice showed not one iota of that anger gave Joanna yet another glimpse of the formidable adversary they were up against.

''The state will prosecute, Your Honor,'' Arbour said.

''Very well. Last day for discovery motions is May 18. Last day for pretrial motions is June 8. That should do it, ladies and gentlemen. Court is adjourned.''

No sooner had the judge left the bench than Tallie Arbour came marching over to the defense table. Scrambling to keep up with her was a six-foot redheaded male trial assistant Logan had identified to Joanna earlier as Tom Smith, also from the D.A.'s office. But Joanna knew Arbour was the one in charge.

"Just who are you trying to kid, Logan?" Arbour asked. "There's no way that you can be prepared to defend this case in less than three months. When June 22 comes along, you're going to be asking for a continuance, aren't you?"

Joanna watched Logan smile as he slowly got to his feet. "Am I, Tallie?"

Arbour glared at Logan, muttered an oath beneath her breath, turned and stalked out of the courtroom, Tom Smith once again scrambling to keep up with her.

"It worked," Joanna said with a sigh of pure relief. "Still, I have a feeling that somehow, some way, the A.D.A. is going to try to be ready to take us on come June 22."

"Bet on it," Logan said somberly.

"You've been up against Tallie Arbour before?"

"Once. Closest time I ever came to losing. Only time Tallie ever did. She's the best the D.A. has. Word is she fought hard to get this case assigned to her."

"You think she was looking for a rematch?" Joanna asked.

"No. She's had plenty of chances to set up a rematch with me before now if trying to even up the score was her intent. Tallie's too professional for pointless contests."

"Prosecutors on cases like this with media-grabbing headlines generally have their careers jump-started if they give a good showing," Joanna said. "Maybe that's what she's after."

"Tallie's already a shoo-in for first assistant district attorney."

"Then why did she take on the extra workload of a case she doesn't need?" Joanna asked.

"I don't know," Logan said. "And that is a cause for concern. Still, we have scored a victory today. And I would be remiss if I did not uphold a sacred New Orleans tradition and take you ladies out to lunch to celebrate."

"What's so sacred about celebrating a victory?" Nikki asked. "Everybody does it everywhere."

"But nobody does it the way we do down here in New Orleans, Nikki. Ever had peanut butter ice cream pie?"

She shook her head. Logan held out his arm to her. "You are about to."

Joanna was very grateful to Logan for treating her daughter with a respect and friendliness that Joanna knew Nikki couldn't resist. He really went out of his way to be charming to her.

They dined at Kabby's, their table right next to an enormous picture window that afforded a breathtaking view of the Mississippi River. Joanna found her steamed clams in white wine with butter, olive oil, basil, oregano and thyme to be delicious. Nikki gobbled down her barbecued shrimp.

Joanna sat back and sipped her coffee, looking out at the perfect sunny spring afternoon. Even the muddy Mississippi looked blue beneath the paddleboats drifting lazily by.

"Why is celebrating different in New Orleans?" Nikki asked after polishing off two servings of peanut butter ice cream pie.

At least her appetite wasn't suffering.

"Because we're always doing it," Logan said with a smile. "Everyone's always drinking too much, eating too much, getting into too much mischief. And in general having a helluva good time. And what's more, we don't even need an excuse to do it."

Nikki leaned forward, smiling at Logan's explanation. "Have you ever lived anywhere else?" she asked.

"When I was young. But I wouldn't want to ever leave New Orleans again."

"Why not?"

"Because in August it's so muggy and hot you need all your energy just to draw the dense air into your lungs. Then comes January, where forty degrees feels like zero because the wet wind cuts through your clothes like a machete. Sometimes the hurricanes hit so hard you can hear the power lines pop like firecrackers and see electrical streamers flying through the air."

Nikki's brown eyes went wide with confusion. "And these are the things that make you *want* to live in New Orleans?"

Logan chuckled at the incredulity in her tone. "Nikki, the

people who live in New Orleans know how to celebrate a storm as well as a sunny day. And those people are the only kind to be around. Why do you think our most famous drink is called a hurricane? Here life is praised and blessed just as it comes—and people just as they come."

"I wish we'd moved here instead of to Bayou Beltane," Nikki said.

"Why do you say that, Nikki?" Joanna asked, sitting forward in surprise at the sudden wistfulness in her daughter's tone.

Nikki didn't answer, just shrugged and looked out at the river. Joanna had seen this reaction often. It always came after she asked her daughter a question about how she felt. Nikki never answered such questions.

Joanna sat back, letting out a deep, silent sigh. Nikki needed help. With so many things. Joanna knew the fact that she had allowed Steven to mistreat her meant she had some deep-seated problems.

And now on top of them, she had to deal with his death and with her being blamed and tried for it.

She must be feeling awful. Why did she hide everything beneath this stoic mask of emotional indifference?

Joanna had hoped that she could breech the gulf that lay between them and give Nikki the help she needed. But it wasn't happening. If Nikki was going to be reached, Joanna knew it would have to be someone else who reached her.

It hurt Joanna to have to admit that it couldn't be her. All her life she had accepted the responsibility of handling whatever problem came along.

But for the first time she realized that being willing to take on a responsibility wasn't enough—she had to be qualified to do it. She wasn't.

Nikki needed someone else.

And Joanna needed to find that someone else. Soon.

TALLIE ARBOUR STOOD in front of the district attorney feeling like a kid who had been called into the principal's office. And not liking it one bit.

"What were you thinking?" he demanded, leaning across the desk to glare at her. "You can't possibly be ready to try the Nikki Gideon case by the end of June!"

"I'll do it," Tallie said calmly.

"What you'll do is get your butt kicked and make us all look like incompetents!" He rose out of his chair and shoved it against the desk. "This case is a heater, Tallie. She's Philip Delacroix's grandchild, for crying out loud!"

"I'm aware of that, sir."

"If she gets off because you were unprepared, the media is going to be accusing us of bribes and who knows what else. Do you understand what that kind of wild talk can do to me in an election year?"

"I'll be prepared, sir. I've been in court all afternoon getting continuances on my other cases. I've pulled Tom Smith off of everything else so he can assist."

"What makes you think that will be enough? You're up against Logan Weston, the luckiest damn lawyer in Louisiana, *and* he's got Delacroix money behind him. Hell, Weston could bring in an army of lawyers to oppose you!"

"He won't. Weston always works alone."

"Who's the lawyer I saw second-seating him this morning?"

"She's the girl's mother—from California. Probably just along for comfort. Look, sir, that chief of police from the North Shore did a damn good job. He has an eyewitness who places Nikki Gideon at the scene. He even got a confession."

"Logan pled her not guilty. He's obviously going to find a way to squelch that confession."

"Even if he does, the medical examiner's report is competent and clear-cut. The murder weapon was found at the scene with the girl's prints on it. I've had the car she was driving brought over here to the Crime Lab Cage so that a thorough forensics can be done by our people. I have everything in my hands to make this case against Nikki Gideon."

The D.A. sat down again. Tallie knew her arguments were beginning to convince him. "What does Weston have?" he asked.

"Whatever it is," Tallie said, "it isn't enough. He purposely put me in a crunch with this June trial date, figuring I'd have to drop the charges because I wouldn't be ready. I'll be ready. Now *he* has to scramble to get ready."

"I still don't know why you fought so hard to get this one, Tallie. What is it about this case?"

"It's personal, sir."

"Now, you listen to me, Tallie. We do a job here representing the people. We do not get on personal bandwagons. If you have some ax to grind, I'm kickin' your butt off this case."

Tallie thought about how best to answer her boss. If she told him the truth, he certainly would pull her off the case. If she didn't tell him the truth and he later found out, there would be hell to pay. And she'd be the one paying it.

Still, the chances of anyone finding out were really pretty slim. She wanted this case too badly to give it up. She was going to play the odds.

"Sir, Logan Weston beat me out the last time we went up against each other only because he got lucky. He's not going to get lucky this time."

The D.A. smiled. He had no problem with competition between his prosecutors and the local hotshot attorneys. Matter of fact, he encouraged it. Tallie knew the D.A. believed it gave his people the incentive they needed to win.

Which was why she was using this as her excuse. That plus the fact that she also knew it stuck in the D.A.'s craw that Weston kept besting his team time and again.

"So you're planning on ending that lucky streak of Weston's, is that it?" the D.A. asked, his eyes glittering.

"Yes, sir."

He came forward in his chair. "Kick his butt, Tallie, and I promise I'll buy you the best damn dinner in New Orleans."

"That would be at the Commander's Palace in the Garden Room," Tallie said, smiling. "You'd better be prepared. I'm ordering the most expensive thing on the menu."

"WHERE'S NIKKI?" Logan asked Joanna as she returned to the dining room in her home, carrying two tall glasses of iced tea.

"She's with a tutor," Joanna said as she set their glasses on coasters among the papers they were reviewing.

"A tutor?"

"The moment her private school heard about her indictment, she was expelled. I'm doing what I can to keep her current on her schoolwork."

Logan detected no change at all in Joanna's calm voice or manner as she slipped into a chair across from him.

"How did Nikki take being expelled?" he asked.

"How Nikki takes everything these days. With a stoic nonchalance that she can't possibly feel."

Just like her mother, Logan thought, but he didn't say it.

Joanna was looking down at the various reports and papers from the D.A.'s office that were spread out before them. She wore a simple blue silk dress that looked anything but simple on her. It swelled gently over her breasts and hips and was gathered beneath a belt that circled her slim waist.

Logan watched her because her eyes were averted. And because he found it too irresistible not to. He'd given her his word that he would not kiss her again. But he hadn't said anything about not looking.

The light from the window shimmered through the rich brown velvet of her hair. Her thick lashes swept shadows across the buff cream of her high cheekbones. Her lips were the color of ripe cantaloupe, natural, unpainted, spread soft and smooth one minute, pursed firmly in concentration the next.

Her head came up suddenly, those clear, vivid cobalt eyes trained directly on him. Logan felt the unexpected contact sparking through his body. Joanna was wrong. Whatever this insanity was between them, it was proving to be anything but temporary.

"Who's Nikki's tutor?" he asked, the only marginally sane question that he could pull out of his singed thoughts.

"Her name's Holly. One of my cousins introduced her to

us a couple of months back. Nikki seems comfortable with her."

"Is that why you selected Holly?"

"That and the fact that she was sweet enough to offer to help. That's saying a lot these days. Flora has been spreading some pretty nasty tales about Nikki. There are a lot of folks in Bayou Beltane who appear only too ready to believe them."

"What kind of tales?" Logan asked.

Joanna took a deep breath and let it out slowly. Her voice remained even, but Logan knew she was controlling it. "That Steven never wanted to have anything to do with Nikki. That it was Nikki who went after him."

Logan laid his hand over Joanna's. "Don't worry. We'll bring out Steven's true character in court. We'll put *him* on trial. He's the one who rightfully should be. We'll show the jury that Steven was responsible for his own death."

Logan felt the enticing warmth of Joanna, both in her gaze and beneath his hand. He also felt the impact of the assurances he'd just given her.

He quickly withdrew both his hand and eyes from hers, quietly cursing himself. He couldn't afford to touch Joanna or give her assurances—no matter how much he wanted to.

"What's Holly's background?" he asked by way of changing the subject. "I assume she's qualified as a tutor?"

"She's way overqualified. Holly's a practicing psychologist who specializes in family counseling."

Logan's eyes returned to Joanna's face. "Don't you think it will be obvious to Nikki what you're trying to do by putting her together with Holly?"

"I told Nikki straight out. She accepted Holly as her tutor on her studies because she knows and likes her. Holly won't pressure Nikki into talking if she doesn't want to. And neither will I. No matter how much I want to."

A sudden, astonishingly sad look overtook Joanna's eyes—a glimpse of all the agony she felt and concealed. And then in the next instant it was once again safely locked behind that solid vault of her cool control.

How had she learned to do that? What had made her learn to do that? And why did this woman's way of bearing her sadness so quietly, so bravely, affect him so strongly?

"There's a lot here to make sense out of before we go to trial," she said after a moment. "I assume you'll be filing a motion to suppress Nikki's confession to Chief Trahan?"

"Already done. The jury will never hear Nikki's emotional outburst. Trahan clearly came to your home suspecting Nikki was involved in Steven's death. Yet he did not advise Nikki of this nor did he read her her rights before he questioned her. Anything she said to him is inadmissible in court."

"Jake was probably trying to be gentle with Nikki. You realize he's married to my sister, Annabelle?"

"That's not going to give us reason to cut him any slack. He didn't cut Nikki any. You've read his investigative reports. He's systematically focused on gathering the evidence against her to put her away for life."

Joanna took a deep breath and let it out slowly, obviously holding on to that tight control that was so much a part of her.

"Annabelle called to say how sorry she was," Joanna admitted after a minute. "She says Jake's doing what he believes he must, but he's not sleeping at night."

"Well then, he should sleep a lot better after I get through tearing him apart on the stand."

Joanna blinked at Logan in surprise. He understood why. For once he hadn't been able to keep the anger out of his tone.

"I can't wait to watch," she said, surprising him in turn. "In case I haven't told you, Mr. Weston, I'm very glad you decided to stay on as Nikki's attorney."

"Then call me Logan. I promise it won't go to my head."

Joanna smiled. "All right, Logan."

The warmth of her smile, the sound of his name in her silky voice sizzled like a white heat through his body. And went right to his head. So much for his promise. What had made him so foolish as to move them to a first-name basis?

Silly question. That approval she wore in her eyes for him had. Still, he was confident he could control his attraction for her.

Joanna was his colleague. Working with her over the last couple of weeks had shown him her intelligence and competence. He'd surreptitiously looked into her record from California. It was exceptional. She'd not only handled but had won several very difficult murder defenses. He liked the fact that she hadn't mentioned her record. She obviously didn't feel the need to boast about her accomplishments.

He liked the way she listened to him, too. Even when she didn't agree, she still abided by their agreement to let him have the final decision. She was true to her word.

He would be true to his word.

He also wanted to show her—and himself—that he could be friendly without being too friendly, that there was a middle ground here where they could interact as colleagues.

Because they had to interact as colleagues. Nikki's life was at stake. He knew it was too late to hand this case over to another attorney. They were going to trial in two months. No one else could hope to come up to speed. Logan forcibly refocused his attention back to the papers in front of him.

"My brother, Drew, has offered his office staff should we require secretarial assistance," Joanna said.

"Why don't you sound more enthusiastic about Drew's offer?"

"I...appreciate his gesture," she said carefully. "His office staff could come in handy."

"But not his legal skills?"

"My brother is a fine attorney when he puts his mind to it."

"And when he's not putting his mind to it, what is he?" Logan asked.

"He's still my brother," she said softly.

"Your brother works for your father, doesn't he?"

"Yes."

"Is that why you're not close to him?"

"It's not important," Joanna said.

But, of course, Logan knew it was. Joanna obviously did

not get along with her father and brother. And he'd just bet the reason was a good one.

"You are discreet about your problems with your family. I respect that. But if there is something that I should know—"

"I'll tell you." Joanna spoke quickly, with a thick verbal period on the end of her sentence.

Logan rather admired her discretion. No matter what her differences with her father and brother, Joanna had a core of family loyalty inbred into her Southern soul.

She reminded him a lot of his maternal grandmother.

Logan could still hear Grandma Siddon's slow-as-taffy tones inside his head admonishing him to always respect his ancestors and stand up for those who shared his blood—whether they be saint or sinner, and particularly if they be sinner.

"The toxicology reports on Steven are not in yet?" Joanna asked, flipping through the papers sprawled across the dining room table.

"No. I'll call again tomorrow to see what's holding them up. I've requested enough samples of everything to duplicate the tests using our own technician. I never blindly accept what police toxicologists report. They can get sloppy from overwork or underconcern."

"I share your view," Joanna said. "Who do you use?"

"A New Orleans lab run by Marvin Dotella."

"Dotella? Isn't he the one whose articles on the science of blood splatter and DNA typing are used as textbooks by most toxicology labs?"

"The very same," Logan said. "His credentials go on for miles. He's very impressive in front of a jury."

"I'm surprised he's agreed to testify for you. I've heard he's unreachable."

Logan shrugged. "We have mutual friends. We did get the forensic reports on your car."

"Anything important?"

"Yes. This."

Joanna leaned across the table to see where Logan was

pointing. With her she brought that intoxicating scent combination of spring and woman and pale pink rose.

"You mean this notation about the grease on the passenger seat?"

Logan once again had to concentrate on collecting his scattered thoughts. "Yes. It matches the grease and general shape of the tire iron that Nikki struck Steven with."

"When Nikki told us about that night, she said she put the tire iron on the passenger seat after she changed the flat tire."

"But why did she put it on the seat, Joanna? And if she changed a flat, why don't the clothes she wore that night show any grease stains?"

"They don't?" Joanna reached for the papers. She found the report and read it. "I don't understand."

"It doesn't fit in with what Nikki has told us."

"You think I lied to you?"

Logan turned in surprise at Nikki's voice. He hadn't heard her arrive. She was standing in the doorway to the dining room, her hand on her hip, her face full of defiance.

Joanna immediately rose. "Logan isn't saying that, Nikki. As your attorneys, we're both just trying to make sense of things. Now, please, won't you come in, sit down and help us?"

Nikki hesitated a moment before she pulled out the closest chair. She slouched against its back, her arms wrapped across her chest in a defensive gesture.

Logan rather admired the fact that Joanna had not let her calm, even tone vary when she spoke to her daughter. By her own actions, she had simply showed Nikki how to act.

"I didn't hear Holly's car," Joanna said once they were all seated.

"She dropped me off down the lane," Nikki explained.

"Would you like an iced tea?" Joanna offered.

Nikki shook her head. "I had a Coke a little while ago."

Joanna looked to Logan. Her expression said it all. She had soothed Nikki's ruffled feathers. She was now ready to hand her daughter over to him for questioning.

"Nikki, I need you to explain some things," Logan said. "There are several details about that night Steven died that are unclear. I believe they could be important to your defense. I know you'll be repeating yourself, but this is necessary. Will you go over them for me?"

"Yeah," she said, her previous sulky tone mellowing. "Sure."

"What time did you leave the house?"

"About ten-fifteen."

"Describe everything you did."

"I took Mom's car keys and—"

"Where were your mother's keys?"

"Where they usually are. In the crystal candy dish next to the Tiffany lamp by the front door."

"Weren't you afraid your mother might hear the sound of the engine starting?"

"No, I always released the handbrake and rolled the car out of the garage until it was way down the lane before starting up the engine."

"So after you started the engine, then what?"

"I drove over to the lake."

"What route did you take?"

"There's only one way to get out there by car. You follow our road out to the highway, go south two miles and then take the second exit. It's a dirt road that leads to the old bridge at the northern end of the lake. On the other side of the bridge is a small cleared section. It's where we always parked—Steven and I."

"Where did you get the flat tire?"

"About a mile down the highway just before the turnoff."

"You stopped to change the tire on the shoulder?"

"Yeah. I opened the trunk and got out the tire iron. I was just about to get out the spare and jack when this truck pulled over to the shoulder and this guy got out."

"What guy?"

"Just some guy. He never told me his name. He put down some flares and then came over to the car and offered to change the flat. I let him. I'd never changed a flat before.

Mom's car is this classic 1959 Mercedes Sedan 220SE. It belonged to my grandmother, and Mom treats it like a family heirloom. I was afraid of scratching the bumper or something.''

"What did this man say to you while he was changing the tire?''

"He didn't say anything. Just kinda whistled and hummed to himself. He was cool. Most adults would have lectured or grilled me about why I was out late and alone.''

"Can you describe this man?''

"A little taller than me. Kinda stocky. His hair was dark, curly.''

"What was he wearing?''

"Jeans. A black windbreaker. Boots, I think.''

"Age?''

"Kinda old. Twenty-five for sure. Oh, and he called me *cher* when I thanked him. 'My pleasure, *cher*,' he said. Cajuns talk like that, don't they?''

"Yes, they do. What direction was he going on the highway?''

"South. Like me.''

"And after he fixed your tire, did you notice if he turned off up ahead or followed the highway into town?''

"He waited for me to start my car and followed me until I turned off. Then he waved and went on.''

"When you first told us about that night, you said you had left the tire iron on the passenger's seat. Is that correct?''

"Yeah.''

"Why?''

"Because the guy used the jack and tire iron from the back of his truck to change the tire. When he put the flat into Mom's trunk and closed it, I was still holding on to the tire iron.''

"Why didn't you reopen the trunk and put it inside?''

"The guy was walking back to his truck. He told me he'd follow me until my turnoff. I didn't want to make him wait while I opened up the trunk again, so I just got in, threw the tire iron onto the passenger seat and drove off.''

"Did this guy see you holding the tire iron?"

"Yeah, I guess. It would have been kinda hard to miss."

"We're going to need to find this man. Is there anything else you can tell me about him?"

Nikki shook her head.

"How about his truck?"

"It looked old. Kinda beat up."

"What year?"

"Don't know."

"Color?"

"Dark, maybe. I can't be sure. It was night. I didn't really look at it closely."

"How about the license plate?"

"Louisiana, I think. Why does any of this matter? All he did was change my tire."

"He can testify that you had a flat."

"The blown tire was in the trunk. The police had to have seen it when they looked over Mom's car."

"The flat could have happened at another time. This man can prove you got it on the night Steven died. He must have seen you holding your mom's tire iron. He can testify that when he closed the trunk, he didn't give you a chance to return the tire iron to it."

"So?"

"So, this man's actions give you a plausible reason for putting the tire iron on the passenger seat of your mom's car."

"Why do I need a plausible reason?"

"Because the prosecution is going to try to ascribe another reason to that tire iron being there. Think about it, Nikki. They found no evidence on your clothes that you changed a tire. They're going to think that you took the tire iron out of the trunk for the sole purpose of using it on Steven Boudreaux."

"But I'd thought everything was going to be all right between Steven and me that night. I didn't know he was going to show up drunk."

"I realize that, Nikki. But the jury is going to look at the evidence and listen to the prosecution's explanation for it."

"But it's not true," Nikki protested.

"That's why we must find this Good Samaritan of yours. He can help explain to the jury what the evidence really means."

"How are we going to find him?"

"Last time you saw him he was traveling down the highway into Bayou Beltane. That could mean he's local. Let's say we advertise and find out."

"In the *Bulletin*?" Nikki asked.

"Would be nice to see Gator Guzman's gossip rag serving a useful purpose for a change," Logan said.

"What kind of ad?" Joanna asked.

"I was thinking of something like 'Wanted. Good-hearted Cajun who rescued me from flat tire at about ten-thirty Sunday night, March 29, on Bayou Beltane Highway. A reward awaits you if you call, et cetera.'"

"I don't know," Joanna said. "This man doesn't strike me as someone who does things for a reward. Consider. He saw a young woman alone on a highway at night, facing a flat tire. He stopped to help like a real Good Samaritan. He kept his distance. He didn't ask questions. He didn't talk about himself. He just did his good deed, saw Nikki safely to her turnoff and went on his way. I don't think the offer of a monetary reward would bring him forward."

"I see your point," Logan said. "Do you have a suggestion as to what might?"

"How about, 'Looking for good-hearted Cajun who rescued me from flat tire at about ten-thirty Sunday night, March 29, on Bayou Beltane Highway. Only you can help me out of a jam with my parents. Please call! Urgent!'"

"Yes," Logan said. "And by using the plural 'parents' that points it away from Nikki. Should we sign it 'Damsel in Distress'?"

"That would be perfect," Joanna said. "But what telephone number can we use?"

"Not one of ours," Logan said. "All it takes is a nosy

someone looking up the number in a reverse directory to find out who it belongs to."

"And I wouldn't put it past Gator Guzman to do just that if he smelled a story behind the ad," Joanna said with a nod. "So how do we get the ad in the *Bulletin* without tipping Gator off that it's from us?"

"I know a lady in New Orleans who will be happy to place the ad and use her name and number."

"Is there a way Guzman would be able to trace this lady to you?" Joanna asked.

"He could. But I doubt he has the connections to do it. And if Gator—or anyone but our Cajun—calls and starts asking questions, believe me, this lady will not let him get a thing out of her."

"She sounds formidable."

"She's my grandmother, a direct descendant of a Confederate general. And it shows."

Joanna's lips curved into a smile.

Logan forced himself to look away from that smile and focus on writing down the text they had discussed. He had no sooner finished than he heard the sound of a car pulling up on the gravel in front of the garage.

Joanna rose and went over to the window. A car door slammed.

"It's Holly," Joanna said. "She's carrying your backpack, Nikki. You must have left it in the car."

"I'll go let her in," Nikki said, getting up and leaving the room to do so.

Joanna sat down again. "It's still early enough to get the ad in tomorrow's *Bulletin*. Shall I bring you the phone so you can call your grandmother and—"

The loud cry of anguish coming from the direction of the front door stopped Joanna in midsentence. Logan sprang to his feet and raced to the front of the house.

Nikki was standing in the open doorway, her back to Logan. Facing her stood a young woman with a red backpack who was glaring down at the doorstep in obvious dismay.

Logan's eyes skittered over the young woman to stare at

the stuffed doll lying at her feet. It had long walnut brown hair and matching eyes and was dressed in jeans and a sweatshirt. It looked like Nikki.

It also had a half dozen sharp pins sticking through it.

CHAPTER EIGHT

"MAY I GET YOU ANYTHING, Holly?"

"Joanna, please don't go all Southern on me and insist on playing the perfect hostess in any circumstance. You've had a shock just as Nikki has. Let's sit down and talk about it."

Joanna nodded and sank gratefully onto the living room sofa.

She and Holly were alone now. Logan had left for Chief Trahan's office with the voodoo doll wrapped in a plastic bag. Nikki had run upstairs and locked herself in her room.

Holly came over to sit next to Joanna. She was a petite five-five with shoulder-length reddish brown hair and gray-green eyes full of caring—the kind of eyes one felt one could trust.

"Tell me what happened when you went upstairs to talk to Nikki just now," Holly said.

Joanna appreciated the genuine note of concern she heard in Holly's voice. From the moment Joanna had met the family counselor, she'd liked her.

"The same thing that always happens, Holly. She refused to talk to me. Did she say anything to you when she saw the voodoo doll?"

"After her initial cry of horror, she fell silent. Whatever continuing shock and fear she feels, she's buried it beneath that protective mask of stoic strength she wears."

"Why would she feel she has to wear such a thing? Has she talked to you at all, Holly?"

"No, Joanna. I think Nikki believes that she has to handle her emotional problems on her own."

"How can we help her if she won't talk?"

"There are some things we don't need her to tell us. The reasons for someone like Nikki tolerating abuse from her boyfriend are pretty well documented. Nikki was obviously willing to trade the affection Steven gave her for the pain. She didn't think she could do any better."

"But that doesn't make sense, Holly. She's pretty, smart—"

"And she's an outsider here in Bayou Beltane."

Joanna looked at Holly in surprise. "Bayou Beltane is our home. With the exception of my mama, all her family is here. How could she be an outsider?"

"Family is important, Joanna. But friends are even more important to someone Nikki's age. When your husband died, you brought Nikki home—at least to what you thought of as home. But Nikki was born and raised in California. When she came to Louisiana, she was leaving her home. She was facing her father's death and the loss of her friends all at the same time."

"I...I never stopped to think of that."

"You were probably too lost in your own grief to think clearly. Kids don't uproot well at her age. Do you remember what it was like when you moved to California as a teenager?"

"It was rough for a while."

"And you didn't have to contend with a small town like Bayou Beltane, where most everyone knows one another."

"Nikki's been an outsider all this time," Joanna murmured, shaking her head, ashamed of herself for not having seen it.

"And probably pretty lonely because of it," Holly said.

"Why didn't she tell me any of this?"

"Nikki's quietness is odd. Most teenagers would have been complaining their heads off. Has she always shut you out, Joanna?"

"The last several years she's barely seemed able to tolerate me, much less communicate with me."

"Was this true even before her father died?"

"Yes, but it's been even worse since his death. I tried to

comfort her. She wouldn't let me come close. Holly, if I had only known, I never would have moved us here. Why won't she trust me enough to share her feelings with me?"

"I don't believe this lack of emotional closeness between you two is because she doesn't trust you."

"Then why won't she talk to me about her feelings?"

"When was the last time you talked to Nikki about *your* feelings?"

"I tell her what I think all the time."

"Not what you *think*, Joanna. What you *feel*."

"I'm not sure I understand what you're saying."

"Joanna, in the months I've known you, I've learned that you're a lawyer, a widow, that you collect antique clocks, don't eat junk food and exercise regularly. You've shared these personal facts with me. But not once have you ever said how you feel about any of them."

"I'm not used to talking about my feelings, Holly."

"Talk to me about them now, Joanna. Tell me about your husband. Your life together. How he died."

Joanna rubbed her palm nervously across the fabric-covered arm of the sofa. "I thought we were going to talk about Nikki."

"This is about Nikki. Trust me."

Joanna did trust Holly. Which was why she took a deep breath, sat forward on the sofa, leaned her forearms on her knees and did as she asked. "Richard and I fell in love slowly, gently, perfectly. We married in my third year of college. Had Nikki in my fourth. It was the Christmas break during my first year in law school when the accident happened."

Joanna stopped, unable to go on as those awful memories from long ago replayed themselves in her mind.

"Yes?" Holly prodded gently.

"Nikki was eleven months old. Richard and I took her out to the ski slopes. It was her first time in snow. She loved it. I stayed with her when Richard went off to ski. An hour later they came to tell me he had...fallen wrong."

"Wrong?" Holly repeated softly.

Joanna took a deep breath, let it out slowly, concentrated on keeping her voice even. "The accident left him paralyzed. He was twenty-seven when he was put in a wheelchair for the rest of his life."

Joanna suddenly felt Holly's hand resting on her own. "Tell me how you felt about it, Joanna."

The sigh that escaped from Joanna came from deep in her soul. "Like my heart had been hit with a sledgehammer. I wanted to cry and never stop. But I couldn't, Holly. For Richard's sake, for Nikki's, I couldn't fall apart."

"So you didn't cry."

"I had to hold together, no matter how much I was breaking apart inside. I had to be Richard's cheerleader and take care of both him and my child. I had to be strong."

"How well did your cheerleading work?"

"Richard told me many times that my strength during those early dark days was what gave him the will to go on."

"Tell me about afterward."

"Richard continued teaching at UCLA and rose from instructor to full professor. He was a terrific husband and father. We had a wonderful life together. I loved him dearly."

"How did he die?"

"A blood clot. It was…very sudden, unexpected, awful."

"And let me guess. You did not break down. You turned to comfort Nikki, to offer her your strength in her time of grief."

"Except she closed her door on me, Holly. Just like she did today."

"Did you speak to Nikki about *your* grief? Did you share *your* feelings of loss for the husband you loved so dearly?"

"I…couldn't burden Nikki with my feelings."

"And maybe that's why Nikki can't burden you with hers."

Joanna looked over into the clear, intelligent eyes that were studying her so intently. "Holly, are you saying Nikki's emulating me?"

"You never let your pain show, Joanna. You accepted your husband's disability and his death with what must have appeared to others as near superhuman strength. When Nikki faced the tragedy of her father's death, she followed your example.''

"I never thought…dear God!" Joanna exclaimed as the full force of Holly's words hit her.

"Nikki is facing another terrible tragedy, Joanna. And once again she is remaining silent. Being strong. Keeping all the terror and hurt and pain to herself in order to spare you. Just as you have always kept your feelings inside to spare her.''

"What have I done to Nikki?"

"Don't let all that Freudian pseudo-psychology in the movies and TV dramas mislead you. Parents make lots of mistakes that don't do permanent damage. What's far more damaging than any mistake you've made with Nikki is thinking that you can't undo it. You can. The important thing between you and Nikki is that you really love her and she knows that.''

"But does she know?"

"You can't fool kids about something that important.''

Joanna sighed heavily. "So what do I do?"

"Give her the gift of your feelings. Let her see that you're vulnerable to the same emotions she's having. Show her you're not afraid to let them out. That being strong doesn't mean having to deny the pain or the fear or the tears. It's all about example, Joanna. Nikki needs a new one to follow.''

LOGAN RETURNED to Joanna's home just as she was waving goodbye to Holly.

"How's Nikki?" he asked as he stepped inside.

"Up in her room. I'm going to talk to her…later."

Logan heard the subtle change in Joanna's voice as she said those words.

He sensed something had happened to make her sound hopeful and wanted to ask her what. But he realized that to do so would be trespassing into personal areas. He had promised himself he would not do that.

Joanna led the way back into the dining room. "How did it go with Chief Trahan?" she asked.

"It seems your father also has been the recipient of voodoo signs. Someone is trying to make trouble and it's pretty obvious who that someone is."

"Flora Boudreaux," Joanna said. "I won't have her terrorizing Nikki, Logan. If it takes pressing charges, I'm ready to do it."

"First we have to wait until the police can tie that voodoo doll to her. I'm curious how she got it to the front door without our hearing her."

"She probably came and went by boat. There's an old ramp at the end of the property. It's the one Steven tied up to that time. The bayou leads right to the Boudreaux place."

"Joanna, I'd like you to give some thought to your taking an apartment in New Orleans while we prepare Nikki for trial."

She looked over at him, clearly not expecting his comment. "Are you getting tired of taking the Twin Span out here?"

"It's not the commute. I think it might be safer for Nikki if she were away for the duration."

"Safer? You mean because of Flora."

"The woman may be dangerous. And she's not the only one."

"Who are you talking about?"

"Flora Boudreaux's story about Nikki chasing Steven, coupled with the fact that we got Nikki's case transferred to New Orleans, isn't sitting well with some of the local troublemakers who are always looking for some reason to start a fight."

"Did Chief Trahan tell you this?"

"When he took my report about the voodoo doll. He's concerned, Joanna. He's been hearing lots of wild talk."

"I can't let a voodoo doll on the doorstep and some wild talk run us out of our home. That would be like telling people we believe in this ridiculous voodoo nonsense and that we let threats rule our lives."

"I understand and respect your feelings, Joanna. In your place, I would probably be doing the same. Still, I would feel better if you'd consider the move."

"You really read this situation as that serious?"

"Let's just say I don't want to make light of it and later be sorry. And before any more of this wild talk starts to sway our potential witnesses, we'd better get their statements."

"Good point. Who do you want to see first?"

"Rick from Rick's Café."

Joanna headed for the telephone. "Let me call Annabelle and see if Nikki can stay with her while we talk to Rick. I don't want to leave Nikki alone in the house while Flora Boudreaux and others are running around loose."

RICK ROSWELL, the owner of Rick's Café, had a full head of dark hair, a bearded chin and the kind of apple-shaped waist that often developed on middle-aged men. Meeting him made Logan glad he forced himself to make the trip to the athletic club several times a week.

Rick greeted Joanna and Logan with a look that said he really wished he'd been out when they stopped by. He waved them quickly into the kitchen, where the scent of spicy jambalaya from a giant, simmering cauldron met their noses.

A young man with a shaved head and curious eyes was stirring the rich cajun stew. Rick didn't introduce them.

When they reached Rick's small office in the back of the café, he closed the door and gestured for them to take the chairs beside a metal filing cabinet.

"There's a lot of talk going around that Senator Delacroix is going to make sure his granddaughter gets off," Rick said, clearly uncomfortable.

"You believe such talk?" Logan asked.

"It's not sitting too well with some of the folks around town. I have to run a business here. I'm not taking sides."

Joanna leaned toward Rick and smiled, pure warmth and grace pouring out of her in equal measure.

"Of course you can't take sides, Rick. Nor will you let wild talk scare you into keeping silent if there is something you know that should be shared. You are by reputation a man who is fair."

Rick basked for a moment in Joanna's smile and portrait of his character. Logan had no idea if it had been accurate, but he was certain that Joanna's description of Rick had been effective.

"Yes," Rick said, "I always try to be fair."

Joanna leaned back in her chair, her smile intact.

She had just wrapped Rick around her little finger in precisely the same way his grandmother Siddon always did, Logan realized—by attributing a man with sterling qualities he simply had to try to live up to.

"So what can I tell you?" Rick asked.

His attitude had clearly changed from reluctance to helpfulness.

"How long did Steven Boudreaux work for you, Rick?" Logan asked.

"Little over a year."

"What was his job?"

"Cook."

"Where did he get his training?"

"No training needed. The recipes are mine—or I should say my family's. All my cooks need to do is know how to follow the recipes and adjust them for quantity. I teach it all to them."

"Were you satisfied with Steven's work?"

"Yeah."

"Was he dependable?"

"Most of the time."

"And the times he wasn't?" Logan asked.

"Typical stuff," Rick said, leaning back in his chair, folding his hands over his ample belly.

"Like?"

"Calling in on Mondays to say he was sick when he was hungover from too much weekend partying."

"How many times during the last year did Steven call in sick for work on a Monday?"

"On average, once a month."

"Other than those twelve Mondays, he showed up on time and did his job?"

"Yeah."

"Did he drink a lot?"

"He came to work sober and he stayed that way," Rick said, his tone taking on a defensive note. "Otherwise I would have canned him. No one who works here is on booze or drugs."

"Did Steven drink when he wasn't on the job?"

"Don't know. That wasn't my business. All I cared about was the job he was doing for me."

"Who were Steven's friends, Rick?"

"Never met any. I can tell you that he was popular with the girls, though. They were always flirting with him when he went up front to wait the counter to cover for the waitresses' breaks. Even had to let one of my young waitresses go a few months back because she couldn't keep her mind on her business with Steven around. These young ones never last long."

"Did that bother you?"

"What?"

"Steven making time with girls when he was supposed to be working?"

"Naw. He brought the girls in. Good for business. Well, except for the waitress I had to let go."

"When you say 'girls,' what age group are you talking about?"

"Around Nikki's age, I guess."

"Do you know who these girls were?"

"I didn't pay attention to any of them."

"But you did pay attention to the fact that Steven was dating Nikki Gideon?"

Rick shifted uncomfortably in his chair as he glanced at Joanna. "Yeah, well, his being with Nikki was common knowledge."

"Why was that?"

"He talked about it all the time."

"What did he say?"

"He said he was making it with her. That they were even going to get married."

"He said this to you?"

"He said this to everybody. I even overheard a couple of girls at a table talking about it."

"What were they saying?"

"Something about not understanding what Steven saw in Nikki. Plain jealousy on their part, of course. Nikki's very pretty. It was obvious what Steven saw in her."

"Do you remember who these girls were?" Logan asked.

"Naw. Just a couple of the local kids."

"Did you ever see Steven with a redhead?" Logan asked.

"I saw him talking to several around the café," Rick said.

"What were their names?" Logan asked.

"I don't know the names of these kids who come in here. If Steven mentioned their names in my hearing, I didn't take any notice."

"But you remember Nikki's name."

"Well, hell. Everybody knows she's Philip Delacroix's granddaughter. She's not someone you would forget."

"So these other girls that Steven showed interest in weren't daughters of the more prominent families in these parts?"

"Just the local contingent of adoring females. I don't know what that kid had, but he had something that attracted them."

"Did he go out with these other girls while he was dating Nikki?"

"He still flirted with the other girls. I don't know if he followed up on any of the obvious invitations they sent back."

"Rick, were you around that last Sunday afternoon when Steven met Nikki here in the café?"

"Yeah. Dottie, my waitress, had gone home early. I was waiting the counter and doing the cleanup in the kitchen, too. There wasn't much of a crowd. There never is on Sunday."

"So you saw Steven and Nikki?"

"Steven was having a Coke when Nikki came in. He went right over to her. I stepped back into the kitchen for a minute. Next thing I knew, the yelling started. I came out front again to see what the hell was going on."

"Who was yelling?" Logan asked.

"Don't know. It had stopped when I got there. Steven was standing between Nikki and another girl. I thought at first that he'd gotten caught dating them both at the same time."

"Something happen to change your mind about that?"

"Yeah, Steven was telling Nikki that he was just giving the other girl a ride and the other girl was agreeing."

"Who was this other girl?"

"Don't know."

"Can you describe her?"

"Medium height. Short red hair. That's all I remember."

"What was she wearing?"

"What they all wear. Jeans and those sloppy layers of tank tops that hang long and loose and look like they're from Goodwill."

"Had you ever seen that redhead in the café before?"

"Not as I can recall."

"Who else was in the café when this conversation took place?"

"Don't think anyone was. Like I said, Sunday afternoons are normally slow."

"What happened then?" Logan asked.

"The redhead left. Nikki sat down with Steven at a table and they talked a little. That was about it."

"Did you see or hear anything else?"

"No, I went back into the kitchen."

"Did Steven and Nikki leave together?"

Rick shrugged. "Can't say. A few minutes later I came back up front and looked over at the table where they'd been sitting and they were both gone."

"What was Steven doing here that Sunday afternoon?"

"Getting an advance on his wages. His pickup had broken down. Garage was insisting on full payment or otherwise he wasn't going to be able to pick it up that next Monday. He was a hundred short. I gave it to him.''

Logan paused a moment, then asked, "Mind telling us what other staff you employ?''

"Cook in the kitchen today is Pete Peterson, just in from Arkansas. Not the brightest porch light on the block, but he seems willing. I just hired him to fill Steven's position. My only waitress with any staying power is Dottie Bell. You going to talk to her?''

"Yes.''

"I'd appreciate your doing it when she's not working.''

Logan stood up and gave Rick his business card. "You've been very cooperative, Mr. Roswell.''

Joanna also rose. She offered her hand. "Thank you, Rick,'' she said. "Most sincerely.''

Rick's ears turned pink as he gently took her hand. "My pleasure, ma'am.''

Logan held the door open for Joanna as they exited Rick's office, wondering if she handled juries as well as she'd handled that café owner.

As they returned to the front, Logan noticed the guy with the shaved head who'd been stirring jambalaya earlier in the kitchen had come forward to wait on customers. A middle-aged woman in a blue waitress uniform was sitting in a booth at the back, sipping coffee, reading the *Bulletin*.

"That must be Dottie," Joanna said, heading in her direction. "She looks like she's on a break. Let's see if she's willing to talk to us now.''

Dottie Bell was not only willing to talk to them but eager to do so. She gestured toward the seat across from her as soon as Joanna had introduced herself and Logan. Dottie Bell had short chestnut hair and warm gray eyes.

"I was a-wondering whether I should call you," she said, folding up the newspaper and setting it next to her coffee cup.

"Why is that?" Joanna asked.

"'Cause unlike some of the folks in this here town, I know

Steven Boudreaux got what he deserved. That one was no good.''

"Tell us about him, Ms. Bell," Logan said.

"You just call me Dottie. I don't stand on no ceremony. I've been waitressing here for going on ten years. I've seen these kids that Rick hires come and go. They last a year or two and then they're gone. Most of 'em are a bit on the lazy side, but there's no real harm to 'em. But this Steven Boudreaux. Now, he was one piece of work.''

"How do you mean?" Logan asked.

"The way he'd go after all the young girls. I can't tell you the times I sat right here at this table and listened to him lay his lines on 'em. Made me boiling mad, it did. He'd take 'em out, use 'em and then dump 'em.''

"You know that's what happened?" Logan asked.

"Should. He bragged about it often enough.''

"Did you ever try to warn the girls?" Logan asked.

"Well, 'course, I tried. You think they paid me any mind? All they cared about was an older, good-looking guy coming on to 'em. All they wanted to believe was what he was telling 'em.''

Dottie paused to take a sip of her coffee. "Way I see it, he chose these young, inexperienced girls 'cause he could impress them. Talking them into the sack probably was no trouble at all.''

"They must have gotten mad later when he dropped them," Logan said.

"Well, I know one who sure did.''

"How do you know?"

"She was sitting right over there at that counter when I heard her tell her friend what a sleaze Steven was.''

"Who was she?" Joanna asked.

Dottie shook her head. "I never knew any of their names, honey.''

"Can you tell us what she looked like?"

"Short dark hair, lots of earrings. I'd know her if I saw her again.''

"Did you see her again after that day she talked about Steven being a sleaze?"

"No, she never came back into the café after that—at least not during my shift."

"You said she was angry?"

"More cynical-sounding. She'd figured out by then that Steven had just been handing her a line. She was trying to laugh it off, to save face in front of her friend."

"Do you remember what her friend looked like?"

Dottie shook her head.

"How often did Steven have these relationships with the underage girls who came into Rick's?" Logan asked.

"Hard to tell for sure. He flirted with so many. Which ones he ended up taking out I can't say."

"Did you see Steven come on to Nikki?" Logan asked.

"Yeah. Surprised me at first. Not that Nikki isn't pretty and all, mind you. But she wasn't like the girls he usually went after."

"In what way was she different?" Logan asked.

"She didn't wear a whole lot of makeup. Steven generally went after the flashier girls." Dottie paused to sneer. "I suppose he read their preening as an eagerness to be mauled and misused. You know what he said to me once when I told him to stop taking advantage of those girls? He said they were asking for it. The bastard."

"Tell us what you remember happening between Nikki and Steven," Logan said.

"Nikki normally came in by herself, sat alone. Like I said, I was surprised at first when Steven moved in on her. But then I realized he wasn't after an easy conquest. He was after money."

"Why were you so sure that marrying into money was the reason he went after Nikki?"

"I overheard him saying it to one of his buddies who stopped by to pick him up one night."

"What did he say, exactly?" Logan asked.

"Can't tell you his exact words. They went something like he couldn't hang out with his buddy that night because he was meeting Nikki later. His buddy told Steven to blow Nikki off. Steven said he couldn't—at least not until he married her. Then they both laughed and left.''

"How long ago was this conversation?'' Logan asked.

"Late in January, I think. I remember Steven was putting on his windbreaker before he went outside.''

"Who was this buddy of Steven's?''

"Some guy called Eddie.''

"Eddie have a last name?''

"Never heard it.''

"What did Eddie look like?''

"Short. Bony thin. Buzz cut. Lots of body art. Pale, spooky eyes. Chain-smoker. Could barely wait to get outside to light up. He came by to pick Steven up several times.''

"Did you see the car this Eddie was driving, Dottie?''

"Couldn't miss it. Pontiac Trans Am, red with black flames painted on the sides. He'd taken the muffler off. Dang thing started up like a cannon firing.''

"Dottie, would you be willing to testify in court to what you've told us about Steven?'' Logan asked.

"Well, I'd be pleased to. It's about time the folks in this here town heard the truth about Steven Boudreaux—about all those Boudreaux.''

"What do you mean, all those Boudreaux?'' Logan asked.

"You wouldn't believe some of the gossip those Boudreaux have been passing around.''

"We've heard that Flora has been saying Nikki chased Steven,'' Joanna said.

"That's not the half of her lies, honey,'' Dottie said, shaking her head.

"What's the other half?'' Logan asked.

Dottie looked around quickly to make sure no one was listening. Then she leaned across the table and lowered her voice.

"That Nikki lured Steven out to Moon Lake that night so she could kill him. And when she bashed him in the head and fled, it was her grandfather, Philip Delacroix, who finished the job by pushing Steven into the water to drown.''

CHAPTER NINE

SENATOR PHILIP DELACROIX wore a deep frown as he leaned back in his chair reading the letter from his political party leader.

In even-numbered years like this one, the legislature wasn't supposed to be convened until the last Monday in April. But the governor was calling a special session to begin in just two days, a full week before the official session.

Philip's party leader had convinced the governor that the "serious issue of the preservation of our beautiful Louisiana wetlands" had to be addressed immediately. And he needed his good buddy, Senator Philip Delacroix, to back him up on a bold new party program to do just that.

Philip threw the letter across the room in disgust.

"You damn hypocrite! You turned hundreds of acres of wetlands into parking lots last year to 'bring in industry and jobs.' I should know. I helped you do it!"

Philip shot out of his chair and stomped around his office. He had important clients to serve. He couldn't just go traipsing off to the capital at a moment's notice.

But he couldn't ignore a party summons, either. This was an election year. Everyone was already falling over one another trying to be first on the bandwagon for those issues that were going to get the voters' attention.

And when Louisiana politicians jumped up on a bandwagon, they expected to see their friends hopping aboard, too. It was that supportive back-scratching ritual for which they were famous. Yep. Just one, big good ol' boy's club.

Philip couldn't afford to give up his membership in that club. He needed his party's support—and those good ol' buddies in the legislature and the governor's office—now more than ever.

His own seat was at stake. The guy running against him this year was young and energetic. The voters were restless, eager for change. And then there was this damn business of Nikki's indictment and trial pulling him down in the polls.

Lately it seemed like one thing after another was going wrong. He knew exactly who to blame. Those damn voodoo hags and their hexes!

The only good news he'd gotten was finding out that Steven wasn't his son. What a relief! He really was going to have to do something about that lying witch, Flora. All those years she'd sucked money out of him for someone else's brat!

But he couldn't do anything about her now. There were too many eyes watching because of the ruckus she was raising over Steven's death. Jackson had probably done the smart thing by not running them out. It could have backfired on Philip's campaign if word had gotten out that he'd been behind it.

Maybe this early call to Baton Rouge wasn't such a bad thing. He could keep in touch with his important clients by phone. And meanwhile his private investigator could be quietly digging into the backgrounds of the judge and prosecutor assigned to Nikki's trial—just to make sure all the bases were covered.

Yes, being out of town for more than a month could actually be of more help to his campaign and Nikki's case than his presence.

He'd done his best to protect her—more than she would ever know. Now, for both their sakes, the smart thing to do was to disassociate himself from her and her trial.

And hope to hell that Logan was as good as they said.

EDDIE'S MUFFLER PROBLEM had made him easy for Logan and Joanna to find. Jake Trahan had looked into the computer files and told Joanna and Logan that an Eddie Zagget of

Slidell had been ticketed and fined for that bad muffler on his Trans Am on three occasions during the last year.

Logan knew Trahan wasn't helping them out of the goodness of his heart. He was doing it because Joanna had told her brother-in-law that Eddie could very well be a material witness for the defense. Which meant that Jake was going to tell Tallie Arbour about him, too.

Logan knew Tallie would have caught up with Eddie sooner or later, anyway. This way at least he and Joanna would get to him first.

Eddie Zagget lived in a vintage raised Acadian cottage with a large front porch on the outskirts of Slidell. Unlike many of the rare rural French Colonial houses, this one was well taken care of and had not been allowed to deteriorate through indifference and neglect.

Logan's knock on the door was answered by a human growl of annoyance. A moment later the growler opened the door with a Dixie beer can in his hand.

"Yeah, what do you want?"

"Eddie Zagget?" Logan asked.

"Who's looking for 'im?"

Eddie was short of height as well as manners. Around twenty, he wore jeans and a T-shirt, with his dark hair sheared off in a buzz cut. The youth was unshaven and didn't smell like he'd seen a shower recently. His pale, almost colorless eyes squinted behind the smoke swirling out of the cigarette that hung from his mouth. Both of his skinny arms were covered in tattoos.

Logan handed him his business card.

"You're that lawyer who called."

"Logan Weston. This is my colleague."

Logan purposely didn't give Joanna's name. They had agreed on the way to this interview that Eddie would probably speak more freely if he didn't know it was Nikki's mother he was talking to. Eddie looked Joanna over in the insulting way that he probably looked over every attractive female under sixty. The offensiveness of it made Logan want to slug the creep.

He restrained himself.

Eddie's eyes returned to Logan.

"Like I told you on the phone, lawyer. I don't got to talk to you. You want to know about Steven Boudreaux, it'll cost you a hundred."

Logan took a hundred dollar bill out of his pocket. But when Eddie reached for it, Logan held it back.

"Up front, lawyer, or no deal," Eddie said.

Logan tore the hundred in two and held out one half to Eddie. "Only a fool pays before he knows what he's getting. This way we both get happy or we both get disappointed."

Eddie hesitated for a moment before snatching the offered half and turning to lead the way inside.

Logan and Joanna followed him into a living room decorated with empty beer cans and full ashtrays. Logan knew he was in no bachelor pad, however. Audubon prints hung on the walls. The rounded edges of the sofa were protected with fabric slipcovers. Eddie might be messing up the place, but this clearly was not his house.

Their host plopped into an easy chair and put up his feet, cigarette in one hand, beer can in the other. Logan and Joanna sat across from him on a sofa.

"You and Steven were friends, I understand," Logan said.

Eddie shrugged. "We hung out."

"Why?"

"Why not?"

It was clear to Logan that Eddie wasn't exactly going to be a fountain of information—more like a well that was going to have to be pumped.

"Where did you meet Steven?"

"High school."

"What did you have in common?"

"We both coughed on the SATs."

Eddie took a heavy pull on his cigarette, then blew the smoke out of his nose. Logan figured it wasn't only his scholastic performance that he was going to be coughing on soon.

"Steven ever talk about his job?"

"Yeah."

"And?"

"He said it sucked."

"What did he want to do with his life?"

"Have a good time."

"What did he consider a good time?"

"Booze and babes. And whatever game was on the tube."

"You work, Eddie?"

"Off and on."

"Now?"

He paused to swig down some beer. "Nope."

"What did you and Steven do when you hung out?"

"I told you. Chugged down a few while we caught a game. Messed around with some babes."

"What kind of babes did Steven like?"

Eddie smiled. It wasn't a nice smile. "Jailbait."

"Why was that?"

"Said he liked teaching them."

"You two bring the babes back here?" Logan asked.

"Sometimes."

"When your parents weren't home?"

Eddie took another swig of his beer. "You said you wanted to hear about Steven. Why all these questions about me?"

"You and Steven were buddies, right? I just want to know what you buddies did together."

"We partied down."

"What were the names of the babes Steven went out with?"

"I didn't keep no roster."

"Steven ever have a steady?"

"For a while."

"Who was she?"

"Nikki Gideon."

"How did he meet Nikki?"

"He picked her up where he worked. That's where he got most of his babes."

"When was this?"

"A while back."

"Last year?"

"Yeah."

"When last year?"

"Sometime in November."

"How steady was it?"

"Told me he was going to marry her. I never believed it. Hell, the babes were always all over Steven. He could have his pick. And did. He'd have to be crazy to shackle himself to some ball and chain, even if it was made of gold."

"Made of gold?"

"Come on, man. Everybody knows Nikki's a Delacroix. The family's rolling in the stuff. Steven kidded himself for a while that he could be rolling in it, too."

"But he smartened up?"

"Yeah. That's when he dumped Nikki."

"When did that happen?"

"February sometime. I knew it was coming. Only surprise was he kept her around that long."

"Why did he dump her?"

"Got tired of her. Like I said, Steven could have any babe he wanted."

"You ever meet Nikki?"

"She was here once for a party. Talk about uptight."

"Tell us about it."

"What's to tell? Vi was getting a tattoo and Steven was scoping her some is all."

"What happened?"

"Nikki freaked. Copped this possessive 'tude. Man, I knew that babe was trouble right then. Steven must've been crazy drunk to keep seeing her."

"How crazy did Steven get when he got drunk, Eddie?"

"What you mean?"

"Did he laugh, cry, clam up, become Mr. Party, what?"

"I look like some freakin' psychologist to you?"

"You were his best buddy, Eddie. I'm laying out a hundred to find out what Steven was like when he tied one on. Doesn't take a psychologist to describe him, does it?"

Eddie paused to pull on his cigarette and swallow some more beer. "When Steven had a few, you didn't cross him."

"Did he get angry at you if you crossed him?"

Eddie snickered. "I knew better than to cross him."

"So who crossed him when he was drunk?"

"Nobody who knew what was good for 'em."

"You talking about Steven's babes?"

"He kept them in line."

"Are you saying he hit them, Eddie?"

"Look, if he slapped them around some, that was his business, not mine."

"You think he did?"

"Yeah."

"Did you see him do this?"

"I heard about it."

"From whom?"

"A couple of his babes."

"Which ones?"

"Steven did them and dropped them so fast I never paid any attention to their names."

"But you paid attention to Nikki Gideon's name."

"I already told you why, man."

"Did Steven hit Nikki, Eddie?"

"Probably."

"You see him do it?"

"Nope."

"But you think he did?"

"She crossed him that night, man. All that yelling about his scoping Vi. Steven had chugged half a dozen beers. Crossing Steven when he was drunk was not smart. Nikki was asking for it."

"What did you think about Steven making a move on Vi?"

"He wasn't. He was just messing around."

"I heard tell that Vi was your steady," Logan said.

"Yeah, well, she's history now," Eddie said in a quick, irritated tone. A frown creased his scalp as he pulled hard on his cigarette.

"Why's that?"

"'Cause I dumped her."

"When was this?"

"Few weeks ago."

"Why'd you dump her, Eddie?"

"'Cause I got tired of her."

"That's not what I heard. I heard she dumped you for Steven."

Eddie came forward in his easy chair so fast that the ashes from his cigarette fell on the carpet. He didn't seem to notice or care.

"Well you heard wrong, man."

"What's Vi's last name?"

"What's it to you?"

"I thought I might have a chat with her about Steven—like I'm having a chat with you."

Eddie frowned and leaned back in his chair. "I don't know her last name."

"That doesn't seem likely, does it, Eddie?"

"Look, man, I don't have to learn their last names. There's always another one to replace 'em."

"Where is Vi?"

"She split when I dumped her. Moved out of state."

"Is that a fact? Do you know that she went to Steven's funeral?"

Eddie scowled but said nothing as he took another pull on his cigarette.

"Why didn't you go to Steven's funeral, Eddie?"

"Who's saying I didn't?"

"Your Trans Am wasn't there."

"So maybe I don't buy into that stuff."

"What stuff would that be?"

"All that afterlife crap. This is it, man. One shot. Get it all now or you don't get it at all."

"Is that why you didn't go to Steven's funeral, Eddie? Because Steven got it all—your babe included?"

Eddie came sailing out of his easy chair so fast that beer shot out of his can.

"Get the hell out of here! Get out!"

Logan dropped the other half of the hundred on the floor as he and Joanna exited through the front door. He figured he'd got his money's worth.

"I'M CONVINCED NOW that Steven only went after Nikki so he could marry into money," Joanna said, trying to keep the outrage at his treatment of her daughter from spilling into her words.

Logan nodded as he drove away from the Zagget house. "Better we tell Nikki than she learns it later when these people take the stand and testify."

"You're right, of course," Joanna said. "But how do I tell her that the only guy who showed her some attention in town did so because he was after money?"

Joanna hadn't expected an answer to her rhetorical question and Logan didn't give her one.

"How did you know about this girl, Vi?" Joanna asked.

"After hearing Nikki's story about the confrontation in the café, I was curious to see who attended Steven's funeral. I sent a photographer to take pictures of both the people and their vehicles. There were two redheads. The one with short hair drove away on a motorcycle registered to Vi Venia."

Joanna knew she was getting a true glimpse into all the hard work and thorough competence that went into that "lucky" label everyone in legal circles liked to attribute to Logan. He was a thoroughly impressive lawyer. And man.

"So that's how you knew Vi attended the funeral and that Eddie didn't. Did you know for certain that Steven took Vi away from Eddie or were you just guessing?"

"It seemed a reasonable explanation for her attending and Eddie staying away."

"It could have been she went just because she knew Steven."

"The picture my photographer shot of Vi Venia shows her crying. He told me she was the only one who shed any tears apart from Desiree Boudreaux. Flora seemed too mad at Nikki not attending to even remember she was supposed to be grieving.''

"Who else was at the funeral?'' Joanna asked.

"Dry-eyed curiosity-seekers mostly. I'll bring by the photos tomorrow so you can have a look. There were some girls Nikki's age. They could have been the ones Steven dated and dumped. My photographer said none of them shed any tears.''

"Logan, we can show those pictures to Dottie. Maybe she'll recognize the girls she told us about.''

"We'll do that,'' Logan said. "How would you like to meet with Vi now? I have her address, thanks to the registration of her motorcycle. We can swing by and see if she's there.''

"I'd prefer to try to set something up for tomorrow. I don't want to feel rushed when we talk to her.''

"You have something else you need to do later today?''

"I'm…having supper with Nikki.''

"Your sister wouldn't be willing to give Nikki supper if you ran late?''

"I'm sure Annabelle would. But Nikki and I always have supper together. And tonight there are…things I have to talk about with her.''

Logan didn't ask any more questions.

Joanna was relieved. There were some things she didn't feel comfortable discussing at the moment—at any moment.

Still, tonight she was going to have to.

"WE'RE HAVING *WHAT* for supper?'' Nikki asked, clearly taken back.

Joanna set the piping hot, extra-large pizza she had just taken out of the oven in the middle of the small kitchen table. There was barely enough room left for the two plates.

"I don't believe it,'' Nikki said, shaking her head. "*You* made a pizza?''

"Nothing to it,'' Joanna said, pretending to misunderstand. "Roll out the dough. Let it rise a bit. Drench it in spicy tomato paste. Load on the four different cheeses and sausage and pepperoni and olives and mushrooms and—''

"You said pizza was full of enough saturated fat to clog every one of our arteries!" Nikki interrupted, her voice continuing to rise in surprise. "Plus which, it has absolutely no fiber and no appreciable protein for building tissue and muscle!"

"That's right," Joanna said as she retrieved two cans of cola out of the refrigerator and set them on the table.

"Cola?" Nikki said in disbelief. "Since when do you buy, much less drink, cola? It's full of sugar and phosphoric acid that eats away at bones and will end up giving us osteoporosis."

"That also is an exact quote, Nikki. I never realized how closely you were listening to me."

Nikki shook her head. "What's going on?"

Joanna sighed as she sat down. "I'm trying to show you how much I care for you."

"By clogging up my arteries and thinning my bones?"

Joanna laughed, grasping for any excuse to ease the tension stretching every tendon in her body. She felt as tightly wound as the springs in the antique 1850 clock that sat in the corner.

"Tonight I just want to share with you food that you really enjoy eating, Nikki. Can you understand?"

Nikki looked down at the pizza, saying nothing, not seeming to know what to say, how to respond.

Joanna wasn't sure, either. She could feel her courage fading. Was she going about this all wrong? How could she have ever let her connection to this person she loved most in the world deteriorate to the point where she had to grope for words?

"No, of course you can't understand," she heard herself say out loud. "How could you? I never really talk to you. You don't know what I feel, how I feel, do you?"

Nikki's head came up. Her eyes were wide with fresh surprise.

"Something's wrong?"

Joanna rested her forearms on the table as she let out a deep sigh. "A lot's wrong. Nikki, I know now I never should have moved us to Bayou Beltane after your father died. I thought I was doing what would be best for us both. But the truth is, I was so heartbroken at losing your dad that I—" she paused to gulp down the painful lump that had collected in her throat before finishing her sentence "—didn't really think about you at all."

Joanna stared into the dark pools of disbelief that were her daughter's eyes. "It had to be awful for you to be uprooted like that," she continued, knowing she had to say it, desperately pushing to get the words out over the tight constriction in her chest and throat. "To lose your friends, to be put in a small town where making new friends would be so difficult. But the fact that you felt you could say nothing, that you had to just endure it, shames me most of all. Why didn't you ever say anything, Nikki?"

Nikki looked down at her hands. In the very long, quiet moment that ensued, Joanna could feel each painful thud of her heart against her rib cage.

"You moved to California when you were sixteen," Nikki finally said. "You never complained. You stood beside your mother."

Her daughter's words more than surprised Joanna. She leaned across the table. "Who told you this?"

"Granny did when we talked about my moving here."

"You talked to your grandmother about moving to Louisiana?"

"I told her I didn't want to go. I told her I'd rather live with her and Emerson in California."

Joanna slumped back in her chair, new despair filling her chest. "Your granny never said a word to me, Nikki."

"She said it would hurt you to know."

It probably would have. But that hurt was nothing compared to what Joanna faced now because she had not known.

"What else did Granny say, Nikki?"

"She said when she left Louisiana, Uncle Drew and Aunt Annabelle insisted on staying behind with Grandfather. You were the only one who stood by her without complaint. She told me I should stand by you without complaint.''

Joanna sighed loudly, deeply, for once making no attempt to suppress the sound. "I wish Granny hadn't told you that. The situations were totally different.''

"How different?" Nikki asked.

"As the oldest child, I had been a witness to your grandfather staying out all night and coming home smelling of other women's perfume. I watched him break Granny's heart with his infidelities. When she met Emerson, I was so happy for her. But your uncle Drew and aunt Annabelle never saw any of this. Which is why they believed the awful gossip.''

"What gossip?"

"That your granny and Emerson had had an affair while she was still with your grandfather and that's what broke up the marriage. Granny and Emerson were socially ostracized here in Bayou Beltane. Their only chance for happiness lay in Emerson transferring to his company's California branch.''

"Why didn't Granny tell Uncle Drew and Aunt Annabelle the truth?"

"She didn't want to turn them against their father. But it hurt her so to lose them! That's why I went with her and Emerson without complaint. I had to, don't you see?''

"Yeah.''

"But I hated moving and losing all my friends, Nikki. I should have realized what I was doing to you when we moved here. I should have been strong enough to stay in California.''

"Mom, you've always been the strong one. Dad told me that, after the accident, you were the one who held us together.''

"I faced the loss of many of our hopes and dreams when your daddy was paralyzed. But I couldn't face the pain of his death. Every time I turned a corner in our house, Nikki, I ran into the ghost of his smile, his laughter.''

Joanna could feel the tears threatening as the memories swarmed around her.

"I never thought I could feel so lost or scared," she continued. "Until now."

"Now?"

"Nikki, if Logan and I don't show the jury that you didn't commit this crime, it—it…"

Joanna felt the hot tears welling in her eyes. Her automatic response was to hold them in, will them away, to regain control. But she overrode that response. She let them come. Nikki had to see and understand what she was feeling. This bridge to her daughter could only be built with her tears.

"It will break my heart if you don't go free, Nikki," she finished. "I love you, baby. And you love pizza and cola. And next to a broken heart, clogged arteries and brittle bones just don't seem that important."

Joanna could feel the tears falling down her cheeks now as she paused to snap open her can of cola with fingers that shook. She raised the container in a toast, not able to see through the continuing wash of salty waves.

"Here's to you, Nikki," she said, her voice rising, breaking. "The best and bravest daughter a mom could ever have."

Joanna paused, bit her lip, trying to speak despite the awful ache in her chest that had thinned her vocal cords into dry leather strips. "And know this, Nikki. If Steven Boudreaux were here tonight, I'd hug the hell out of him for showing you even some of the acceptance and affection that I denied you by bringing you here. And then, so help me God, I'd cut the bastard's heart out for hurting you."

Joanna never got a chance to drink her toast. She was choking too badly on the tears flooding into her throat—and drowning her heart. This was what she had always feared, why she always held them back. She was out of control.

Blind, sobbing, shaking, helpless, caught up in grief and anger and love too strong, too long held back, she wept.

Somewhere in the middle of it all, she felt an arm wrap around her shoulders. And then she heard Nikki's voice near her ear.

"It's all right, Mom. I'm here. It's going to be all right."

Joanna raised her head. She blinked, her vision clearing for one crystal moment.

And as she saw the sweet tears streaming down her daughter's face, she began to believe that maybe someday it could, would really be all right.

LEONCE LACOUR leaned back in his chair at the Mandeville Real Estate office, flipping through the *Bayou Bulletin* as he waited for a couple from Montana to finish their bickering.

Normally his problems ended when his clients decided to buy. But not this time. The Mrs. had fallen in love with the quiet brick traditional on a cul-de-sac in the River Oaks estates. The Mr. had to have the contemporary with the pool and separate in-law suite in Westwood—with special emphasis on that separate in-law suite. Apparently his wife's mama was coming with them on this move to Louisiana.

It was late. Leonce and the bickering couple were the last ones in the office. Leonce was right certain he wouldn't be getting a sale tonight.

And from these two, probably never.

The real estate agent was not normally an impatient man. But this was definitely a night for boiled crawfish, cold beer and the double-time beat of a washboard and guitar to the zydeco two-step. Leonce sure wished these two would settle on something.

Then a personal ad in the *Bulletin* caught Leonce's eye.

Looking for good-hearted Cajun who rescued me from flat tire at about ten-thirty Sunday night, March 29, on Bayou Beltane Highway. Only you can help me out of a jam with my parents. Please call! Urgent!

Damsel in Distress

Could it be? Leonce wondered. March 29. Yeah, it was just about three weeks ago, when he was driving back from seeing his very pregnant sister, that he'd stopped to fix that pretty girl's flat.

But what kind of trouble could that *petite fleur* be in with her folks? Maybe he just better call and find out.

Leonce was reaching for the telephone when it rang.

"Mandeville Real Estate," he answered. "Leonce Lacour at your service."

"Leonce. Thank heavens it's you!"

Leonce slipped out of his professional tone and into a half drawl laced with Cajun the instant he recognized his younger sister's voice. "'*Tite ange,* this is a surprise. How'd you know I'd be here so late?"

"Leonce, the *bébé*'s coming! Lon left on a trip to Albany last night and I can't get hold of *grand-mère!*"

"The *bébé*'s coming?" Leonce repeated, sure he must have heard wrong.

"*Oui.* And three weeks early!"

"*Bon Dieu, avoir pitié!*" Leonce whispered. He rose to his feet, his stomach suddenly feeling as though it were full of hot sauce.

"Now, don't you worry none," he said in his most reassuring voice. "You call your doctor and tell him you're on the way. I'll be there to pick you up in no more than fifteen minutes. You hear me now, *ange?*"

"Fifteen minutes," his sister breathed in obvious relief.

Leonce hung up the phone and quickly gathered up the Montana couple on his way out the door. "Sorry, folks, but I gotta go. My sister, she's having a *bébé!*"

CHAPTER TEN

LOGAN AND JOANNA FOUND Vi Venia working a cash register at a Winn-Dixie in Slidell.

Vi had a Barbie doll body, all breasts and bones. Her complexion was sallow and her eyes bloodshot. Her black roots drew attention to the fact that her red hair had not been a selection of genes but rather of the brightest bottle at the Clairol counter. The registration record on her motorcycle said she had turned eighteen the week before. To Logan she looked a decade older.

"My mama told ya where I'd be, huh?" Vi asked after Logan had introduced himself and Joanna.

"Yes," Logan said.

"Figures. She hated Steven. Probably thinks yer gonna lay some heavy-duty slime on me about him. That what ya here for?"

"Actually, we've come to ask you about him," Logan said.

Vi turned to Joanna. "Yer Nikki's mama, huh?"

"Yes, Vi," Joanna said calmly, evenly.

"Big mistake letting her take up with Steven," Vi said.

"Why's that?" Logan asked, a little surprised at the candor.

Vi turned back to him. "'Cause she didn't know nothin' about handlin' him."

"How did you handle him?" Logan asked.

"Just like I handled my old man afore my mama packed us up and out. When a man like that drinks, ya git scarce. Or ya git to be his punching bag."

Vi turned away a moment to ring up a couple of purchases.

Logan and Joanna exchanged glances. It was clear that Vi had had far too much of the wrong experiences.

No wonder she looked so much older than she was.

"Tell us about you and Steven," Logan said when her transactions were completed.

"What's to tell? When Nikki dumped him in February, I saw my chance and moved in."

"He told you Nikki dumped him?"

Vi snickered. "No guy like Steven admits to gittin' dumped. They play it all cool like and pretend they did the dumpin'."

"But you knew."

"'Course. I seen him waiting for her private-school van every day afterward. Didn't worry me none, though."

"Why not?"

"'Cause I figured she'd caught on that she wasn't gonna reform him. Thinking she could had to be the only reason she kept him around as long as she did. Nikki's pretty, comes from money. She don't gotta put up with the kind of grief a guy like Steven brings ya."

"What kind of grief is that, Vi?"

"Look, girls like Nikki got no idea what's going on with a guy like Steven. He acts like an angel while he's lying his way into their pants. Then when he don't got to be on his good behavior no more, he hits the bottle and that ol' booze demon just comes a-pouring out."

"And knowing this about him, you went after him, anyway?"

Vi shrugged. "I told ya. I could handle him. I got experience with the type."

"Weren't you going out with Eddie before you went out with Steven?"

"Sorta. Eddie's only got one thing goin' for him, though. His mama travels out of town a lot, leaving him free to filch her booze and throw a bash. I met Steven at one of them."

"How did Eddie react to your going out with Steven?"

"Real whiny, like the loser he is."

"I understand Eddie and Steven were good buddies. Why didn't Eddie go to Steven's funeral?"

"Probably 'cause he was mad at Steven for making it with me. I heard them shouting up a storm about it the Sunday morning that Steven died."

"What did they say?"

"Steven's pickup was in the shop till Monday. All I got is a bike. We drove over to Eddie's on it to use a bedroom for…well, you know what for. His mama was out of town."

"So what did Eddie say?"

"He told Steven to shove it. They argued 'bout it, cussing each other back and forth. Then Steven and me split. He was real mad at Eddie. Good thing for Eddie Steven hadn't been drinking."

"Has Eddie called you since Steven's death?"

"Yeah. He asked me out last week."

"What did you say?"

"In his dreams. After having Steven, no way I'd go back to Eddie the dweeb."

"Other than Nikki, did you meet any of the other girls Steven dated?"

"Nope. After Nikki dumped him, I moved in hard and fast. I wasn't gonna give nobody else a shot."

"What did you find that was special about Steven?"

"He was hot."

"Define *hot.*"

"Ya don't define *hot.* Yer just hot…or yer not."

"Did he ever drink around you, Vi?"

"Yeah."

"Ever get nasty?"

"He give me a cut lip once when I made the mistake of staying around too long. Like I've been telling ya. When Steven drank, he got mean. Just like my ol' man."

"I understand you were in Rick's Café that Sunday afternoon when he and Nikki had a confrontation."

"Yeah."

"What happened?"

"I'd dropped Steven off to get some money from his boss,

then came back later to pick him up. Only I walk in and there's Steven smiling at Nikki like a damn lover. I didn't know what lies he was telling her, but I could see she was close to believing them. So I walked over and put my hand on his shoulder. Nikki freaked, just like I figured she would."

"You did it on purpose," Logan said.

"Yeah. I'd do it again, too. Steven didn't belong with Nikki. He belonged with me."

"Didn't you tell Nikki you were there just to get a ride from Steven?"

"Steven would have dumped me for sure if I hadn't."

"So you lied."

"Look, he met *me* outside afterward. We went over to the bayou and did it butt naked, rolling around in the mud, over the rocks and brush, 'cause we had nowhere else to go. We both got scratched up some, but it was worth it. She'd never have done that for him. It was just a matter of time."

"What was a matter of time?" Logan asked.

"Way I figured it, even if she took him back for a while, she'd dump him again sooner or later and I'd be there. I just never figured she'd…"

Vi stared at her jagged, bitten nails. When she didn't continue, Logan prodded gently.

"She'd what, Vi?"

Her eyes rose to Joanna's. "Don't take no brain to figure out what went down. He got drunk and knocked her around. I'm not blaming her or nothing. Only if it'd been me…"

"You would have handled him," Logan finished for her. He knew she had obviously loved Steven, ugly warts and all.

"Yeah," she said, reaching for some tissue to catch the tears that had begun to flow. "Bastard oughta have been with me—not her. He was no damn good. No damn good at all."

"LOGAN, IS THERE SOME reason you've become interested in seeing where it happened?" Joanna asked as Logan drove over the bridge into the clearing next to Moon Lake.

"I need to get a clearer picture in my mind of the events that night," he said as he parked the car.

Without getting out of the vehicle, Joanna looked around her. It was a beautiful spot on this spring afternoon. The temperature was in the mid-seventies. The sun was high, its mirror image nestled deep in the silver-white water. Through the open window, the scents of boxwood and wisteria reached her nose. Every plant along the shoreline appeared to be bursting into bloom. Birds flittered and sang above in the canopy of trees. The light humid breeze felt like silk against her skin.

"It doesn't seem possible that this place has ever seen death," Logan said, beside her, perfectly reflecting her reaction to the lovely scene before them.

"And yet it's seen two," Joanna said, her voice soft.

"Yes," Logan said. "I read the account in the *Bulletin* of the woman who died here sixty years ago."

"Did you also read that my grandfather was defense counsel on that case?" Joanna asked.

"His only murder-case defeat, as I recall."

"There was no hard evidence against his client. My grandfather seemed to have every one of the prosecution's points countered. He should have gotten an acquittal. And yet his client was found guilty."

Joanna's words hung suspended in the air, like a dark cloud hovering over the beautiful sunny day.

Something had gone wrong with the case her grandfather had tried. Justice had not triumphed. Mistakes happened in this imperfect legal system within which they worked. If another mistake happened in this trial against her daughter…

"We can't think about losing, Joanna," Logan said calmly, firmly, almost as though he had read her mind.

She knew he was right. Dissipating her energy in fear was not the way to protect her daughter. She would need every ounce of her strength for the fight to come.

"Joanna, remember Nikki told us she didn't see Steven's truck that night?"

Joanna nodded. "That's why she thought at first that Steven had left."

"Both Rick and Vi said Steven's pickup was in the shop being fixed. How did he get out here to meet Nikki Sunday night?"

"Someone gave him a ride?"

"His good buddy, Eddie, was mad at him. I can't see Vi offering to drop him off here to meet Nikki."

"He must have come by pirogue, like he came by our house that night to pick her up. Except I don't remember Chief Trahan's report saying anything about finding a boat."

Logan leaned into the back seat and drew out a folder from his briefcase. He thumbed through the papers, found the report he had secured through a discovery motion, and skimmed it.

"Here it is. They found his pirogue several hundred feet downstream. It had apparently been pulled away from its mooring and blown by the storm that night."

"Why didn't they find it the night they found his body? The storm hadn't hit yet."

"That's a good question, Joanna. Let's see if we can answer it."

Logan took a moment to study the papers he held. "According to Trahan's report, a Claudia Landry saw Nikki in your car, speeding across the bridge, heading back toward the highway. Landry drove her car into the clearing and discovered Steven's body floating in the water. She says nothing about seeing a boat."

"It could have been tied to a tree farther down the bank, out of sight of the clearing," Joanna said. "Let me see our copy of the crime-scene photos again."

Logan opened another folder and drew out the photographs.

"Looks like the police did take pretty extensive photos of the bank in both directions," Joanna said after studying the shots. "No sign of a boat."

A frown appeared on her brow. "Logan, isn't it strange

there aren't any footprints along this muddy bank where Steven fell into the water and where he was dragged out?"

Logan searched through all the photos. "You're right. That doesn't seem possible. Not with what we know."

He compared several of the photographs.

"Joanna, look here," he said, pointing at them. "This is Steven's body shot from various angles as it lay on the bank. It was obviously photographed with a strong strobe light at night. You can see the darkness at the edges of the blowup."

Joanna nodded.

"Now look at these two photos," he said. "This first one is a shot of the broken chain and the crystal-heart pendant of Nikki's that was found snagged on a tree limb. And this second is of the tire iron."

Joanna studied the pictures. "Yes, the tire iron was found on the ground behind a tree. That's where Nikki told us she dropped it."

"But notice the difference in the lighting? A strobe light was used here, too, to fill in, but these two pictures don't have dark edges. They were taken in daylight."

Joanna nodded as she saw the differences Logan was pointing to. "Which means they didn't find Nikki's crystal pendant and the tire iron until the next morning. Does that bother you?"

"No. What bothers me is why all these other pictures taken over by the edge of the water are also missing that faint black edge."

Joanna took a closer look at the photos. "You're right," she said after a moment. "They photographed Steven's body on the night he died, but they didn't photograph the lakeshore until the next morning. And I think I know why. Jake's report says he found Steven's body at eleven-thirty. Right?"

"Right."

"He was knocking on my door at midnight to talk to Nikki. That was just about the time the storm hit."

"I see what you're saying, Joanna. You're thinking that he allowed the shooting of the rest of the scene to take place the next morning because of the severity of the storm."

"No, not Jake Trahan. He'd never do a slipshod job. He'd have his people out in a hurricane to preserve a crime scene if that's what it took."

"So you think the photographer was out here alone when he got caught in a deluge, and made the decision to finish up in the morning without telling Trahan?"

"That's exactly what I think."

"Which means they never got a picture of the bank that night," Logan said. "Maybe that's why they missed seeing the pirogue. Let's go take a closer look, Joanna."

They got out of the car and walked over to the edge of the water. Joanna was certain Logan was right about the photographer not shooting the bank that night when she saw both her and Logan's shoe prints clearly registering on the soft earth.

"No doubt about it, Logan. The police slipped up."

"And you can be sure I'll make them pay dearly for it, too, Joanna. What do you know about this woman who found the body and called the police?" Logan asked.

"Claudia Landry? She's a nice little gal. Runs my cousin Remy's bait shop. Claudia's in her early twenties, a bit klutzy and somewhat self-effacing, but I believe quite intelligent. Why do you ask?"

"What was she doing driving out and parking at Moon Lake alone in the middle of the night?" Logan asked.

"Many people drive out here to see the moon on the water."

Logan pulled a pocket calendar out of his shirt pocket, consulted it for a moment, then slipped it back. "New moon was the twenty-seventh. There was no moon on the night of the twenty-ninth. Just high winds and a brewing storm."

"Yes, I see your point. It does seem strange for her to have not only come out here that night, but to have gotten out of her car and walked along the bank."

"And how could she have seen a body floating in the lake on a dark night?"

"Actually, it wouldn't have been dark, despite the lack of a moon. The bridge is well lit at night for safety. The reflection of those lights probably would have been sufficient for her to see Steven's body if she were close to the edge of the water."

"Still, there's something very strange here. Joanna, picture yourself in Claudia Landry's place. You're alone at the lake late at night. The wind's howling. A storm's brewing. Why are you walking along a muddy bank at the edge of the water?"

"That is a good question. She'd have to be a pretty gutsy gal to have chanced the slippery mud."

"Whatever she is, I'm going to have some serious questions for her when she takes the stand."

Joanna turned to look at his profile. "We're going to have to put on a defense, aren't we?"

"Tallie Arbour is too good to rest the state's case on anything less than an avalanche of evidence. Way I see it, we'll establish Steven's character—or lack thereof—with Dottie's testimony about how he made plays for the underage girls who frequented Rick's."

"We'll need at least a couple of them to testify."

"We'll get them. Then we'll hammer home the fact that Steven deliberately pursued and seduced Nikki, with the sole intent of trying to marry into a wealthy family."

"Both Dottie and Eddie can testify to his statements of that intent," Joanna said.

"Yes. And Eddie and Vi can also be subpoenaed to testify to Steven's propensity to get vicious when he got drunk. Since I'm sure he treated other girls he dated in like fashion, when we find them we'll find even more ammunition."

"You'll put Nikki on the stand to tell her story?"

"Never, Joanna. Tallie's deadly against even hardened criminals. She'd chew Nikki up on the cross-examination. Nikki's self-confidence is pretty fragile, and she's still suffering from guilt over Steven's death. Tallie would use both to have Nikki believing it was all her fault again and saying as much to the jury. No, we'll let the other girls' testimony about Steven's abuse paint the picture about how he acted with Nikki that night."

"Will it be enough, Logan?"

"We'll just have to make sure it is enough. Joanna, I need you to do something for me."

"If I can, of course."

"Come back to the car and let's reenact the events as Nikki told them to us. I want a clear picture of what happened."

When they reached the car, Logan opened the trunk and took out his tire iron. Joanna watched as he retrieved a clean linen handkerchief from his pocket and wrapped it around the tire iron before handing it to her.

The care he took to keep her hands from becoming soiled said so much about the man he was. As their fingers brushed in the transfer of the tire iron, Joanna felt a warm, feminine stirring deep inside her.

"I don't remember, Joanna. Did Nikki say she had opened the trunk of your car before Steven came up behind her, or was she just getting ready to?"

"She was in the processing of doing so," Joanna said.

"Which means she would have had the keys in her hand. Here. Take mine."

Joanna switched the tire iron to her right hand in order to free her left hand to take the keys.

"Why are you using your left hand for the keys?" Logan asked.

"Nikki's left-handed," Joanna said. "I assume she would have used her dominant hand to open the trunk."

Logan nodded. "That means she struck the blow using her weaker arm. It makes sense. The wound was not that serious. Okay, you're facing toward the trunk. I'm Steven. I come up behind you and grab your shoulders."

Logan grasped Joanna as he spoke.

Joanna pulled back instinctively. Despite the warmth of the spring day, a shiver snaked down her back and into her legs.

They were play-acting. But she couldn't forget that this had been real for Nikki. All too real.

"Now, what happened next?" Logan asked, seeming to search his memory.

Joanna had no problem remembering. She could still hear Nikki's voice inside her head describing that night. She was afraid she would always hear it. She repeated her daughter's words aloud for Logan.

"She could smell the liquor on him. She told him to let go of her. He wouldn't. His words were slurred, incomprehensible. She tried to pull away."

"Go ahead," Logan said.

Joanna stepped sideways. Logan's grip on her shoulders tightened. Joanna was doing her best to remain calm and in control, but it was getting more difficult by the second.

It had been bad enough hearing all this the first time. Being here in the place where it had happened, playing her daughter's part—retracing her very steps—was bringing it all back.

"What happened next?" Logan asked.

"His fingers were entwined in the chain around her neck, the one holding the crystal heart her dad had given her," Joanna said. "It was cutting into her skin. She told Steven he was hurting her. He still refused to let her go."

"That was when she hit him with the tire iron. Go ahead."

Joanna forced herself to maintain her focus and remember the reason for doing this was to understand everything so that they could help Nikki. But her stomach constricted, making her feel cold and sick as she feigned a blow to Logan's temple.

"He staggered back," Logan said, releasing his hold. "That must have been when the chain broke in his hand."

The image of the beautiful chain and exquisite crystal heart that Richard had given Nikki on her thirteenth birthday flashed through Joanna's mind. The only thing to match the beauty of that gift had been the smile on her daughter's face. Now that happy memory would forever be overlaid with this terrible new one.

The outrage of it ripped through Joanna like a silent scream.

"She next ran toward the trees for cover," Logan said.

Joanna nodded as she turned toward the trees, her legs stiff, unresponsive. The handkerchief was damp with her palm's perspiration. Her heart was thudding unevenly.

I knew I was going to have to hit him again if he came after me. Her daughter's scared words echoed in her ears.

Joanna's brain spun with the effort to remain in control. By the time she reached the tree where the tire iron had been found, she stumbled against it.

She desperately tried to hush her daughter's voice in her ears, tried to will away that night of terror from her own soul. She dropped the tire iron and covered her face with trembling hands.

"Joanna? What is it? What's wrong?"

She opened her eyes. Logan stood beside her, his face full of concern.

She took a deep, unsteady breath. "It's become too... real."

Logan's arms came around her. Joanna leaned fully into the warmth of his chest, resting her head against his shoulder. She took the comfort he offered without a moment's thought or hesitation.

And it felt wonderful. It had been so long since anyone had held her like this, since she had wanted anyone to hold her like this. By the time she recognized that the trembling had been replaced by a distinctive tightening and feminine softening inside her, it was already way too late.

She looked up into Logan's face, suddenly overwhelmed with the alarming realization that she was a woman being held closely by a man she admired, respected, desired.

And he desired her. It was burning in his tawny eyes, in the tightening of his arms around her and in the pounding of his heart over her breasts.

She was struck with the startling and absolute certainty that if she so much as wet her lips or breathed in too deeply, Logan would kiss her again. And more. Much more.

A surge of longing washed through her, leaving her face

warm, her knees weak. She remained absolutely, perfectly still, unable to move a muscle, to draw in another breath.

Then she saw and felt the change taking place in Logan—the cooling of the heat in his eyes, an easing of the tightness in the hard muscles of his arms wrapped around her.

In the next moment he had released her completely and stepped several feet back.

"Forgive me, Joanna," he said, his deep voice rumbling like sudden thunder through the still air. "I'll take you home now."

As she followed Logan back to the car, Joanna found herself confused by many things—not the least of which was his apology. Had he given it to her because he had taken her through the reenactment of her daughter's terrible struggle against her attacker? Or because he had held her and reenacted their struggle against this attraction that lay so strongly between them?

Whatever his apology was for, he had kept his word to her. He had not kissed her again.

She felt reassured. And oddly disappointed. She told herself she was not thinking logically. She wasn't.

There wasn't anything logical about the way she felt toward Logan Weston. Just an ever-expanding wonder at all the feelings he generated in her.

She knew she had been wrong to think that there was anything temporary about the insanity that had led them to that first kiss. Very wrong.

WHEN JOANNA INVITED Logan to join her and Nikki for supper, Logan almost accepted. At the last moment, good judgment prevailed and he stopped himself. But he could no more have stopped himself from holding her that afternoon down by the lake than he could have prevented his heart from beating.

Seeing her control slip had been one of the headiest experiences he'd shared with her yet. He'd always found

Joanna's cool self-possession exciting. Her momentary lack of it had been sheer seduction.

He knew the time had come to face his feelings. He wanted this woman too much to keep telling himself he could never have her. He had to have her.

There was a way. And that way was to get Nikki acquitted.

Once it was all over and Joanna was no longer even remotely considered his client or his colleague, he was going to do his damnedest to disarm each and every one of her defenses and make love to her.

A lot of love to her. A month's worth. A year's worth. Hell, whatever it took to satisfy this damn ache he'd been carrying around ever since the moment he'd met her.

She preceded him to her front door. He tried not to notice the contracting of the slim muscles in her calves, the gentle curve of her hips or how the bright sunlight turned her dark brown hair into a delectable color feast of chocolate and cinnamon and rich vanilla.

She put her key in the lock, opened the door and then turned to face him. The deep blue of her eyes and the rose pink of her lips both caught a bolt of sunlight that hit him straight in the solar plexus.

He was so struck with her beauty that he never saw it coming.

The next thing he knew a wooden coffin was falling from the gallery above, missing Joanna by mere inches before landing with a deadly thud on the bricks of the front porch.

CHAPTER ELEVEN

"JAKE, THAT DAMN COFFIN was rigged by a wire to fall as soon as the door was opened," Joanna said into the phone, her tone barely civil. "Anyone standing directly beneath it when it fell could have been seriously injured."

"How large was this coffin?"

Joanna continued to fight for control as the image of the hateful thing flashed through her mind. "Four by eight inches. Made of pine. Hollowed out. Inside it was another doll made to look like Nikki. There were pins sticking out of its chest, its legs, its head. It was clearly meant as a threat, Jake. Even nastier than the last one."

"I'll send someone over to pick up the coffin and doll right away. Try not to touch it."

"Touch it? I wouldn't go near it with a ten-foot pole. I beat Nikki home by less than two minutes today. Do you realize how close she came to being the one coming through that door? Jake, this has to stop. Now."

Joanna heard the police chief exhale heavily in her ear. "I haven't been able to trace the last voodoo doll to anyone yet."

"We both know where they're coming from," Joanna said, her voice becoming as cold as the anger solidifying in her stomach.

"Knowing and proving are not the same thing, as you know very well, Joanna. Until I have some concrete evidence—"

"What are you telling me, Jake? I'm supposed to sit back and wait until Flora Boudreaux decides how she is next going to terrorize my daughter?"

"Joanna, take it easy. I'm doing the best I can."

"It's not enough, Jake. Nowhere near enough."

Joanna hung up the phone. She was furious—that kind of sick fury that came from being caught in a situation where she felt helpless and ineffectual. She knew Jake was doing all he could under the circumstances. But knowing that didn't make the events she had to live with any easier to accept.

"Go pack your things," Logan said. "I'll find you and Nikki a place in New Orleans."

Joanna turned startled eyes to him as the unbending quality in his deep voice registered.

"Logan, we'll be letting them win if we leave."

"No, you'll be letting them win if you stay. Joanna, never wage war on your enemies' terms. The minute Nikki is no longer in Bayou Beltane, they'll have lost their target and their ability to terrorize you both."

Joanna took a deep breath and let it out with a sigh. "I hear what you're saying, but—"

"While you pack, I'll call and arrange some rooms for you."

He was out the door and heading toward his car phone before Joanna could catch her breath. If he had been anyone else, she would have been offended by the presumptuousness of his words and actions. But he wasn't anyone else. And he was right.

As soon as she made the decision to leave she felt empowered. It was as though she had taken back the reins of control over the situation and was no longer a helpless victim.

The only thing she worried about now was how Nikki would respond to being uprooted again. Joanna headed up the stairs to tell her daughter.

Her conversations with Nikki had definitely improved since the evening Joanna had let down her defenses. But she had to remind herself each time she spoke to Nikki to talk of feelings as well as facts. It still didn't come easy.

"I *feel* badly about asking you to do this, Nikki," she emphasized, after explaining why she and Logan felt it necessary. "I hate making you move again, even for a little while."

"It's okay, Mom. I don't care if we ever come back here."

"You feel that strongly?" Joanna asked, surprised.

"No one my age in school or around town ever liked me."

"Not even your cousin, Cade?"

"Family doesn't count, Mom. Steven was the only one nice to me, and as it turns out, he wasn't really...nice."

"Does it hurt a lot that he's gone?"

"It hurt a lot more before I heard what Dottie Bell and Eddie Zagget said about his only wanting to marry me for money. I guess I was kinda dumb to think it could be for anything else."

Joanna gently rested her arm on Nikki's shoulder. "I know I'm family so I don't count, but I think you're terrific."

Nikki didn't say anything or look at her mother, but she didn't pull away this time.

"You really don't mind about the move?" Joanna asked as she withdrew her arm, not wanting to press the physical contact.

"Mr. Weston said people in New Orleans accept you as you are. Is that true?"

"I don't know, Nikki. But if you want to stay in New Orleans and find out when this trial is over, we will."

Nikki's eyes flew to Joanna's face. "You mean that, Mom?"

"We'll even move back to California if you want."

"But you said it was important for you to be here in Louisiana around family and stuff."

"You're my family, Nikki," Joanna said, feeling tears coming into her eyes, letting them stay. "There's no one more important to me in the world than you."

"You're getting mushy again, Mom."

"Yeah, I guess," she said, reaching for a tissue to blot her eyes. "Didn't know you had such a mushy old mom, did you?"

A smile pulled at Nikki's mouth. "It's okay. Way I figure

it, you're starting through the change, so I'm going to have to make allowances.''

Joanna's head came up with a jerk. "Through the *what?*"

Nikki's smile got bigger.

Joanna grabbed a pillow off the bed and threw it at her. Nikki caught it and threw it back. When Logan came upstairs a few moments later to investigate the squeals and howls, he found them in a full-fledged pillow fight.

"I CALLED EVERYWHERE," Logan said as they walked up a narrow staircase with a rickety banister to the second-story apartment in a stuccoed, pinkish building in the French Quarter. "All the hotels are booked. This was the only rental available and it requires a six-month lease."

Joanna felt the soles of her shoes sticking. She tried to assure herself that all the stairs needed was a good, thorough scrubbing.

"I didn't realize there was such a shortage of available rooms in New Orleans," she said.

"Normally there are plenty," Logan said. "But this is the eve of the JazzFest, the second-biggest bash for which this party town is famous."

"It's when all the jazz musicians come here from around the world, isn't it?" Nikki asked.

Logan nodded as they continued their ascent. "And all the people who want to hear them. You like jazz, Nikki?"

"Funky jazz. And some futuristic. Steven used to play it all the time. He said it was cooler than rock."

Nikki's voice dropped with the mention of Steven's name. Joanna realized that memories of Steven would probably be painful for her daughter for a very long time.

And for herself.

But that playful pillow fight she and Nikki had shared earlier had done much to lift Joanna's spirits.

"The JazzFest takes place on the last weekend in April and the first in May each year," Logan explained as they continued to climb. "It'll begin tomorrow and go through Sunday. Then it will pick up again next Thursday through

Sunday. Until it's over, there will be no vacancies any-where.''

They had reached the door to the upstairs apartment, and Logan put the key he'd gotten from the landlord into the lock. He opened the door and stepped aside to allow Joanna and Nikki to precede him.

As soon as Joanna stepped into the dark, dank place, she understood why it hadn't been rented.

It was a single room, twelve by fourteen, with a bath at one end and a kitchen at the other. The aged gray paint was peeling off the walls. Dark, ancient drapes covered the only window. A thick scent of mildew hung in the still air.

Joanna walked over to the window and drew back the drapes to let in some light. She choked on the dust she disturbed. Neither the drapes nor the window looked like they had been cleaned in decades.

The light filtering through the thick dirt on the panes revealed an equally thick coat of dust over the bare wooden floor. The frayed and dirty furniture resembled rejects from Goodwill.

Nikki stood in the middle of the floor, shaking her head in disgust. Joanna shared the unspoken sentiment. She'd have to scrub down the place and have it repainted and replace the drapes and get some decent furniture to make it even marginally presentable. Still, if that's what it took…

But it was going to take a lot more. That became immediately apparent when she walked into the kitchen, flicked on the light, and a dozen cockroaches immediately skittered across the counters into the dark recesses beneath the chipped cabinets.

Joanna shuddered involuntary.

She felt Logan beside her, taking her arm, gently turning her around. "Let's go. You and Nikki aren't staying here."

"But you said there wasn't anything else available in New Orleans."

"There is one other place," Logan said.

They took St. Charles Avenue past beautiful Greek Revival mansions of the Garden District. When they reached the lower section, Logan pulled in front of a red-brick Georgian house that also combined the Creole features of a lacy and intricate wrought-iron fence and balcony railing.

As they stepped through the gated entry and up to the front door, Joanna read the brass plaque embedded in the red brick.

Logan Clayton Weston III, Attorney at Law.

"This is your law office," she said.

"Part of it is, yes."

He opened the door and beckoned Nikki and Joanna into a lovely hallway of pale peach wallpaper above terra-cotta tile.

"On the right is my office. On the left is a small apartment, which I will be occupying. You and Nikki will be upstairs. This way."

Logan gave Joanna no chance to respond. He took the graceful crescent stairwell to the second story two steps at a time, leaving Joanna and Nikki to follow.

Joanna did so with mounting curiosity. When she reached the top and stepped inside, she was charmed by what she saw.

The two-bedroom, two-bath apartment on the second floor was a subtle, pleasing blend of light neutral colors. Its twelve-foot windows opened out onto the balcony. Creamy canvas blinds were drawn over the French doors. The clean-lined, pale glow of the cypress furniture was sheathed in a matching canvas upholstery. The throw rugs over the highly polished bleached ashwood floors were simple sisal.

Books lined every available space on one full wall; an anachronistic fireplace in biscuit bricks decorated another.

The neutral, blended tones were as practical as they were pleasant. For this was an apartment where sunlight turned everything to white gold and made every other color obsolete.

Logan came out of the master bedroom a moment later, an armful of garment bags in his hands. "I'll be back with your luggage in a few minutes."

"No, we can't possibly stay here," Joanna said, trying to

sound absolutely firm. As much as she loved the place, the idea of putting Logan out of his home was unthinkable.

"There's nowhere else to go," Logan said, his tone the epitome of reasonableness. "At least not until after the JazzFest is over. Here we can concentrate on the case instead of commuting. Nikki will have her own bath, and her bedroom is equipped with extra power for her computer and a Prologic, full-rack surround sound. Check out the speakers, Nikki."

It was as underhanded an exit line as Joanna had ever heard.

The instant he whizzed out the door, Nikki whizzed into the second bedroom. When a loud rock tune exploded through the doorway and Nikki yelled, "Oh, cool!" Joanna knew it was all over. They were staying.

Logan insisted on cooking dinner for them that night, while showing Joanna and Nikki around the kitchen. He made his favorite foolproof stew, court bouillon. His version of it involved lots of shrimp, oysters, tomatoes, carrots, potatoes, celery, rice, three kinds of onions and a whole lot of spices.

Joanna mixed up a batter for buttermilk biscuits that turned a golden brown in the oven and added immeasurably to the good smells around the kitchen. Nikki was in such good spirits she actually volunteered to make a green salad.

When they sat around the dining room table to share the meal, Nikki ended up doing most of the talking, much to Logan's surprise. She had gone through Shari's entire CD collection and apparently shared his daughter's tastes. Nikki chatted on happily about the different rock groups between bites of food.

Logan knew kids who talked were generally happy kids.

But it was more than just being happy with her new room and Shari's sound system. Nikki seemed relaxed here, freer and more open than Logan had ever seen her before. He didn't know why that was, but he took it as a good sign. When her conversation finally began to wind down, he asked her a question to keep it going.

"How do you like the food here in Louisiana?"

"It's the best. But mom's always worried about all the saturated fat and stuff. Dad was under doctor's orders to stay away from animal fat. Mom sure approves of your court bouillon, though. She's eaten a whole plateful."

Joanna smiled. "Nikki's right. It was marvelous."

Logan looked away from the smile on Joanna's face because he was enjoying it and the warmth in her voice too much.

"In California we used to go out to eat every Friday night," Nikki said. "We took turns picking the restaurant. Mom and Dad always used to groan when it was my turn."

"Why was that?" Logan asked.

"'Cause I'd always pick pizza."

"Your pizza-loving gene must have skipped a generation."

"Actually, Dad liked it, but he couldn't have it 'cause of his high cholesterol. It also bothered him that the wheelchair-access ramp at the pizza parlor wasn't designed right. There was this sharp turn instead of a gradual one. It was always a hassle for him to get around it."

Logan looked over at Nikki, trying not to show his surprise. "I didn't realize your dad had been in a wheelchair."

"Yeah. He had an accident when I was just a baby. He couldn't move his legs or hips or anything like that."

Joanna's husband had been paralyzed from the waist down? Logan looked at Joanna, unable to restrain himself in view of the shock of the news. She was calmly sipping her coffee, her expression serene, her eyes looking toward the reflected light of the setting sun, which was gliding through the windows.

"His arms and chest were real strong," Nikki was saying, blissfully unaware of the import of the information she had just imparted. "Dad lifted weights every day. He could lift me up and hold me over his head even when I got big."

Nikki's voice faded into the background. Logan had wondered what kind of a marriage Joanna had had.

Now he knew.

Since Nikki was a baby, Joanna had lived with a husband whose disability prevented them from a physical union. No wonder she came across as being made out of pure steel emotionally.

She would have had to have been.

Logan immediately dismissed the possibility of Joanna having had another man during those years. He knew the kind of woman she was. She had been totally loyal to her wheelchair-bound husband.

He was as certain of it as he was certain he drew breath.

"Mr. Weston, didn't you hear me?"

Logan looked over at Nikki with a start, realizing his thoughts had been receiving all his attention. "Sorry, Nikki. I got distracted. What did you say?"

"I asked if you lift weights."

"Three times a week at a gym," he answered absently, picking up his cup of coffee and taking a sip.

"Mom's into exercising, too. She gets up at the crack of dawn every day to do aerobics."

I'd be doing them all day and night if they were my only physical outlet, Logan thought.

"Do you have a kitchen downstairs?" Nikki asked.

"Yes," Logan said, surprised at the change of subject.

"But you could still come up and join us for meals?"

Joanna's attention immediately shifted from the light of the muted sunset to her daughter's face. "Nikki, we've just taken over Logan's home and crowded him into his own guest quarters. What do you say we give him some breathing room?"

Her voice was calm, the smile on her lips taking away any possible sting from the gentle reprimand in her words.

Nikki shrugged. "Yeah, right."

Despite her agreement, Logan could tell Nikki was disappointed.

She was really a sweet kid once you got to know her.

He leaned toward her and smiled. "Anytime you need a cook, you knock on my door."

The genuine smile that curved Nikki's lips warmed Logan's heart. But when he caught a glimpse of the smile Joanna was sending him, it nearly singed the hair off his legs.

"THIS IS NOT GOOD NEWS, Joanna," Logan said as he leaned over his office desk and handed her the forensic report.

"What's wrong?" Joanna asked as she took it from him.

For nearly two weeks they had been in his office every day, building their case. This was the first time Joanna had seen a frown on Logan's face.

"Look at the blood alcohol concentration," Logan said.

Joanna scanned down the report to the BAC-level entry.

"The BAC is .04 percent?" she read aloud. "That's way below the level for legal impairment. Steven was clearly drunk when he attacked Nikki. Something's wrong with this report."

"I agree there has to be," Logan said. "I'll call Dotella today and get him to do a reevaluation."

"Any word from the Good Samaritan who changed Nikki's tire?"

Logan shook his head. "He must not have been a local man. Our chances of finding him are nil now. I've pulled the ad."

Joanna took a deep breath and tried to control her rising disappointment.

"When is our appointment with that girl who Dottie identified from the funeral photos as one of Steven's conquests?"

"Katlyn Morvant's parents begrudgingly agreed to bring her by today at two. They are still insisting she didn't even know Steven, much less have a relationship with him."

"Their daughter's lied to them," Joanna said.

"Which means if we want the straight scoop out of Katlyn, this interview has to be a formal deposition."

"Who's your court reporter?"

"His name's Bruto. He comes across just like an enforcer for the mob. No one would ever guess he's really a very kind, mild-mannered, hard-working family man with a wife and two kids. If his legal swearing-in of Katlyn doesn't scare the absolute truth out of her, I doubt anything will.''

"Do her parents know this is a formal deposition?"

Logan smiled. "Not yet. Thought I'd surprise them.''

KATLYN MORVANT WAS TINY and trim, her makeup expertly applied, her pretty oval face framed by short, straight black hair that ended just above the three rings in each ear. She eyed Joanna and Logan with a cocky air. It was the same look her father, Clancy Morvant, was sending them.

Clancy was the principal at the Bayou Beltane grade school. He was a short, fussily dressed man with dark moussed hair. His excessive attention to grooming, ruddy complexion, bold red tie and the way he strutted around reminded Joanna of a bantam rooster on display in front of a henhouse.

Clancy explained that his wife, Bitsy, had been too busy to come. They had two younger children, still in grade school, and Bitsy was having to attend to their needs.

For the first several minutes after he entered Logan's office, Clancy stood arrogantly mouthing off in his best school principal's bluster about having his lawyer file a lawsuit for harassment if Logan insisted on putting his family through any more of this ''nonsense.''

Logan relaxed back in his chair and listened politely.

Clancy's final admonition, ''I will put up with no more!'' was delivered with a finger wag at Logan, as though he were a recalcitrant student who had been brought to *Clancy's* office for a reprimand. Clancy then turned to his daughter.

"Katlyn, tell this fool to his face that you didn't even know Steven Boudreaux and we'll get out of here."

"I didn't even know—'' Katlyn began.

"Excuse me, Miss Morvant," Logan said, deliberately interrupting her as he leaned forward in his chair, ''but I'll need your statement to be properly recorded.''

"Properly recorded?'' Clancy repeated. ''What do you mean?''

Logan pressed the intercom and spoke into it. "We're ready for you now, Mr. Bruto."

"Bruto?" Clancy Morvant repeated.

The door to a private room off Logan's office swished open and a six-foot-eight giant lumbered into their midst. The Morvants turned around and stared at him in disbelief. Joanna actually felt her mouth dropping open.

She had never seen such an enormous, scary-looking man. His hair was pitch black, his eyes sooty slits, his skin deeply pockmarked, his features so misshapen and off center that he could have been a stand-in for Frankenstein.

Logan had said Bruto looked like an enforcer for the mob. He hadn't exaggerated. Joanna could imagine this man making cement shoes for his enemies. Easily.

"This is Mr. Bruto, my court reporter," Logan said. "He will be administering the oath."

"Oath?" Clancy repeated, his previous bluster ebbing substantially with every breath.

"A man is dead, Mr. Morvant," Logan said, his voice extra deep, solemn. "Clearly you understand why my inquiries into his death must be conducted with all due legal formality?"

Clearly, Clancy Morvant had understood nothing of the sort. The color was visibly draining from his face. He fell into his chair. Katlyn descended to the edge of hers, grabbing the armrests for support.

Bruto said not a word of greeting but stomped over to the recording machine sitting on the edge of Logan's desk.

Every eye was on him as he heaved one heavy leg over the chair and hit the seat like a sack of falling cement. He positioned fat, sausagelike fingers over the recording machine's keys. His eyes bored into Katlyn Morvant's face. His sandpaper voice scraped against everyone's eardrums.

"Raise your right hand and repeat after me."

Katlyn sat frozen in her chair, seemingly unable to move.

"Miss Morvant?" Logan said.

Katlyn turned toward her father. All her cockiness was gone, replaced by a pleading look in her eyes.

"What in the hell are you trying to do to my daughter?"
Clancy asked, the protective father in him surfacing despite
the fear that stretched his vocal cords so tightly he squeaked.

"This is a formal deposition, Mr. Morvant," Logan said
very firmly. "Your daughter will be testifying just as if she
were in a court of law. Indeed, her testimony today may be
admitted into the record of the upcoming trial. Now, please
do not interrupt again or I will have to ask you to leave.
Mr. Bruto, you may proceed."

Clancy Morvant fell back into his chair, newly stunned.
Joanna almost felt sorry for him. Up until this moment, he
had not had a glimmer how far out of his league he was.

"Miss Morvant, raise your right hand and repeat after
me!" Mr. Bruto commanded.

Katlyn jumped, her hand visibly shaking as she raised it.

"Do you solemnly swear under penalty of perjury that the
testimony you are about to give will be the truth, the whole
truth and nothing but the truth?"

Katlyn swallowed three times before she could get even a
croak to come out. "I do."

"State your complete name and address for the record."

After two more enormous gulps, Katlyn complied.

Logan leaned forward. "Katlyn, you are now under oath.
Anything and everything you tell me must be the absolute
truth. If you lie, you will be guilty of perjury. Do you understand what perjury is?"

Katlyn nodded her head.

"You'll have to answer out loud, Katlyn," Logan said.
"Mr. Bruto cannot hear a nod, and he is taking down your
every word. Now, do you understand what perjury is?"

Katlyn's eyes darted to Mr. Bruto. His were aimed at hers
like two black bullets, cocked and ready to be fired.

"Perjury is lying under oath," she said quickly.

"Perjury is also a felony and may carry a prison sentence
of ten years," Logan added. "If you lie to me today, be
assured that I will petition the court to hand down the heavi-
est sentence prescribed by law. Do you understand?"

Katlyn's face was white beneath its makeup now. Stark white.

"Do you understand, Katlyn?" Logan repeated.

"Yes."

Logan shot his questions out like machine-gun fire. "How old are you?"

"Seventeen."

"When were you seventeen?"

"Last December 15."

"When did you meet Steven Boudreaux?"

"Last October."

"Do you remember what day?"

"No."

"Where did you meet him?"

"At Rick's Café, where he worked."

"Were you alone when you met him?"

"No, I was with my friend Cara."

"Did Steven ask you out?"

"Not the first time."

"When did he ask you out?"

"About a week later, when I came into the café without Cara."

"Did you go out with him?"

Katlyn hesitated, gulped some more as her eyes darted over to her father's. "Yeah."

Joanna heard Clancy Morvant's half-strangled gasp. His ruddy complexion had turned a sickly olive. It was clear to Joanna that up until this moment, Clancy had believed his daughter's previous lies about not even knowing Steven.

"Where did you go on your first date?" Logan asked.

"To a movie."

"Did your parents know you were with Steven Boudreaux?"

"No. I told them I went to the movie with Cara."

"Did Cara know you were with Steven?"

"Yes. She said she'd cover for me if they asked."

"Why did you lie to your parents?"

Katlyn's hands were white from the intensity of her grip on the chair arms. Her eyes pleaded with Logan.

"Does my father have to be here for this?"

Joanna looked over at Katlyn's father. Clancy Morvant was staring at his daughter. He looked like a man watching two cars careering headfirst toward each other, knowing the crash was imminent, and also knowing he was powerless to prevent it.

"Mr. Morvant," Logan said in a tone far more gentle than he had previously used on the man. "There is some coffee in the waiting room if you would care for a cup at this time."

Clancy Morvant nodded numbly as he rose unsteadily to his feet. He shuffled out into the waiting room, closing the door behind him.

Joanna was rather appalled. She knew Clancy Morvant hadn't left to make it easier on his daughter. He had done it to make it easier on himself. He didn't want to hear the truth. Maybe that was part of the reason why Katlyn had never told it to him.

Once he was out of the room, Logan picked up where he'd left off with his questioning of Katlyn.

"Why didn't you tell your parents you were going out with Steven Boudreaux?"

"'Cause they wouldn't have ever let me go out with him. They only let me go out with the dorks from high school and then only to school stuff. They treat me like a child."

"Did you and Steven go anywhere together after the movie?"

"Yeah, we...parked."

"Where?"

"In a vacant lot a couple of blocks from the theater."

"What did you do there?"

"Made out."

"By made out, do you mean he kissed you, touched you intimately?"

"Yeah."

"Did you have intercourse with him?"

"No."

"How many more times did you go out with him?"

"Half a dozen."

"Where did you go together?"

"All he wanted to do was…park."

"At the vacant lot behind the theater?"

"He drove us out to Moon Lake. Said it was more private."

"Did you tell your parents you were with Steven Boudreaux on these six other occasions?"

"No."

"Who did you tell your parents you were with when you were with Steven Boudreaux?"

"Cara. I said we were studying together at her house."

"Did Cara know who you really were with?"

"Yeah."

"Did you have intercourse with Steven on any of those subsequent dates?"

Katlyn exhaled deeply. "Yeah."

Now that it was out, Katlyn seemed actually relieved. Some color was coming back into her cheeks. She released the death grip on the arms of the chair and leaned back.

"Did you wear protection, Katlyn?"

"Oh, yeah. Steven came prepared. He acted like he was being all thoughtful and protective of me. And I was so dumb I actually believed it."

"But you don't believe it now?"

"Hell, no. Steven was only interested in protecting himself. He didn't care about me or anybody else."

"How did it end with you and Steven?"

"I told my folks that I was sleeping over at Cara's one Saturday night. I was going to spend it with Steven."

"What happened?"

"After we had sex, he got drunk. And then he got mean. Started knocking me around. I jumped out of his pickup and ran three miles to a phone to call Cara to come get me."

"Were you angry at Steven for his behavior?"

Katlyn's dark eyes flashed. "What do you think?"

"What I think is not the issue, Katlyn. This deposition is a record of your actions and thoughts."

"All right, I *thought* that bastard loved me. He said he did. But it was all a line. All he ever wanted was…"

Katlyn swallowed, not finishing her sentence. Logan gave her a moment before pressing. "What did he want, Katlyn?"

"Sex. And once he had enough, he didn't give a damn."

"Did you see Steven again?"

"The next day I walked into Rick's and told him it was over. I told him I didn't put up with that crap from anyone."

"How'd he take that?"

"He said I had asked for everything I'd gotten. Then the bastard laughed and just walked away."

"You must have been pretty angry."

Katlyn's hands balled into fists on the armrests. "I could have killed him."

"When next did you see him?"

"Couple of weeks later when Cara dragged me into Rick's for a Coke. Steven was sitting at a corner table coming on to Nikki Gideon."

"You know Nikki Gideon?"

"I know about her."

"What do you know about her?"

"She talks funny and thinks she's something 'cause she's Philip Delacroix's granddaughter."

"Who told you this?"

"Everybody."

"Who's everybody?"

"Just everybody."

"Did you ever talk to Nikki to find out what she was like?"

"What for? I already knew."

"Did you ever see Steven again?"

Katlyn shook her head. "I stopped going to Rick's after that. I didn't want to see him."

"Do you know anyone else who Steven dated?"

"Know? We've got a club going."

"Excuse me?"

"There are five of us that I've been able to find so far. Sophomores and juniors, mostly. We all did it with him until he got drunk and got mean. He fed us all the same line about keeping our relationship quiet so we didn't get in trouble with our mamas and daddys. He was so full of it."

"What do you mean, Katlyn?" Logan asked.

"He knew none of us could tell our folks what he did to us 'cause then we'd have to admit to them what we'd been doing with him. That's how he kept getting away with it. Man, he was such a selfish, lying bastard."

"If you felt that way about him, Katlyn, why did you go to his funeral?"

Katlyn leaned forward suddenly in her chair, her eyes bright, her face flushing. "I'll tell you why. 'Cause I was glad he was dead, and it felt real good watching him get buried. I only wish I had been the one with the guts to put him in that grave."

"WELL, WE HAVE THE NAMES of four more of Steven Boudreaux's young victims," Joanna said after the Morvants and the court reporter had gone. "And every one of them is underage. I know the evidence is important, but it makes me sad to think these youngsters are going to have to take the stand and bare all."

"I'm not real pleased about it, either," Logan said, coming over to sit on the corner sofa in his office next to her.

"Do you ever worry about Shari?"

"No less than twenty-four hours a day," Logan admitted. "She was only five when her mother and I divorced. We both overindulged her. Best thing that ever happened to Shari was her mother's remarriage. She was presented with two younger brothers and the need to learn to share."

"But you never remarried."

It was a statement. Still, Logan knew Joanna would only have made it if she were interested in knowing why. His pulse throbbed to a quickened beat as he met her eyes.

"I've been too busy concentrating on building my practice and raising my daughter."

"Both full occupations in and of themselves," Joanna said. "I just wish I were better at the parenting one. Compared to it, being a lawyer is a cinch."

"I know what you mean. I finally decided that the only thing a father can do for a daughter is instill in her such a strong sense of self-esteem that when a bastard like Boudreaux comes along, she immediately knows she's too good for him."

Joanna sighed. "I wish I had done that for Nikki. I uprooted her right after her father died. I made her easy prey for a vulture like Steven Boudreaux."

Logan covered Joanna's hand with his because he couldn't stop himself. The quiet strength of her voice was at such odds with the heartbreaking sadness in her eyes.

"Nikki is going to come out of this just fine, Joanna. This experience will mature her in important ways and put her on guard against all the guys like him still running around in this world."

Joanna looked directly at him, a warmth and a wish caught up in the deep blue of her eyes. A sudden sharp ache of longing pulsed through Logan's body. He could feel himself flowing toward her, not consciously making a move and yet knowing the distance between them was irrevocably melting away.

Until nothing stood between them but his promise.

He kept reminding himself that the measure of a man was his word. Without it, he was no man at all.

He had never willfully broken his word in his life, but he was so close to breaking it now that his hands had begun to shake with the intensity of the struggle.

Logan was barely breathing as he waited to see which one of them would make the next move.

CHAPTER TWELVE

"DADDY?"

Shari's voice hit Logan's eardrums like the crack of a gunshot.

He released Joanna's hand and rose to his feet. He glanced at his wristwatch and took a deep breath, trying to forget as he stepped forward to greet his daughter how close he had just been to kissing Joanna.

"Hi, Shari. You're early."

He planted a kiss on her forehead.

"Looks to me like I was just in time," Shari said, not even attempting to keep her voice low.

Logan was still trying to digest his surprise at his daughter's comment when Joanna stepped forward and offered her hand.

"Hi, Shari. I'm Joanna Gideon. I've heard a lot of nice things about you. It's a pleasure to finally meet you."

Shari took Joanna's hand with something less than enthusiasm. There were several socially acceptable responses to Joanna's pleasant greeting. Much to Logan's dismay, Shari didn't choose to use any of them.

"Hello," she said sullenly.

Logan had never witnessed his daughter act with so little civility before. He was astonished, confused and unprepared.

Joanna, however, did not seem to take offense. She sent Shari a smile with more wattage than Bourbon Street on a Saturday night. "You are as lovely as your father described."

Shari's thank-you was barely audible. "I'll wait across the hall until you're finished with your business," she said.

When she'd left, Logan turned back to Joanna.

"I apologize for my daughter's lack of civility. I don't know what has gotten into her."

"You've given up your home to Nikki and me. We're spending a lot of time together working on this case. You had to cancel going to the JazzFest with Shari last weekend because of it. Your daughter is no doubt feeling neglected. If I were she, I wouldn't be feeling too cordial toward me, either."

"She's canceled on me a dozen times to be with her friends."

"But you know it's different when we cancel on them, Logan. Kids always take it as a personal rejection. They see our lives as revolving around theirs."

"I suppose if I thought about it hard enough I'd realize I pulled this kind of stuff on my parents when I was her age."

Joanna chuckled. "The only solace we parents possess is knowing that one day our kids will have kids of their own who will put them through the same kind of hell they put us through."

Logan smiled as they walked out of the office and he closed the doors behind them. "Thanks for being so understanding about Shari."

"You've been more than understanding with Nikki—and have completely won her over, I might add. If I didn't stop her, you realize she'd be insisting on your taking every meal with us?"

"So you're the one who I have to complain to for not getting invited to breakfast and dinner and having to wait until supper for a home-cooked meal?"

Joanna laughed as she headed for the stairs. "Guilty as charged."

"You realize that Nikki invited us to supper tonight?" he called up to her.

Joanna's tone was thoughtful as she responded. "Shari may wish to spend the evening alone with you."

"No, we'll be there," Logan said, watching Joanna ascend

the stairs with that effortless grace that always remained a part of her no matter how long and difficult their days were.

When she reached the top of the staircase she turned around and smiled down at him. No matter how many times he saw it, Logan knew he would never get over the beauty of that smile.

"Seven-thirty, then," she said.

She slipped inside the upstairs apartment and closed the door. Logan stood staring up at the empty space on the landing, feeling the smile on his lips.

"You like her."

Logan turned with a start. Shari stood in the open doorway to his downstairs apartment, her arms crossed, her face frowning.

"Yes, I do," he said quietly as he stepped forward.

"Why?"

Logan took hold of his daughter's shoulders and twirled her around. He gave her a gentle shove into the apartment and closed the door behind them.

"Well, let's see. She's brilliant, beautiful, and she refused to find fault with you for greeting her in a manner totally devoid of warmth and breeding. I'd say those are pretty good reasons for starters."

"The JazzFest has been over for a week now," Shari said in a sulky voice. "Why are she and her daughter still here?"

"Because I've asked them to stay. We don't have much time to prepare our case. Having Joanna and Nikki here is proving pivotal to getting things done."

"I'm not going up there tonight. This is supposed to be our weekend together. I'm not going to spend it with *them.*"

"Shari, you heard me tell Joanna that we'd have supper with her and Nikki. Are you going to make me break my word?"

"I didn't give *my* word."

"I can't believe what I'm hearing. This isn't like you at all. What's going on?"

"My bed's not comfortable."

"That uncomfortable bed you're complaining about is the

one I gave up so you'd have the privacy of a room to yourself. I'm on the sofa, remember?"

"You gave *my* bedroom away and you never even asked me!"

Logan forced himself to take a deep breath and slowly let it out. He knew his getting angry was not going to help. He controlled his emotions and voice to project a reasonable tone.

"Shari, at the most you spend two or three nights a month here with me, and that's only when I don't get bumped by one of your friends or dates."

"So?"

"So, Nikki Gideon has been through hell and is bravely facing what is sure to be more hell to come when she goes on trial for her life. Is it really so hard for you to let her use your room during the next couple of months?"

The reasonableness of his tone seemed to be working. At least Shari deigned to look a bit embarrassed.

"You like this Nikki Gideon?" she asked.

"Yes, I like Nikki. I think you'd like her also, if you gave her a chance. Now, I would be very pleased and proud to show off my beautiful, talented and charming daughter to Joanna and Nikki Gideon at supper tonight. Will you come?"

Shari thought about it for what seemed like a very long moment before her mouth finally twisted into a smile. "Well, now you know I will, Daddy."

"That's my girl," Logan said, trying not to show her too much of the relief he felt. He'd never seen this side of Shari before. He was beginning to think that most of the growing pains of the teenage years were felt by the parents.

"Can we spend the rest of the weekend together, just the two of us?" Shari asked.

"A whole weekend with your old man, huh? You must be getting really hard up for a date."

Shari laughed. "Yeah, you wish. I know you'd like to lock me up until I'm thirty-five."

"And who told you that?"

"I overheard you tell Mama that over the phone last month."

"If you don't stop eavesdropping on your mama's and my conversations, I just might lock you up until you're thirty-five."

Shari laughed. She didn't look a bit worried.

BY THE TIME JOANNA SERVED the salad she knew that supper was going to be a complete disaster.

Shari Weston had shoulder-length, dark gold hair framing features as delicately and fortunately arranged as any out of a fashion magazine. Her eyes were big and blue and had probably already caused death by melting for many a teenage boy.

Unlike her lack of civility that afternoon, tonight Shari was all smiles and gracious ease, offering to help Joanna in the kitchen, assuring Nikki that she was welcome to stay as long as she liked and use anything in her room.

Her effervescent conversation modestly revealed she was on the honor roll and serving a second term on the student council. She was altogether a pretty, smart, sweet, doting daughter.

And with every proud look Logan sent Shari, Joanna's heart sank a little further in her chest. Because Nikki seemed to retreat further and further into a sad little shell.

It wasn't until tonight that Joanna realized how attached Nikki had become to Logan, how much she looked forward to his presence—and attention—during these meals they shared together.

How much Nikki had been treating Logan as the missing dad in her life.

And how unlikely it was that Logan would ever fill that void.

For Shari was using her warm, sweet smiles and pet names and frequent arm touches with her daddy to make it obvious to Nikki—and Joanna—that Logan belonged to her. It was the Southern female's faultlessly clever—and outwardly innocent—way in which she laid claim to her menfolk. An iron hand of possession encased in the casual caress of a silken glove.

And Nikki wasn't the only one feeling the fallout.

Joanna made herself face it. She, too, had been getting too close to Logan.

She loved that lazy, fluid smile on his lips, so opposite to, and yet so perfectly blended with, the sharp glint of solid gold intellect in his eyes. The way the muscles moved in his tanned forearms when he rolled up his sleeves on warm afternoons. That subtle, sophisticated sense of humor that was reflected in his sexy smile. The sandalwood soap that seemed so much a part of his clean male scent.

When he had stopped himself from kissing her that afternoon—despite the fact that he so obviously wanted to—she had responded to his restraint by nearly losing her own.

She probably would have kissed him if Shari hadn't arrived.

But Shari had arrived, so jealous of her dad's attention and affection that she was orbiting around him like a death star.

Joanna told herself she was glad. Shari's presence was an important reality check. She had needed one.

Joanna didn't have time to concentrate on anything but Nikki's defense. Her growing feelings for Logan were inappropriate and definitely a distraction she couldn't afford.

She needed all her energy to fight for Nikki. And Nikki needed her. Particularly tonight after this disastrous dinner. Before Joanna could serve dessert, Nikki had excused herself, saying she did not feel very well.

Joanna did the only thing she could do in the situation. She ended the evening as graciously and early as possible.

And then she made her way to her daughter's door. She got no response to her first knock. She tried again. "Nikki? Please, I just want to know if you're all right."

When Nikki finally opened the door, her sad face said it all. "I'm okay, Mom."

"May I come in?"

Nikki shrugged. When Joanna stepped inside, she saw the

light from Nikki's computer screen. Joanna had always been proud of Nikki's aptitude with computers. But she was beginning to be tormented by the suspicion that Nikki turned to them because she felt so left out when it came to human interaction.

"Are you really okay?" Joanna asked.

Nikki dragged herself over to the edge of her bed and slumped down on it. "She's perfect, isn't she."

"I understand she's lousy at computers," Joanna said, knowing exactly who Nikki was referring to.

"He's so proud of her."

Joanna came over to sit next to Nikki on the bed. "He's her dad, Nikki. Of course he's proud. You remember how proud your dad always was of you?"

"I still miss him, Mom."

Joanna let out a deep sigh as she wrapped her arm around her daughter's shoulders. "Me, too, honey."

"Mr. Weston reminds me of Dad. I know they don't look alike or anything, but he's real nice to me and all."

Joanna forced herself to say what she knew she must.

"Logan is your attorney, Nikki. He likes you very much. But attorneys are warned against having personal relationships with their clients. It makes them less effective in the job they have to do."

"He...he doesn't make me feel like everything I do is wrong the way Grandfather always does. He talks to me like I'm an adult. He even listens to what I say."

"I like all those things about Logan, too," Joanna said. "But we have to remember that he is the best lawyer you could possibly have. We cannot ask any more of him. And I suspect we've been doing just that. It might be best if we try to distance ourselves some. What do you think?"

"I'm not going to invite him to supper anymore."

Joanna's heart sank at the sound of loss in her daughter's voice. She'd been wrong to let Nikki get so close to Logan. Once again she'd set her daughter up for disappointment.

How many more mistakes was she going to make with her

daughter before she finally got this damn parenting thing right?

"Nikki, what do you say we spend this weekend finding the best beauty parlors, boutiques and fast-food restaurants that New Orleans has to offer?"

Nikki turned surprised eyes toward her mother. "You're kidding. *Fast-food* restaurants?"

"Oh, what the hell. I'll double the aerobics next week."

The first smile of the evening lit Nikki's face. "You know, Mom, you are getting so close to being cool."

When she saw the look of mischievous pleasure that went along with her daughter's compliment, Joanna's heart lightened so much she burst out laughing.

Just when she had thought she had blown it all it turned out that she had done something right.

"SORRY FOR KNOCKING so early," Logan said as he took in Joanna's robe and slippers. "But I had some news that wouldn't wait."

"Come in," Joanna said, treating him to the warm fragrance of a woman just out of her bath as she turned. "The coffee's made."

Logan followed her into the kitchen, his gaze traveling from the sheen of her freshly brushed hair to the provocative swells her bottom made beneath the silk peach of her robe.

When he realized he wasn't seeing a panty line, perspiration broke out on his palms.

This was the first time in two weeks that he had been up here. Ever since their dinner with Shari, Logan had noted a definite change in Joanna.

She was much more formal in their working hours, assiduously keeping her emotional and physical distance. The invitations to supper had ceased entirely. It appeared as though she and Nikki were suddenly entertaining one or more of her cousins from Bayou Beltane every night or being entertained by them.

Logan knew why Joanna was doing this, of course. Working together, being together had drawn them too close together—at least too close for her comfort.

He tried to tell himself that her decision to back off was for the best. She was living up to the bargain they had struck when he agreed to stay on as Nikki's attorney.

But no matter what he told himself, he was feeling cut off from her and Nikki's lives and was oddly angry about it. He missed the easy laughter and companionship of their previous working relationship. He missed the back-and-forth banter during the suppers the three of them had shared. He didn't like the new barriers she had put up. He wanted to break them down.

But he wouldn't.

He couldn't.

Logan sat down at the kitchen table, releasing an internal sigh. Joanna poured him a cup of coffee. As she leaned over, the lapel flap of her peach silk robe dipped open just enough for him to catch a glimpse of the top of a creamy white breast.

As he suspected, she was naked beneath that robe.

An ache akin to searing pain pulsated in his brain and body. He forcibly reminded himself of his promise once again as he looked away and clasped his coffee cup.

He'd once convinced himself he only had to wait until Nikki was acquitted before he could make love to Joanna. He no longer believed that. Joanna had retreated during these past few weeks. They were growing farther apart with each passing day. By the end of Nikki's trial, who knew how far away she might be?

And now here he sat, possessing news so bad it might mean he would never be able to get Nikki free. And if he didn't, there would be no future for any of them.

The escalating frustration of those thoughts ticked inside Logan's brain like a time bomb.

He ignored the cream and sugar that sat on the table and took his coffee as it came—as hot and as black as his mood.

"We have a problem," he said. "A big one."

"What?" Joanna asked as she sank into the chair across

from his. Her voice and expression remained calm, just as he knew they would. But her eyes were alert and focused on his own.

He took a deep breath, trying to think how best to give her this news, knowing there was no easy way to say it.

"The toxicology report is back. The police lab did not err. The blood alcohol concentration in Steven's blood was .04 percent."

"But how could it be?"

"There's only one way, Joanna. Steven wasn't drunk on the night that he died."

Joanna said nothing, just stared down into her coffee cup. She was calm, taking the news like the professional she was. But Logan knew what it must be costing her. He would have given anything not to have to be telling her this.

"Joanna, I need to talk to Nikki again."

Joanna raised her head slowly. "She spent last night with Shelby, one of my cousins. She won't be back for hours."

Joanna rose from the table, seeming unable to sit still another second. "Why did Steven attack Nikki? He showed no propensity toward physical violence when he was sober. What happened that night?"

"I've told Marvin Dotella to run every test there is to see if we can come up with an answer. But there are so many, it'll take weeks of working around the clock before he'll know anything—if there is anything to know."

Joanna wrapped her arms around herself suddenly as though chilled. When she spoke again, her raw-silk voice trembled ever so slightly. "If he wasn't drunk, how can we prove Nikki struck him in self-defense?"

The sadness in Joanna's eyes slashed through Logan like a knife. Before he knew what he was doing, he had come around the table and pulled her to him.

"We'll find a way," he whispered against the perfume of her hair, hearing the promise in his words, feeling the jump of his pulse at her nearness, silently cursing himself for both.

Still, he knew at this moment he would say and do anything he could to take her sadness away. Absolutely anything.

"Logan, how can we ever make the jury understand what we don't?"

He wrapped his arms more completely around her, telling himself he did it as a gesture of comfort. But he knew his motives were far from noble. The soft warmth of her pressing against him was heaven.

"There's an explanation, Joanna. We'll find it."

He was going to have to release her before he did something he'd regret. But at the moment, he'd sooner cut off his arms than let her go.

Just a moment more, he told himself. *I just need to hold her a moment more.*

Joanna's chin lifted. She looked up at him.

Logan knew he had been thinking about something important, but he suddenly had no idea what it was.

All he could concentrate on was the desire swirling deep in the lovely blue of her eyes, the soft swell of her breasts brushing lightly against his rib cage, her warm, sweet scent filling his nostrils.

"Joanna." He didn't even know he had said her name until he heard it echoing in his ears like a plea.

Her arms wound around his shoulders. She stretched up to softly brush his lips with hers. She tasted as sweet and hot as freshly spun taffy.

Logan tightened his hold, leaning into her softness, letting her feel the heated hardness of his body as he took the smooth, warm contours of her mouth with all the unappeased hunger that had been churning inside him for so long.

When she melted into his embrace, exultation swept through Logan with such power that it left him shaking.

Joanna felt herself being swept up in arms as strong and solid as oak and held as effortlessly as if she weighed no more than a glad sigh. Logan pressed his mouth even more deeply into hers, spreading the pleasure inside her body like a hot wind.

Since the moment she had felt the force of his mouth on

hers, she had lost every thought in her head; indeed, the capacity to think at all.

All she was aware of was the all-consuming need for him that crowded into her throat and tore through her body.

Her hands circled to the back of his head. She felt dizzy from the demand of his kiss, the scent of heated desire coming off his skin, the hot feel of his scalp through the cool strands of his hair.

He carried her into the bedroom and sank down next to her on the mattress. His hands pushed aside the silk robe she wore, eager and yet tender as they bared her skin for his touch.

The sound of something ripping was followed almost immediately by the feel of Logan's bare chest against her breasts. She sighed in pleasure as she grasped his strong, muscled shoulders and rubbed her aroused nipples against the taut resilience of his skin.

The incoherent murmurs escaping from her throat into his was the only language she had to tell him of the dear havoc he was unleashing inside her with his every touch.

His strong hands rubbed her back and then circled around to her breasts. He cupped them as the pads of his thumbs flicked across her nipples. Joanna's blood beat faster with the sensations singing through her.

Logan's mouth replaced his thumbs as he suckled each nipple in turn, sending sharp, sweet quivers through her core. Joanna arched her back, wild with a longing for him to take all of her.

Logan's hand moved low, his fingers brushing seductively against the sensitive curls between her thighs.

Joanna's murmurs erupted into plaintive moans. He seemed to understand each and every one of her sounds, using them to guide him. He opened her thighs and stroked her with heated intimacy.

Even if she could have found words to describe the wondrous sensations spiraling through her, Joanna knew she could not have spoken them. She needed every breath just to keep her lungs expanding in her chest as he stroked her silken folds, so sensitive to her texture and moistness that she writhed beneath the exquisite torture he wrought.

When she could stand it no longer and was whimpering for him to bring it to an end, he intensified the pressure with unerring skill.

The release came in a sudden, blinding surge, making her cry out as the heat rose from everywhere in her body, spiraling until it had concentrated and exploded within the sensitive folds beneath his touch.

Joanna was calling his name over and over—yet another incoherent sound escaping from her throat that he read and understood completely.

She felt his thighs pressing against hers and then his hardness nudging against her wet, tender depths.

And suddenly she was afraid.

She wanted him inside her, desperately, just as far as he could go. But it had been so long. He was bound to misinterpret the tightness he would soon encounter.

She opened her mouth to tell him, but his clamped down on hers hard. His tongue danced with hers in a growing hunger that caused him to growl deep in his throat. She had no resistance. She gave herself up to the sweet incendiary sweeps that threaded beads of new pleasure through her blood.

She ran her hands down his knotted biceps, feeling the sweat that coated them. He was holding himself up, keeping the brunt of his considerable weight from crushing her. But she could feel his stomach as hard as warm stone as it slipped over her belly.

Slowly, gently he began to fill her. His restraint registered in her thoughts and expanded her chest with wonder. Somehow he knew.

She lifted her hips to meet him, no longer afraid, feeling herself moistening, softening, opening, molding around him.

When she had fully opened for him, he trust into her, and she heard his jubilant cry surging inside her as well. His mouth was as hot as fire and as firmly fused to hers as ever.

It was glorious, intense, a total mindless joining that

Joanna embraced just as hard as the man she held in her arms.

They rode their straining hearts to a stunning release and then lay back, their bodies and breaths still joined, pulsing in unison at the most bold and basic of life's celebrations.

Only when the beating in their blood had slowed did Logan release Joanna's lips from the claim of his own.

She had never shared such an intimate kiss. With it he had both told her things and learned things from her that went beyond any words they could have exchanged.

And she had loved every part of it.

But now it was time for words, and she knew from the determined look in his eyes that he was getting ready to say some hard ones.

"I broke my promise to you, Joanna. I'll never forgive myself for—"

She raised her fingers to his lips to silence him, loving the fact that he was once again taking all the blame.

"No, Logan. You didn't break your promise. I kissed you. I was the one who put aside all ethical behavior and crossed the line. I provoked this. It's my fault."

"Fault?" Logan wrapped his arms around her tightly and sighed deeply against her cheek. "If I hadn't made love to you this morning, Joanna, I swear to you I would have gone mad. I've wanted you since the moment I saw you and every second since. I'll live with my lamentable lack of ethical conduct. But I can't live with your being sorry that this has happened."

The sincerity of his words and the obvious distress in his voice circled warm and comforting around her heart. She kissed the edge of his ear, the only spot she could reach. "I'm not sorry, Logan."

He leaned back to look at her face. The morning sunlight shifted through the gold in his hair and eyes. But it was the shine of his smile that was the most blinding. He scattered soft, sweetly tender kisses across her cheeks, chin and answering smile.

She sighed, feeling that incredible languor that came in

the aftermath of intense lovemaking. She had forgotten until this moment how wonderful it could be, how much she had missed it. She cherished it all the more because she had waited until she could share it with the man she loved.

She was not surprised to realize she loved Logan. Looking back, it seemed inevitable from the first moment he had ridden to her and Nikki's rescue in that courtroom in Bayou Beltane.

Her knight in shining legal armor.

When she remembered how Logan had insisted on treating her with such first-rate reserve and respect despite the undercurrents of raw lust that had been running rampant between them these past few months, she was ready to fall in love with him all over again.

His kisses softly traced a path down her throat. She knew she could drift in this mindless lassitude forever if she had not needed to know where they were going. But she did need to know. It was too important for her not to know.

"What do we do now, Logan?" she asked.

His smile turned almost wicked as he leaned over her breast and licked her nipple. Joanna felt the warm wet caress stirring new flames within her. She let out a little breath of surprise that she could feel so responsive again so soon.

"Logan, I didn't mean—"

"But I do," his voice purred as his marvelously warm, clever hands roamed over her body.

A small, happy sigh bounced out of her throat, far too fast for her to catch. She tried for the rebound.

"Logan, there's so much to—"

"Yes, there is," he said, stretching her arms above her head to rest on the pillow as he leaned over her other breast and expertly drew its nipple into a tight throbbing bead. Joanna gasped at the bolts of pleasure shooting through her body.

Every ounce of her feminine instinct told her that Logan was deliberately evading her attempts at conversation. She was trying to face what the future might bring. He was assiduously avoiding it with this gentle seduction.

Because he knew they had no future?

The thought tormented Joanna. It wasn't that she had harbored any expectations. She had never acknowledged her love for him until now. She had had no time to develop expectations. But the evidence was there to see. And she wasn't blind to it.

Logan had been divorced for twelve years. Busy practice and raising Shari aside, she knew if he had wanted something permanent with a woman again, he would have made it happen.

He hadn't. There could be only one reason. He wasn't looking for anything permanent.

Joanna was not a casual person. She had given herself to only one other man in her life, and he had been her husband. If this was to be just an affair, she had to know now so that she could stop it before it was too late.

"Logan, there are things we have to…ohh…"

His lips drifted down her belly with openmouthed kisses. Her body hummed and sparked to his every touch, leaving her naked with need. She tried to summon her strength to stop him before he went any further, so she could say what she must.

But suddenly his moist, heated mouth settled fully against the apex of her thighs. Every hesitation, every thought in her head, melted right along with the rest of her. It was too late.

CHAPTER THIRTEEN

"BUT STEVEN HAD TO HAVE been drunk," Nikki said. "He smelled of liquor. He was babbling, grabbing at me."

"I believe you," Joanna said.

She rose from her position beside Nikki on the living room sofa and began to pace. "There's another explanation for that low blood alcohol concentration. And we're going to find out what it is."

Logan had assured Joanna of that himself just hours before.

The memory brought a chill to his heart. He had had no right assuring Joanna of anything. Nothing was sure in life and certainly not in a court of law. And that blood alcohol concentration was not something that could be dismissed.

He was caught in the same trap he had fallen into all those years before. He was personally involved with his client. And he was making promises that he had no way of insuring he could keep.

Logan looked at Joanna. Her lips appeared a little swollen beneath their light covering of lipstick. He imagined there were a lot of places on her this afternoon that were tender and sore from his ardent ministrations of the morning.

He had shamelessly taken advantage of her and he knew it. But her frank sensuality and open desire for him had been so genuine that they'd undone him completely. She had not held back from him. And because of it, he found that he had not been able to hold back from her.

He had given himself to her more completely than he had ever intended.

On some level he had always known this deep, driving

desire for her that throbbed through him was far more elemental and essential than mere physical need. But he had never realized until now how outmatched all his good intentions had been against its power. There was nothing that could keep him from her now. Nothing.

Except his failure to keep his word.

If Nikki went to prison for life, Joanna would not be spending hers with the man whose empty promises had let her and her daughter down. Even if somehow they could forgive him, he knew he would never be able to forgive himself.

"How are you going to defend me?" Nikki asked.

"You're innocent under the law," Logan said. "It's up to the prosecution to prove to the jury that you were the one who hit Steven and that he died due to that blow. I'm going to be there to prevent them from doing that."

"I don't understand. You know I hit him."

"Nikki, what I know is that it would not be smart to give the prosecution any help. And we're not going to. The burden of proof rests with them. Let's make sure it remains as heavy as hell on their shoulders. How would you like to help?"

"I can help?"

"One of the key factors to your acquittal is selecting unbiased people to sit in judgment. I've been provided a list of the prospective jurors. We need to find out as much about them as possible before we see them in court."

"How do we do that?"

"By combing through voter registration records, civil and criminal proceedings and property holdings to see whether any of the names of the prospective jurors appear."

"It sounds like a lot of work."

"It's labor intensive, but often pays off. You ready to become an official member of the defense team?"

Nikki smiled. "Yeah, sure. Just show me what to do."

Logan found that Nikki needed very little instruction. She was a fast learner and worker and entered the data on his computer like a pro. But more important, he could tell it made her feel better to be able to contribute something. She lit up at the slightest praise.

All she really needs is a little acceptance and she'd blossom, Logan thought.

That and to be acquitted of murder.

JOANNA WAS NOT comfortable with the new courtroom strategy Logan was adopting. It was logical, but did not fit the facts as they all knew them. That made her uneasy. Still, in view of the blood alcohol results, she recognized they had little choice.

Joanna took the lead in choosing the jury. She went for well-educated people, reasoning that they possessed the capacity to pay attention during long stretches of inactivity—exactly what was required in higher institutions of learning and courtroom cases.

She also went for middle-class people, assuming they would be less likely to resent Senator Delacroix's wealth and take it out on his granddaughter.

And finally she looked for parents of teenagers. If anyone could understand the craziness of those years and forgive it, Joanna believed firmly it would be them.

She felt incredibly weary when they left the courthouse late on the third day, after the jury had been seated.

"It's time to celebrate," Logan said.

Nikki turned to him. "The trial doesn't start until tomorrow. Why would we celebrate tonight?"

"This is New Orleans, Nikki," Logan said, draping his arm casually across her shoulders. "We don't need a reason to celebrate, remember? However, if you insist on having one, how about being alive on such a perfect evening?"

Joanna looked around her, noticing for the first time how lovely an evening it was. The air was warm and velvety, as seductive as a sultry whisper.

But it was Logan's continuing kindness and attention to Nikki that made this evening and other recent ones special.

His idea to make her an active participant on her own

defense team had been met with an enthusiasm in Nikki that Joanna hadn't seen in years.

She knew she was letting Nikki get too close to Logan again, but she couldn't make herself intervene this time. Nikki needed every small pleasure she could get during this difficult time. And so did she.

Logan took them out to dinner at Arnaud's in the French Quarter, a pleasing place with lots of leaded-glass windows, mosaic tile floors and greenery everywhere. After a marvelous supper of classic Creole cuisine capped with bananas Foster, flambéed at the table to Nikki's delight, Joanna felt as though tomorrow were a million miles away.

When they reached home, Nikki went up to bed with a tired yawn. Logan took hold of Joanna's hand and led her into his apartment. He closed and locked the door behind him.

They had been apart since that morning more than a week before when they had made love. Joanna had insisted. She feared it was the wrong time for Nikki to have to deal with any more changes in her life. She had explained her concern to Logan, asking him to keep the change in their relationship to themselves. He had agreed with a quiet nod, raising not one word of complaint.

Joanna had wished he had complained. She had wished he'd said something, anything, to indicate that he felt what had happened between them was too important to keep quiet.

His hands were quivering now in eagerness as he parted her blouse, pulled down her slip and bra. He buried his face between her bared breasts. "I've missed the scent and feel of you, Joanna," he said, his voice little more than a husky whisper.

She inhaled a deep, unsteady breath as her hands dove into the gold dust of his hair and she arched her back, offering her breasts to him. He dropped to his knees and suckled her nipples greedily. Her womb tightened into an aching knot of need as she cried out his name.

His hands slipped beneath her skirt and up between her thighs. She convulsed around his probing fingers, moist and more than ready. Logan carried her quickly to the sofa. They took each other with a hunger that was way too impatient.

And incredibly exciting in its intensity.

"Stay with me tonight," Logan whispered afterward as he held her tightly to him, as though he would never let her go.

Joanna wanted to stay. She wanted to go on feeling his arms hold her like this forever. But her practical streak was never far away.

"What if Nikki knocks on my door and I'm not there?"

"When was the last time Nikki knocked on your door in the middle of the night?"

Joanna smiled. "She was eight, I think."

Logan kissed her neck. "I rest my case. Don't worry. I'll have you up and out of here before Nikki awakes."

Joanna was sure there were a lot of good reasons to refuse. But at the moment, wrapped in Logan's arms, she couldn't think of one of them.

LOGAN POURED COFFEE for Joanna as they sat together in his small downstairs kitchen. She was wrapped in his blue terry-cloth bathrobe. The ends of her hair were still wet from her shower. Her eyes were still only half open. And no wonder. Neither of them had gotten much sleep.

Still, he'd never felt better and she had never looked more beautiful.

"I make a mean omelette," he offered.

Joanna sipped her coffee as she shook her head. "No, thank you. Nikki and I will be having breakfast together just as soon as I can summon the energy to get myself upstairs to fix it."

Logan smiled as he came around the table to stand behind her. He leaned down to nibble at a delightfully sensitive spot he had found at the back of her neck. She sighed in pleasure.

"Nikki shouldn't be up for an hour. We have plenty of time to—"

A sound reached him from the next room. Logan straightened immediately as he recognized it as the door to his apartment being unlocked.

"Daddy, you up?"

Shari's voice opened Joanna's eyes full and wide. She shot to her feet. Logan rested his hands on her shoulders and gently eased her back into her seat.

"I'm in the kitchen, Shari," he called out. Logan knew the apartment was too small to try to conceal Joanna's presence. He wasn't embarrassed for his daughter to find Joanna here. Still, he could sense Joanna was. He kept his hands resting on her shoulders in reassurance.

Shari came bouncing in seconds later. As soon as she saw Joanna sitting at the table in her father's robe, however, she came to an abrupt and stunned stop.

"Good morning, Shari," Joanna said, sending her a smile. She rose slowly. "Nice to see you again. I hope you'll excuse me. It's time I made Nikki breakfast."

Logan watched her glide out of the room with all the self-confidence and grace of the lady she was. He felt a strong possessive pride he knew was dangerous but couldn't squelch.

"You're sleeping with her?" Shari's voice was shocked.

Logan ignored her question. "Orange juice?"

Shari didn't answer, just stood staring. Logan poured a glass of orange juice and placed it in front of her.

"So what brings you by?" he asked, sipping his coffee and keeping his expression bland as he watched her face.

"The trial is front-page news," Shari said, dropping the morning edition on the table between them. She still looked and sounded stunned. "I wanted to tell you, wish you luck."

"Thank you, Shari."

Logan could hear the opening and closing of the door to the apartment. He realized it was Joanna leaving.

Shari suddenly leaned across the table, her eyes focused on him, her voice rising in horror.

"Daddy, her daughter's a murderer!"

"Nikki Gideon is not a murderer. Her boyfriend physically attacked her, and she defended herself. Her only crime was making the mistake of getting mixed up with the wrong guy."

"She should have known better! You've always told me I was responsible for the friends I chose. That I would be known by the company I keep! Why does Nikki Gideon get excused from her mistakes? Because she's from California where they don't know any better? Or because you're sleeping with her mama?"

Logan looked straight into his daughter's eyes. "Sit down, Shari."

Shari started, obviously taken aback by the look her father was sending her and the uncharacteristic command in his voice.

"I said sit down," Logan repeated.

Shari sat. Logan leaned across the table toward her.

"Shari, I love you. But that does not mean you have censure or approval over my relationships with others. Or the right to criticize anyone because of where they hail from. Your mama and grandma may be old New Orleans society. But make no mistake, your grandfather was born and bred in Quincy, Illinois."

"So what does that have to do with anything?"

"Just this. Two weeks after I was born, your grandfather moved us to Illinois to live. I was seven years old before we moved back here to New Orleans. I was like a foreigner in another country. And that's exactly how the kids treated me."

"But you really weren't from away. You were born here in New Orleans."

"Shari, I was a freaky blond Yankee who talked funny and didn't know squat about how to eat crawfish or use hot pepper sauce. I got called a lot of names and ended up fighting my way through every recess. I hung out with other outcasts, some pretty nasty and destructive. They were the only kids who would accept me. I probably would have grown into a full-fledged hellion if your grandma Siddon hadn't taken me in hand."

"What did Grandma do?"

"She taught me how to talk and be Southern, so I didn't stick out like a sore thumb. Then she put me in private school where nobody knew me and I'd have the chance of a fresh start. Once I made friends there, everything turned around for me.''

Logan rose to his full height and stared down at his daughter. ''When you're accepted, Shari, it's a damn sight easier to make the right choice in your friends.''

''You're saying Nikki didn't make the right friends because she wasn't accepted here in Louisiana?''

''Imagine what it would be like for you to be uprooted tomorrow, taken to the other side of the continent, sent to school where everyone took an instant dislike to you just because of your accent. Do you know how grateful you would feel if some guy finally paid you some compliments and attention?''

''I guess I never thought...I suppose I wouldn't be so picky about the rest of him.''

''And now you know where Nikki was coming from.''

Shari was silent a moment, biting her lip. ''I'm sorry about what I said. I didn't understand.''

Logan came around the table and gave his daughter a hug. ''We all make mistakes, but the biggest one is not owning up to them. I knew you were better than that.''

''Do you think Nikki would want me to be her friend?''

''Wouldn't be a bit surprised. Did I tell you she's a whiz at computers?''

Shari smiled. ''I've been looking for a friend like that.''

Logan laughed as he gave her another hug.

He thought he heard the opening and closing of his apartment door again. But when he went into the living room to check, no one was there.

THE JUNE MORNING was already hot and humid. By the time they reached the courthouse, Joanna felt as wilted as a day-old lettuce leaf. She walked beside Nikki down the gleaming corridor, with Logan on the other side. A few lawyers lumbered by carrying briefcases. Uniformed NOPD officers lounged outside courtroom doors, waiting to be called in to testify.

Nikki's case had gotten a lot of media attention on the news the night before and in the morning's newspaper. The thought of being barraged by the press and having to field reporters' questions had not thrilled Joanna.

But no one paid them any particular attention. It was comforting to see everyone looking as lethargic and laid-back as the heat of the day seemed to demand.

When they turned down the final corridor, Joanna saw that she had counted her blessings too soon. There was an energy buzz circling around the bustling crowd that stood at the entry to their courtroom.

"This is the day the spectators and press will be allowed inside," Logan explained. "We'd best go in through the judges' corridor from now on." He changed direction immediately and Joanna and Nikki followed.

They were seated at the defense table a couple of minutes later when uniformed officers of the court opened the doors.

The members of the press surged inside. On their heels came the throng of people who quickly filled up the spectator seats. Joanna recognized many Delacroix family members, all of whom sent her a smile of support. She also saw Flora Boudreaux and Gator Guzman with quite different expressions on their faces.

She wasn't surprised. Shelby had kept her informed of the continuing saga of the case against Nikki in the *Bayou Bulletin*. Guzman had already convicted Nikki a dozen times over.

For her own sanity, Joanna could concentrate only on Nikki's acquittal.

Tallie Arbour looked crisp, unwrinkled and raring to go. Her opening statement to the jury was full of energy and all the points she was eager to make.

"Ladies and gentlemen, all the state has to prove to you is that Nikki Gideon took the life of Steven Boudreaux. But I am going to do more. I'm going to prove to you why she did it.

"Nikki Gideon was having an affair with Steven Boudreaux. That affair started to turn nasty when Nikki discovered that Steven was cheating on her. Filled with a jealous rage, she put a tire iron on the seat of her mother's car before she drove out to Moon Lake to meet Steven. When she saw him, Nikki picked up that tire iron, got out of the car and struck him with it. Seriously wounded, dizzy, disoriented, Steven staggered over to the lake, fell in and drowned.

"This was a deliberate, brutal, premeditated, calculated attack, ladies and gentlemen, and it robbed a young man of the rest of his life. Nikki Gideon is before you today on the charge of second-degree murder. After you hear the testimony the state presents, I know you will be convinced that you must return a verdict of guilty as charged against her."

Tallie Arbour retook her chair at the prosecutor's table with an air of superb confidence. She seemed so sure of victory. Joanna had a feeling that Tallie truly believed Nikki was guilty.

Now came Logan's turn. He rose to his commanding height. His deep, beautiful voice carried to every corner of the courtroom.

"Your Honor, ladies and gentlemen of the jury, it is my pleasure to stand before you today as the advocate for this young woman, Miss Nikki Gideon."

He paused to stop and smile at Nikki, bringing the jurors' attention to her, letting them see the returning smile on Nikki's face as she looked up at him so trustingly.

Then Logan stepped out from behind the defense table so their focus would follow him. "Ms. Arbour has just made many statements about what she hopes to prove to you, but none of what she said is proof. It is very important for you to keep that in mind. Accusations are nothing. Proof is all."

Logan approached the jury in a smooth and easy stride.

"Everything Ms. Arbour has just described to you as being true is based on nothing but a series of circumstances and a lot of creative interpretation. Please remember that interpretation—no matter how creative—is not proof."

Logan paused a moment to let his words sink in, looking at each one of the jurors in turn.

"I ask you to listen carefully to what you *won't* hear during this trial. You will not hear any *proof* that Nikki took the life of Steven Boudreaux. What you *will* hear are all the mistakes a misguided and overzealous police and prosecutor have made, mistakes that have resulted in this seventeen-year-old girl being so unjustly accused.''

Logan turned from the jury box and walked to the middle of the courtroom. ''Ladies and gentlemen, Nikki doesn't have to take the stand and swear to you that she didn't do this. She has already done so by pleading not guilty. She is presumed innocent under the law. The state must prove her guilty or let her go. When you *don't* hear the prosecution prove her guilty, you will have all you need to set Nikki Gideon free.''

He paused again to look into their faces.

''It's a wonderful experience to know you can right the scales of justice and help someone who has been wronged. Ladies and gentlemen, you're going to have such an experience. When you find Nikki innocent of these false accusations against her, you will know what it feels like to serve justice out of your very own hands. And that wonderful feeling will stay with you for the rest of your lives.''

And with a final blinding smile, Logan turned and slowly walked back to the table where Joanna and Nikki waited.

It had been one of the best opening defense statements Joanna had ever heard. Logan had come across as completely believing in Nikki's innocence. His obvious sincerity had the courtroom murmuring in appreciation.

Tallie stood up looking a little irritated as she called Claudia Landry to the stand as her first witness. A uniformed officer of the court brought her in from where she waited in one of the separate rooms for witnesses. About twenty years old, Claudia was short with long, tangled dark hair. She stumbled on her way to the witness box. Her hand shook slightly as she raised it and swore to tell the truth with a noticeable waver in her voice.

Tallie Arbour asked her full name and address and other basic incidentals in a gentle manner, obviously aware of Claudia's nervousness and trying to put her at ease.

"Ms. Landry, I'd like to direct your attention to the night of March 29 of this year. Will you please tell this court what you did?"

"I took a drive."

"About what time was this?"

"Sometime after ten-thirty."

"And where did you go?"

"Moon Lake. I go there sometimes when I want to be alone."

"What time did you get to Moon Lake?"

"Around eleven."

"And what, if anything, did you see, Ms. Landry?"

"I saw Nikki Gideon driving away in her mother's car."

"You recognized Nikki Gideon?"

"And the car. A big old dark blue Mercedes Sedan."

"And Nikki Gideon was driving it?"

"Yes. She passed me on the bridge."

"What bridge is that, Ms. Landry?"

"It's the one that takes you over the lake to the clearing on the other side. Nikki Gideon was driving away from the clearing. I was driving toward it. We met on the bridge. There's just enough room for two cars. She was going pretty fast. I done my best to steer straight to avoid hitting her. We missed each other by inches."

"And what happened after Nikki Gideon passed you on the bridge?"

"I drove into the clearing and parked my car. After about fifteen minutes, I got out to walk along the bank. That's when I seen a man's body floating facedown in the water."

"What did you do?"

"I waded in and dragged him onto the bank. I turned him over. He didn't have no pulse. It was…too late."

"Did you recognize this man when you saw his face?"

"Yes. He was Steven Boudreaux."

"What did you do then, Ms. Landry?"

"I ran to my car and drove to a Winn-Dixie off the highway. I used the pay phone there to dial 911."

"Then what did you do?"

"The 911 operator told me to go back to Moon Lake and wait for the police. The chief of police arrived five or ten minutes later. I told him everything. He sent me home."

"Thank you, Ms. Landry. I tender the witness."

Logan approached Claudia Landry with a straight, focused step. When he spoke, his voice was even, businesslike.

"Ms. Landry, how did you know Steven Boudreaux?"

"From Rick's Café, where he worked."

"Did you know him well?"

"No, not well."

"Ever talk to him?"

"Once when I, uh, accidentally bumped into him and spilled some shrimp on his shoes. He called me a few names."

"Steven Boudreaux wasn't very nice, was he, Ms. Landry?"

"Objection, Your Honor," Tallie said.

"Sustained," the judge ruled.

Logan had expected it to be. Still, he'd wanted the idea planted in the jury's mind. "How well do you know Nikki Gideon?"

"Her mama introduced us once when she brought Nikki into the bait shop where I work."

"So you saw Nikki Gideon only that one time?"

"No, I seen her again."

"When?"

"One day when I came into Rick's she was sitting with Steven at a corner table. I'd heard they were dating."

"There was a lot of talk about their being a couple?"

"Yes."

"Why was there so much talk?"

"Because Nikki's Philip Delacroix's granddaughter, I guess."

"Do you know who started this talk?"

"No."

"Could it have been Steven Boudreaux trying to enhance his image?"

"Objection, Your Honor," Tallie said. "No foundation has been laid for such an inference."

"I withdraw the question," Logan said quickly, having succeeded in planting the thought in the jury's minds.

"Other than seeing Nikki talk to Steven in the café that one time, did you ever personally see them together?" Logan asked.

"No."

"You never saw Nikki and Steven on a date?"

"No."

"You just saw them sitting together at a table in Rick's?"

"Yes."

"And you assumed from the gossip you heard that they were dating?"

"Yes."

"Ms. Landry, how was it that you ended up at Moon Lake on the night of March 29?"

Claudia Landry shifted uncomfortably in the witness chair before answering. "I go there sometimes when I want to get away from…things."

"What things were you trying to get away from on the night of March 29?"

"Your Honor, I object," Tallie said. "How can this question possibly be considered relevant?"

"It goes to establish the state of mind of the witness, Your Honor," Logan said.

"I'll allow it," the judge responded. "You may answer the question, Ms. Landry."

"My brothers had come by my houseboat and was hounding me for money. I had to get away from them."

"Were you upset when you left your houseboat, trying to get away from your brothers?"

"Yeah."

"Are you aware that Moon Lake is on Philip Delacroix's land?"

"That's why I picked it. I figured if my brothers come after me they wouldn't think to look there."

"You testified that you parked at the lake and remained

in your car for fifteen minutes. What were you doing during that time?"

"I'm going to night school. I brung along a flashlight to read my notes for a test I had the next day. Then I started feeling cramped in the car and decided to stretch my legs."

"What was the weather like that night?"

"The wind had kicked up and it was clouding over real fast. I knew a storm was coming."

"Knowing a storm was on its way, you still got out of your car and walked along the edge of the water?"

"It was windy, but it wasn't raining or anything yet."

"So you walked along the water's edge and saw a body floating in the lake. How long did you wait before wading in and dragging that body up the embankment?"

"I...don't know."

"You don't know?"

"I don't know how long I stood there before I could get my feet to move."

Logan's voice suddenly deepened with gentleness, understanding. "Forgive me, Ms. Landry. I forgot what a very harrowing experience that must have been for you that night."

She nodded, saying nothing.

"Had you ever waded into Moon Lake before?"

"No."

"But you knew the water wouldn't be too deep?"

"I never even thought about that."

"Was the water cold?"

"And slimy," she said. "But not so bad as a swamp. I grew up on a swamp."

"Still, you were very brave to have gone in."

"Truth be told, Mr. Weston, I was scared to death. But I...well, I had to be sure he was dead."

Joanna knew Claudia wasn't giving herself enough credit. True bravery was doing what had to be done despite the fear.

"Ms. Landry, did you see a boat tied anywhere at the lake?"

"No. But then, I never looked."

"Before the night of March 29, how many times had you seen Joanna Gideon's car?"

"I guess a dozen."

"You know it well?"

"Sure. It's got an old-fashioned shape. In real good condition, too. Engine just purrs, not like my old clunker. I always noticed her car when it went by."

"Do you know how many other dark Mercedes sedans with boxy, classic shapes are owned by residents of Bayou Beltane?"

"Your Honor," Tallie said, clearly upset as she rose to her feet. "That question has no relevance."

"On the contrary, Your Honor," Logan countered. "The witness's ability to distinguish a certain car is part of her testimony. The defense has the right to test her awareness of other cars matching its description."

"I'll allow it," Judge Wooten said.

Logan turned back to the witness. "I ask you again, Ms. Landry, do you know how many other older, dark Mercedes sedans are owned by residents of Bayou Beltane?"

"No."

"Would you be surprised to learn there are three?"

"Your Honor, defense counsel is presenting his word as fact to this witness and the court."

"If the prosecution wants the facts, I have them right here, Your Honor," Logan said, slipping a sheet of paper out of his breast pocket. "I submit into evidence Defense Exhibit One, this document from the state licensing board listing the three older, dark Mercedes sedans owned by Bayou Beltane residents."

The judge scanned the document that Logan handed to him and had it entered into evidence. "Objection overruled," he said.

Tallie sat down. Logan returned to his witness. Joanna was once again impressed by Logan's preparation. And presentation.

"Ms. Landry, I repeat, would you be surprised to learn there are two other dark Mercedes sedans owned by residents in Bayou Beltane, all possessing the similar classic, boxy shape of Joanna Gideon's car?"

"Yes."

"Why does that surprise you?"

"I didn't know there were any others than hers."

"On the night of March 29, Ms. Landry, you stated you thought Joanna Gideon's car passed you on the bridge in a direction leading away from Moon Lake, is that correct?"

"Yes."

"How fast was it going?"

"Very fast. It whizzed by."

"So you only had time for a very brief glimpse?"

"But the bridge is lighted pretty good."

"Of course, you were concentrating on steering your own car to avoid a collision at the time, correct?"

"Well, yes."

"So your eyes had to be on the road to insure your own safety?"

"But I still recognized the car. It's real distinctive."

"How can you be sure it's so distinctive if you haven't seen the other two dark Mercedes sedans owned by people in Bayou Beltane?"

"Well, I..."

"Can you be sure, Ms. Landry?"

"I don't know. I ain't seen them."

"And that is my point, Ms. Landry."

"Objection, Your Honor," Tallie Arbour said, coming to her feet again. "Defense counsel is testifying."

"Sustained," Judge Wooten said.

"Tell me, Ms. Landry," Logan said, "how good a look did you get at the driver of this car that passed you?"

"I knew right off it was definitely not Joanna Gideon."

"So you just assumed it had to be Nikki because you had already made the assumption that Joanna Gideon had the only dark Mercedes in town?"

"No, it *was* Nikki behind the wheel."

"You testified that you had only seen Nikki Gideon twice before you allegedly saw her that night, is that correct?"

"Yes."

"When was the first time you saw Nikki?"

"Year and a half ago, when Joanna brung her into the bait shop."

"And the last time?"

"In December, when I saw her with Steven in Rick's, right around the time the talk about her and Steven started to spread."

"And after seeing Nikki Gideon only two times, over a year apart, you recognized her behind the wheel of a car whizzing by you at night while you were doing your best to keep your eyes on the road and avoid a collision?"

"You make it sound like I could've made a mistake."

Logan paused for a moment, looking intently at Claudia Landry's face. When he addressed her again it was in a soft, gentle voice that nonetheless carried to every corner of the courtroom.

"If you made a mistake, Ms. Landry, I think it was perfectly understandable. You were upset over the situation with your brothers. You'd had a terrible shock, discovering that body, wading into the icy, slimy water to drag it to shore. Finding out he was dead. Recognizing him as someone you knew. Isn't all that true?"

"Yes."

"And couldn't it also be true that, upon recognizing him, you immediately thought of Nikki Gideon, the young woman whom gossip had linked him to?"

"I could have."

"Could that also have been the moment when you decided the car that had passed you on the bridge those twenty minutes before must be Joanna Gideon's car and the driver Nikki Gideon?"

Claudia Landry bit her lip, not answering.

"Ms. Landry, can you honestly say from your heart as you sit in this witness box under a solemn oath that you could not *possibly* have made a mistake in identification that night?"

"I...I didn't think I did."

"But you could have?" Logan asked, his voice very gentle.

"I...I guess I could have."

"It might not have been Joanna Gideon's car you saw?"

"I...don't know."

"It might not have been Nikki Gideon in the driver's seat of that car?"

"I...don't know. I don't know who it was."

A thrilled murmur shot through the crowded courtroom.

"I realize that was not easy for you to admit, Ms. Landry," Logan said. "Thank you for your honesty. That's all the questions I have."

Joanna saw the smile on Logan's face as he walked slowly back to the defense table. And no wonder. He had just invalidated the testimony of Tallie Arbour's eyewitness.

"No, no!" a shrill voice suddenly wailed from the spectators' section. "Don't let him do this! Don't let him get the murderer of my baby off!"

Joanna swung around in horror to see Flora Boudreaux yelling like a banshee from the back of the courtroom. She had risen to her feet. Her features were twisted. Joanna could feel her hatred as though it were a physical thing as she glared at Nikki.

CHAPTER FOURTEEN

LOGAN WAVED FROM THE DOOR of the café and then joined Joanna and Nikki at a table spread with muffuletta sandwiches.

"It's all right," he said as he took a seat. "I convinced Judge Wooten to ban Flora Boudreaux from the courtroom for the remainder of the trial. We won't have to deal with any more of her dramatic outbursts."

"It was obviously done for the benefit of the jury," Joanna said.

"Fortunately, you put intelligent people in that box. Even if they feel sympathy for her, I believe they'll still understand that punishing an innocent young woman is no way to show it."

"Hopefully," Joanna echoed.

"I feel kind of sorry for Claudia Landry," Nikki said, her forehead puckered in a frown.

Joanna smiled. "I do, too. Another five minutes on that stand answering Logan's questions and she probably wouldn't have even been sure *she* was there that night. That was a hell of a cross-examination. Remind me never to be on the wrong side of the witness box from you, Mr. Weston."

Logan gave Joanna's knee a squeeze under the table.

"But I was there, Mom," Nikki protested. "She saw me."

"You didn't know who passed you on that bridge, Nikki," Logan said. "It all happened too fast. I very much doubt Claudia Landry recognized you or your mother's car."

"If she didn't, how did she know it was me?"

"When she recognized Steven," Logan said, "she just

assumed it had to be you she saw on the bridge. It happened too fast for her to be sure. That's what I wanted her to admit on the stand."

"But—"

"Remember, Nikki," Joanna said. "It's the prosecution's burden to prove every point. If we don't challenge them, then they have a much better chance of getting the jury to interpret the evidence their way. And that means the jury will be made to believe that you were with Steven at the lake that night so you could kill him."

"So you're not going to tell them I was there?"

"Nikki," Logan said, "at this point our motto is Admit Nothing and Challenge Everything."

"Speaking of challenging things, have you heard anything more from Dotella?" Joanna asked.

"He's run all the obvious tests to see if Boudreaux had any drugs in his system. Unfortunately, they've all come back negative. Now Dotella's starting on the less-than-obvious tests, but it's hard to know which ones to run, there are so many. He's also looking into something he noticed on the autopsy photos."

"What?" Joanna asked.

"Some scratches on Boudreaux's legs. Dotella's opinion is that they were probably caused by a twig or stone. But he's a thorough man. He's asking permission to run the autopsy photos through the university's powerful microscope. Before he's finished, he'll know exactly what caused those scratches. And that is our second motto on this case. Leave No Stone Unturned."

TALLIE ARBOUR CALLED Jake Trahan to the witness stand when court convened after lunch. He described responding to the 911 call made by Claudia Landry and what he and his team had subsequently discovered.

Tallie placed the crime scene photos into evidence. Steven's face in death looked young and innocent. Tallie passed the photos among the jurors so she could get the victim's pathetic image planted firmly in their minds.

She interrupted Trahan's testimony to call Dr. Joseph Irwin to the stand.

Irwin, a medium-size man with an oversize mustache, was the medical examiner who had performed the autopsy on Steven Boudreaux. His pretentious air was evident in the bored expression on his face and his dismissive tone of voice.

He gave a detailed account of the injury to Steven's head, the destruction of cells, the resulting bleeding into the brain, all the more chilling because of his staccato delivery.

"Dr. Irwin," Tallie asked, "would this injury be consistent with a blow from a tire iron?"

"Perfectly consistent."

"And how might a person behave who had sustained such a serious injury?"

"He would probably be dizzy, disoriented."

"So after such an injury, he might be subject to stumbling, a loss of balance?"

"Most likely, yes."

"Might he even lose consciousness?"

"He might."

"And if this person were to lose consciousness or his balance and fall into Moon Lake, would he have been able to save himself?"

"Objection, Your Honor," Logan said. "Assumes facts not in evidence."

"Your Honor, it's a fact that Steven Boudreaux fell into that lake," Tallie protested.

"Your Honor, I beg to differ," Logan countered. "Steven Boudreaux may have been found in Moon Lake, but there has been no evidence to show how he got there. Ms. Arbour's statement that Boudreaux fell in has no basis in established fact."

"But, Your Honor, it's so obvious—"

"Not to me, Ms. Arbour," Judge Wooten said, interrupting. "Mr. Weston's right. Objection sustained."

The assistant district attorney's attempt to sneak that one past him had been smooth. Logan had firsthand experience

with how tough Tallie was. He wasn't letting his guard down
a second.

"Dr. Irwin, was Steven Boudreaux drunk that night?"

"No. He had consumed less than a can of beer."

Tallie smiled over at Logan. She obviously had discovered
Steven got violent when he drank. She had just made sure
Logan couldn't come back with that defense.

"Those are all the questions I have for Dr. Irwin," Tallie
said. "I would now like to resume my interrupted examination of Chief Trahan."

"One moment, Your Honor," Logan said rising. "I would
first like to cross-examine Dr. Irwin."

Shrugging as though she saw no point to objecting, Tallie
returned to the prosecutor's table. Her confidence showed no
signs of abating. Logan knew she was putting on a good
performance for the jury. She had to be sweating this one.

"Dr. Irwin," Logan said, facing him squarely. "How did
Steven Boudreaux die?"

"He drowned."

"So this blow to his head that you have just described in
such minute detail over the last thirty minutes for the benefit
of this court did not result in his death?"

"No."

"Dr. Irwin, if Steven Boudreaux hadn't drowned, would
this blow he received have resulted in his death?"

"No."

"Then why did you dwell on it?"

Dr. Irwin patted his mustache in self-important pique.
"Because it is my duty to speak to anything out of the ordinary in regards to the physical condition of the deceased."

Logan walked over to the autopsy exhibits that had been
entered into evidence. He picked up several of the photographs and brought them to the witness stand. He handed
one to the medical examiner.

"Dr. Irwin, what is that a picture of?"

"It's a close-up of the deceased's bare legs."

"And what are these marks on his legs?"

"Cuts. Scratches. A couple are deep."

"When and how did the deceased get these cuts and scratches?"

"He got them a few hours prior to death. I don't know how."

"They are out of the ordinary. Why didn't you mention them?"

"Because they didn't *cause* his death."

"But you just testified that the blow to his head was not the cause of death, either, isn't that right?"

Irwin's mustache twitched in annoyance. "Yes."

"And yet you dwelt on it for over thirty minutes. Dr. Irwin, did you examine these scratches and cuts on Steven Boudreaux's legs under a microscope?"

"There was no reason to. I had already determined the cause of death to be drowning."

"Isn't it true that you discovered no direct physical evidence in the autopsy of Steven Boudreaux to indicate that his drowning was anything but accidental?"

"There was the blow to his temple. I have to consider its contribution to his death."

"Dr. Irwin, did you discover any evidence that Steven Boudreaux's drowning had *anything* to do with that blow to his head?"

Irwin's mustache had begun to twitch again. "Not directly."

"Indirectly?"

"As I explained to Ms. Arbour and this court, that blow could have made him dizzy. It could have caused him—"

"You keep saying it could have, doctor. But isn't it true that you *don't know* whether it did?"

"One can never be certain in cases like these."

"So, you're not?"

"Not…absolutely."

"And isn't it also true that Steven Boudreaux *could have* drowned from any one of a dozen reasons—all totally unrelated to the blow that he received to his temple?"

"I don't see how."

"But then you don't know for sure, do you?"

Irwin's mustache was really twitching with irritation now. "No."

"Thank you, doctor," Logan said, sounding like a dentist who had just pulled a particularly stubborn tooth. "That is all."

JOANNA HAD ALWAYS KNOWN that Jake Trahan was going to be a good witness for the prosecution.

She wasn't wrong. When Tallie Arbour called him back to the stand that afternoon, Jake carried with him an air of sincere reluctance that came across loud and clear. It was so obvious that he was only doing what his job required of him.

Joanna knew it was a good thing that Logan had gotten Jake's conversation with Nikki on the night of Steven's death barred from being entered as evidence. Such a damning admission of Nikki's being repeated by this man who came across as so damn honest would have proved a disaster.

As it was, Jake's finding of Nikki's crystal heart pendant caught in a bush by the shore and the tire iron behind a tree with Nikki's fingerprints all over it was damning enough.

Tallie was smiling broadly when she tendered the witness to Logan.

Joanna watched as Logan approached Jake Trahan. There was a wariness to his walk this time, like that of one predator approaching another.

"Chief Trahan, did it ever occur to you that Steven Boudreaux's death had been an accident?"

"No."

"Not even after the autopsy proved he had drowned?"

"I believe the blow to his head led to his drowning."

"But you have no proof of that, do you?"

"The medical examiner said the blow probably made Boudreaux dizzy, and that he probably fell in and drowned because of it."

"And that was good enough for you? You want to send a seventeen-year-old girl to prison for life based on a *probably?*"

"Your Honor, I object," Tallie said. "Counsel is not asking questions of this witness. He's attacking him."

"Sustained," Judge Wooten said.

Sustained or not, Joanna knew Logan was painting a different picture of Jake Trahan to the jury—one that didn't quite fit the reluctant-law-enforcer image he had so recently projected.

"Chief Trahan, when did you locate the crystal heart pendant and the tire iron that you described as being found at the scene of Steven Boudreaux's death?" Logan asked.

"On the morning after we found his body."

"Why not on the night you found the body?"

"A fierce storm was brewing, about to break. After Steven Boudreaux's body was photographed and taken away by the medical examiner, we had to give up looking for the night."

"Just packed up and went home, did you?"

"Based on Ms. Landry's statement to me, I went to talk with Nikki Gideon. The detective who was doing the photographing stayed on to finish up the pictures of the crime scene."

"What is the name of this detective?" Logan asked.

"Jackson Boudreaux."

"Boudreaux?" Logan said as though surprised. Joanna knew he had known all along. "Chief Trahan, is this Jackson Boudreaux any relation to Steven Boudreaux, the deceased?"

"They were brothers."

A small murmur erupted among the spectators.

"Wait a minute, let me get this straight. You had the *brother* of the deceased working on this case with you?"

"It was not by design, Mr. Weston. It was Jackson's duty night. He responded as I did to the call. When I verified the identity of the deceased, I told Jackson to go home. He told me that was not necessary and stayed on to help."

"And you let him."

"I was shorthanded. The storm was imminent. There was a lot to do to preserve the crime scene."

"And you never thought there might be a conflict of interest in letting the deceased's brother work on this case?"

"Bayou Beltane is a relatively small town, Mr. Weston. Every time you turn around you find yourself running into kin. You can't let that stop you from doing your job."

Joanna knew Jake was speaking from his heart. He had never let it stop *him*.

"Did you secure the scene before you left?" Logan asked.

"We wrapped the traditional yellow tape around a hundred-foot radius to warn trespassers away."

"What time did you return in the morning?"

"At ten."

"The storm had passed?"

"The first one. Another came along a few hours later."

"Were you alone at the death scene?"

"Jackson Boudreaux assisted me in the search for evidence."

"Did you arrive together?"

"He was already on the scene when I drove up."

"Who found the crystal heart pendant and tire iron?"

"I found the pendant. He found the tire iron."

"The *brother* of the deceased found what is being purported to be the murder weapon?"

"Yes."

"Chief Trahan, could the crystal heart pendant and the tire iron have been left in the clearing at Moon Lake at a time other than on the night of the death of Steven Boudreaux?"

"It's possible."

"Could they have been left there on the next morning before you arrived?"

A nerve twitched in Trahan's jaw as he got the implication. He did not hedge with his answer, however. "Yes."

"So you don't know for certain that either of these items were left at Moon Lake on the night of Steven Boudreaux's death?"

"That's correct."

"Chief Trahan, did you suspect anyone other than Nikki Gideon as having contributed to Steven Boudreaux's death?"

"No."

"You decided Nikki Gideon was somehow responsible from the start and did not consider any other possibilities?"

"I believed she was guilty, yes."

"Based on what?"

"On the evidence that I and my detective had gathered."

"Your detective being the crime scene photographer, the finder of the alleged murder weapon, the *brother* of the deceased?"

"Yes."

Although Logan had made no accusation, the implication in his words was clear enough. Joanna knew he was keeping the fact that Steven Boudreaux's brother had been at work on the case in the forefront of the jury's attention.

"Chief Trahan, how did Steven Boudreaux get out to Moon Lake on the night of his death?"

"By pirogue. We found it down the bayou the next day."

"Why didn't you find it on the night of his death?"

"He must have tied it farther up the lake, out of sight."

"You're sure it was out of sight?"

"Pictures of the area were taken with a strong fill-in strobe. Nothing was missed."

"And when did you take these pictures?"

"At the time we found the body."

"Why do you take such pictures, Chief Trahan?"

"Criminal procedure requires that the crime scene be photographically preserved immediately after a crime has been discovered."

"So all of the pictures entered into evidence by Ms. Arbour were taken right after you found the body?"

"Except for the ones of the tire iron and the pendant. We photographed them where we found them on the following morning."

"Just those pictures were taken that next morning?"

"Yes."

Logan paused in his cross-examination to retrieve the crime scene photos from the evidence exhibits held by the court clerk. He approached the witness with them.

"Please look again at these six shots of the embankment at Moon Lake, Chief Trahan, and tell this court when they were taken."

Joanna watched Jake take the photos from Logan's hand and study them carefully. It wasn't long before his mouth stretched into a thin, tight line and the twitching in his jaw became quite pronounced.

"They appear to have been taken at the same time as the photos of the tire iron and pendant," he said.

"That would be on the *morning following* Steven Boudreaux's death, isn't that right, Chief?"

"Yes."

"Then you were wrong before when you said that the only pictures of the scene that were taken the next morning were the pictures of the pendant and the tire iron, is that correct?"

"Yes."

"So this area of Moon Lake where Steven Boudreaux jumped or dived into the water or his boat capsized—or who knows what else—was not photographed on the night of his death, was it?"

"No."

"Could the intervening storm have washed away valuable evidence of what happened there that night?"

"Yes."

"Chief Trahan, can you honestly tell this court that you know what happened out there at Moon Lake that night?"

"I believe I have already done so."

"No, what you've done is let a medical examiner's pompous talk of possibilities make you jump to conclusions."

"Your Honor—" Tallie began.

"And then as if that wasn't enough," Logan interrupted, "you permitted the deceased's own brother to screw up the photos that might have told us the truth! Thanks to you, Chief Trahan, none of us will ever really know for certain what in the hell happened!"

"Objection, Your Honor!" Tallie screamed.

"Sustained," Wooten responded. "Mr. Weston, that will be enough."

"It certainly will," Logan said with disgust as he walked back to the defense table. "I have no further questions."

Joanna knew a person had to experience a hostile cross-examination from a lawyer of Logan's ability to fully appreciate how shattering it could be. She wouldn't have wanted to be Chief Trahan at that moment for anything.

Logan had said he would tear apart Trahan's testimony against Nikki when he got him on the stand. And bless his big, beautiful heart, he had.

"WHO DOES TALLIE HAVE on her list of witnesses for tomorrow?" Joanna asked Logan as she leaned back in her chair later that night in his office.

"Rick Roswell, Eddie Zagget and Vi Venia."

"They'll be difficult cross-examinations. I wish we could just admit to the relationship between Nikki and Steven."

"Joanna, if I could, I'd put on the stand every one of those young women who Steven so callously abused, and give the jury a feeling for who should really be on trial. But that strategy went out the window the day we got the results of that blood alcohol concentration proving Steven wasn't drunk."

"I know. We could establish a pattern of Steven getting physically abusive when he was drunk. But not when he was sober. Why did he turn violent that night, Logan?"

"Dotella's still trying to come up with an answer. But we can't count on his tests giving us something we can take into court. We have to go with what we've got. And that means we have to try to minimize Nikki's ties to Steven. Because the closer their relationship, the closer that puts her to the scene of his death."

"Logan, I hate to play devil's advocate here, but Tallie Arbour is obviously going to have Rick Roswell, Eddie Zagget and Vi Venia all testifying to Nikki and Steven's relationship."

"Think about it, Joanna. All Rick heard was Steven boasting. Eddie saw Nikki at a party with Steven once. And outside of that same party, the only other time Vi saw Nikki and Steven together was at Rick's Café. There is no proof that Steven and Nikki had an intimate relationship."

"But Steven talked to everyone about marrying Nikki."

"He was a guy making minimum wage trying to impress people by boasting he was marrying into wealth. After my cross-examination of those three tomorrow, Tallie will be left with nothing but vague innuendo."

"After seeing you in action today, I have no doubt about it. I guess Jake Trahan's mistake was believing Jackson Boudreaux would brave the storm to finish up taking those photographs like he was supposed to."

"No, Trahan's mistake was ever believing that Nikki could be guilty of a cold-blooded murder."

Joanna's heart swelled with the warmth his words were bringing to her. She looked directly into his eyes. "I wish I could tell you how much your belief in Nikki means to me."

Logan covered her hand with his, the pad of his thumb gently stroking her knuckles. "You just did."

"Mom!" Nikki called excitedly from the hallway. She was approaching fast.

Joanna immediately rose to her feet. By the time Nikki burst into the room, she had steeled herself to face whatever she must. "What's wrong, Nikki?"

Nikki was actually smiling. "Wrong? Nothing's wrong. Shari just called. She's going to come over and hang out for a while. She's got some new CDs she wants me to hear. I asked her to stay overnight. That's okay, right?"

Joanna smiled and took a relieved breath. "More than okay."

"She's going to bring pizza. She knows this place where they make it with Cajun shrimp. She says it's to die for. You haven't started dinner or anything yet?"

"No, and I'm sure you'll also be delighted to know there's a six-pack of cola in the refrigerator."

Nikki grinned. "I was. Only it's a five-pack now." She was off in a flash.

"Thank you for that, too, Logan," Joanna said softly.

"So that *was* you I heard in the living room this morning," he said, rising. "I thought you had already left the apartment."

"I had to go back in the bedroom for my stockings. You defended Nikki with such understanding, Logan. It took all my restraint to keep from coming in and hugging you and your Shari for the sweet way she responded."

Logan wrapped his arm around Joanna's shoulders. "You know exactly the right thing to say to a father."

Joanna rested her head against his shoulder. "You're so good at being a parent. Why did you stop at Shari?"

Joanna instantly felt the tension in Logan as his arm fell from her shoulders and he turned away. "What is it?" she asked, straightening up in alarm. "What did I say? Please, tell me."

There was a look in his eyes that made Joanna's stomach suddenly hurt. She wondered too late if she had asked too much.

Logan didn't look at her. His eyes were trained on the framed LSU law degree that hung on the wall behind her. But she could tell he wasn't really seeing it. He was seeing something that settled on his features like a chill. His voice was oddly flat when he finally spoke.

"When my wife first handed Shari to me in the hospital, she confessed that she'd been an unwed mother when she was seventeen. She'd been forced to give up the child. She wept as she told me that not a day went by that she didn't think of her first baby. She begged me to find it so that we could adopt and raise it together with our Shari."

A new element entered Logan's voice, something that spoke of limits reached—and exceeded.

"I was a young, cocky attorney, Joanna. I thought I could do anything. I promised to get her child back. It took me a year to track down the private adoption agency that had placed my wife's baby. For four years I filed petition after petition with the court, trying to get the adoption records opened. To protect the child and its adoptive parents, the court denied my petitions. The records remained sealed."

"What a terrible disappointment," Joanna said softly.

"My wife realized my promises hadn't meant a thing. She would never see her child. We faced each other like the victims of a hurricane, looking around at the personal devastation, all too aware that our love had not survived the storm."

Logan paused before turning his eyes back to Joanna.

"And I learned that an attorney who represents someone he's personally involved with is facing a living hell if he fails."

Joanna could have wept at the bleakness that had dulled the liquid gold of his beautiful eyes.

"Logan, you're not going to fail Nikki or me."

His hands grasped her shoulders. "Joanna, I cannot promise Nikki will go free. I cannot promise anything."

"I don't need promises, Logan. I just need you to be the lawyer—and the man—you are."

He released her suddenly, turned and left his office.

Joanna heard the door to his apartment open and close behind him. She knew he was not coming back. She had meant to show Logan her belief in him by her words. But now she knew she had said the wrong thing.

Logan did not want her believing in him.

LOGAN WAS SATISFIED with his cross-examinations of Rick Roswell, Vi Venia and Eddie Zagget that next morning. As he had predicted, there was really no evidence of Nikki's intimate relationship with Steven Boudreaux—only Steven's boasting of it.

If things continued to go this way, there was a chance that he would have enough reasonable doubt established and it wouldn't be necessary to present a defense. He hoped to hell that was the case. He had no defense to present.

He kept trying to forget the look on Joanna's face when she'd told him he would not fail her and Nikki.

Everything he had fought so hard against happening between them had happened. Until this trial was over, until everything was resolved with this case, he knew he could never go to her again, never hold her in his arms.

The danger was too great. For disappointment. For heartbreak. For them both.

"The state next calls Leonce Lacour to the stand," Tallie said.

The unfamiliar name hit Logan's ears like a warning blow. He picked up the list of potential witnesses on the prosecutor's docket and quickly scanned it.

"Leonce Lacour's not listed," Joanna whispered.

Logan immediately stood. "Your Honor, Leonce Lacour is not on the prosecution's list of witnesses."

"What's going on here, Ms. Arbour?" Judge Wooten asked.

Tallie didn't look worried, a fact that was beginning to worry Logan. "Your Honor, may we approach?" she asked.

Judge Wooten beckoned both prosecuting and defense counsel up to the bench. He placed his hand over the microphone to maintain the confidentiality of the conversation.

"Your Honor," Tallie began, "the state was not even aware of Mr. Lacour's existence until he contacted our office just before trial convened this morning."

"This is most improper, Ms. Arbour," the judge said. "You cannot pop a surprise witness on the defense this way and you know it."

"Your Honor, defense has known of this witness for months."

"I've never heard of Leonce Lacour until now," Logan said.

Tallie turned to him, a deadly gleam in her eye. "No? Then why did you place an ad in the *Bayou Bulletin* asking him to come forward?"

Hot knives of understanding stabbed into Logan's temples.

"What ad is this?" Judge Wooten asked.

Tallie pulled the ad out of her jacket pocket and slipped it onto the pad in front of the judge. He scanned it quickly.

"I see no evidence that this ad came from defense counsel," Judge Wooten said.

"That's his grandmother's telephone number, Your Honor," Tallie said.

"Mr. Weston, did you place this ad?" Judge Wooten asked.

"Yes, sir," Logan said. It was all he could say.

Tallie's voice was sweet, almost mellow in victory. "Your Honor, although the ad did not bring Mr. Lacour forward, Nikki Gideon's picture being run in the *Bayou Bulletin* recently did."

"Then how did you know about the ad?" Wooten asked.

"Lacour told us. He is ready to testify that he is the Good Samaritan who changed the tire on Joanna Gideon's car on the night Nikki Gideon was driving it to Moon Lake to kill Steven Boudreaux."

"Your Honor," Logan said evenly, trying not to show his continuing alarm, "Ms. Arbour's behavior is insupportable. She admits to having known about this witness since before court this morning. Yet she informed neither you nor me until this dramatic moment she chose to spring him on us."

Tallie was smiling. "Spring him on you, indeed. You've known about him for months, Weston."

"I didn't know Leonce Lacour by name nor—"

"But you knew about his existence and obviously what he could testify to," Judge Wooten interrupted. "Otherwise you would never have run this ad. I'm going to let Ms. Arbour put Leonce Lacour on the stand at this time. I'll give you a continuance afterward to prepare for your cross-examination. Now, both of you step back and let's get to it."

Leonce Lacour looked exactly as Nikki had described him—about five-nine, with dark, curly hair, big arms and shoulders. Lacour testified that he had pulled off the side of the road to help a young woman in trouble. He knew the model, make and color of the car Nikki drove, the clothing she wore. He even described the way she leaned against the fender while he changed her tire, twirling a tire iron in her hands. Then afterward he saw her turn off on the road leading to Moon Lake, placing her at the scene right at the time of Steven's death.

With his every word, Leonce Lacour buried Logan's de-

fense strategy alive, and as a consequence, Nikki's chances
of an acquittal.

Then Lacour came to the part of his story where he mentioned seeing the ad run in the newspaper.

"I intended to answer the ad to help out the girl with her
folks, only my sister's *bébé* came and I forgot about everything else," Lacour said. "Then yesterday I saw Nikki Gideon's picture run in the *Bayou Bulletin*. I recognized her as
the girl I helped that night. Thought I ought to tell the police."

A disturbed murmur broke out in the courtroom as Lacour
delivered this final blow to the defense.

Now everyone knew that Nikki Gideon had indeed been
present at Moon Lake on the night of Steven's death. And
that her defense counsel, Logan Weston, had also known it
all the time, despite all his clever cross-examinations that cast
so much discredit on the previous witnesses and evidence.

Leonce Lacour's testimony was absolutely damning.

Judge Wooten adjourned court right afterward, granting
Logan the continuance he had promised. Logan spirited
Nikki and Joanna quickly out through the judge's chambers
before the reporters could descend.

And all the time the weight of what had just taken place
felt like an anvil on his heart.

Until this moment, Logan didn't think there could be anything worse than when he had failed to reunite his wife with
her child. Now he knew there was. His failure today was
going to send Joanna's child to jail for the rest of her life.

CHAPTER FIFTEEN

"IT WENT PRETTY BAD TODAY, didn't it, Mom?" Nikki asked as she and Joanna sat together at supper, both of them just picking at their food.

Joanna had never lied to her daughter. She wasn't about to start now. "Yes."

"Yeah, well, no matter what happens, Mom, I want you to know that I...it's...I mean, I know I really screwed up this time and you still...stood by me, believed in me. It's meant a lot."

Tears gathered in Joanna's eyes as she circled around the table to give Nikki a hug. When her daughter returned it, the tears rolled down Joanna's cheeks and her heart filled with gratitude.

"I just hope the prison clothes don't have horizontal stripes," Nikki said. "I'd hate to look hippy."

Joanna chuckled through her tears. "Don't go giving up yet, Nikki. If anyone can turn this around, Logan can. And I believe he will."

"Are you in love with him, Mom?"

Joanna hadn't been ready for that question. She hoped Nikki was ready for the answer. She released her daughter's shoulders and straightened, pulling a tissue out to dab at the moisture around her eyes.

"Yes, I sure am. So what do you think?"

Nikki smiled. "I think it's cool."

Joanna smiled back, very relieved at Nikki's totally calm acceptance. And very proud of the woman her daughter was becoming.

When the telephone rang just then, it was Shari calling.

Joanna handed the phone to Nikki and discreetly left the two teenagers to talk over the events of the day.

As she made her way down the stairs to Logan's offices, however, Joanna's lightened heart grew heavy again. The time had come to discuss their very serious legal predicament.

As Joanna approached Logan's office, she heard the sound of raised voices. She increased her pace in concern when she recognized her father's distinctive, sharp-tongued tone.

"Weston, listen. My detective just called me with the news. Tallie Arbour's daddy was that cop who shot an innocent woman while he was pursuing a couple of felons. You must remember the case. I used him as an example of police incompetence during my senatorial campaign twenty years ago. I got him drummed off the force in disgrace!"

"It's irrelevant, Senator," Logan said quietly.

"Are you dense, boy? Tallie Arbour only took this case as a personal vendetta against me! You can claim she tampered with evidence, bribed witnesses, anything you want. She's totally vulnerable to any attack once this information gets out. Call the D.A. tonight. Threaten to let the press have the story. Mark my words, he'll not only pull her off this case, he'll can her butt. And you'll get the mistrial you need."

"That isn't the kind of law I practice, Senator," Logan said quietly.

"The kind of law you practice had Arbour wiping up the court with you today!" Delacroix shouted. "Now, you'll use what I've given you or I'm firing *your* butt right now!"

"Logan's not your lawyer to fire," Joanna said, quickly stepping into the office.

Her father swung toward her, his face glowing hot with anger. "Stay out of this, Joanna."

"Not a chance. I don't doubt Tallie Arbour took this case against Nikki to try to get back at you. Louisiana is strewn with the carcasses of promising careers you've trampled to dust in your ride to power. But however personal Arbour's agenda, she has not bribed witnesses nor tampered with evidence. We will not make such untrue and unfair accusations against her."

"You fool! Your daughter's life is at stake!"

"Nikki will not be defended with lies! Now, I would appreciate it if you would please leave. Logan and I have a lot of work to do."

Philip Delacroix stomped toward the door.

"And Father," Joanna called after his retreating figure, "before you think about contacting the D.A. and reporters on your own with this information, you might want to remember that year I worked for your law firm—and all the things I could share with both the D.A. and the press."

Philip Delacroix glared at Joanna with eyes as cold and sharp as ice shards. "You're no daughter of mine," he said. And then he was out the door, slamming it behind him.

Joanna sank into the nearest chair, her knees giving out on her. She stared at that slammed door, knowing in her heart that she had really lost her father a long time ago. Still, the pain shot through her as though brand-new. She was vaguely aware of Logan kneeling beside the chair, putting his arm around her.

"Joanna?"

She swallowed the painful lump in her throat.

"When I was a little girl I absolutely adored him, Logan. I used to sneak into the courtrooms just to watch him in action. He was so handsome, so eloquent, so courageous as he defended his clients. I wished with all my heart that one day I'd grow up to be a lawyer just like my daddy. Now I thank the good Lord every day that I did not get that wish."

Logan held her, rocked her gently as she softly sobbed. She knew she was crying for the father she had molded out of her little girl's need and imagination—a father of honor and bravery and conviction. A father who had never really existed.

When the tears finally stopped, Logan led her to his bed and made very slow, sweet love to her, the kind of love to heal old wounds and spread balm over new ones.

Love gentle enough to break Joanna's heart.

As LOGAN LAY IN BED that night, he felt the rhythmic rise and fall of Joanna's chest against his side, signaling the deepness of her sleep. But he couldn't doze off. His every last good intention had been overruled by his overwhelming need to hold her tonight, to comfort her, to love her.

He couldn't stay away from her.

He had no fight left. He knew he would take whatever moments were still left to them. He was powerless against his feelings for this woman—this strong, sweet, incomparable woman.

When the phone rang, he picked it up quickly and answered it softly so as not to disturb her.

"Logan, it's Marv Dotella. I think I have it."

Logan straightened. "Have what, Marv? Tell me."

"Nope, this is something you have to see for yourself. Come on down to the lab."

"I'll be there in ten minutes."

Logan hung up the phone and slipped out of bed, careful not to disturb Joanna. He could not get her hopes up—not on a mere possibility. He would say nothing—not unless and until he had something concrete to offer to her. The last thing he ever wanted to give this woman was an empty promise.

THERE WAS A HUSHED expectancy in the courtroom Monday morning when Logan walked in and joined Joanna and Nikki at the defense table. He had not seen either of them since Friday night, so busy had he been preparing for this morning.

As he looked over at Joanna's face now, he expected to be greeted with disappointment or reproach for his having left her. But she wasn't looking at him with disappointment or reproach. She was looking at him with trust.

She had the courage to believe in him when even he lacked that courage.

He was sure, absolutely sure, that he had never seen a more beautiful pair of eyes with a more beautiful emotion pouring out of them.

And it scared the hell out of him.

Because he might let her down.

The judge made his entrance and court was called to order. Logan snapped his attention back to the matter at hand. He knew that he was about to face his most important day in court. What he did here right now would determine the fate of them all. He had to do it right. Absolutely right.

"Mr. Weston, are you ready to proceed with the cross-examination of Leonce Lacour?"

Logan rose slowly and addressed the bench.

"I have no questions for Mr. Lacour."

The excited roar that broke out in the courtroom had Judge Wooten pounding his gavel. "Order," he commanded, "or I'll have all the spectators removed."

No one wanted to be put out at an exciting time like this. The throng instantly hushed.

The judge turned to Tallie. "Ms. Arbour?"

Tallie rose, seeming as startled as the rest of the courtroom at Logan's decision not to attempt to discredit Leonce Lacour's testimony—a testimony that all but convicted his client. A pleased smile of victory touched her lips.

"The state rests, Your Honor," she said.

"Mr. Weston, will you be putting on a defense at this time?" the judge asked.

"Yes, Your Honor, I will."

Logan called Katlyn Morvant to the stand. She told the court about her relationship with Steven and his physical abuse of her when he drank. Then Logan called the other four teenagers Steven had similar relationships with and they told similar tales. And with each one the jury's faces darkened with disgust.

Tallie asked no questions. Since Steven hadn't been drunk on the night of his death, she obviously felt the testimony of the girls irrelevant. Logan called Vi Venia back to the stand. She described making love with Steven on the leaf litter of the woods alongside the bayou on the afternoon of his death.

"We were both pretty scratched up," Vi admitted.

Having set the stage, Logan next called Dr. Marvin Dotella to the stand.

Dr. Dotella smoothed his sparse, gray-blond hair back as

he stood tall and swore to tell the truth. He gazed at Logan with alert gray eyes as he modestly recited his professional credentials for the court.

Those credentials spanned thirty years and included authoring several textbooks on various techniques he had pioneered that were now standard procedure in the field of forensic toxicology. He was readily accepted by the court as an expert.

"Dr. Dotella," Logan began, "did you run a number of toxicology screens on Steven Boudreaux's blood at my request?"

"Yes, I did."

"Are these normal toxicology screens?"

"No. These screens would be performed only if the cause of death could not be determined and certain evidence pointed to their efficacy."

"And what evidence did you find that caused you to run these screens?"

"A photographic enhancement of the autopsy photos revealed two puncture wounds behind the deceased's right ankle."

"And what, if anything, did you do after finding these puncture wounds?"

"I ran a blood test and found a number of neurotoxins in Steven Boudreaux's blood telling me he had been bitten by *Micrurus fulvius* within the twelve hours preceding his death."

"Is there a common term for that Latin phrase?" Logan asked.

"The layman's term for *Micrurus fulvius* is coral snake."

Logan could hear the excited whispers beginning among the spectators.

"Is a bite from this snake a serious matter, Dr. Dotella?"

"Very serious. The deadly coral snake is one of the most venomous of species in the United States."

The whispers were replaced by a low, speculative murmur spreading throughout the throng. Judge Wooten gave a rap with his gavel and it immediately ceased.

"How would someone get such a bite?"

"The snake spends most of its time buried in soil or leaf litter, under logs or stumps. If it's disturbed, it will strike."

Logan looked over at the faces of the jury to be sure they had connected the snake's habitat with where Steven had been on the afternoon of his death. Their expressions told him they had.

"What might a victim of such a snakebite experience?"

"The envenomization has a curarelike inhibitory effect on neuromuscular transmission. This results in various neurologic abnormalities. Paresthesia, ptosis, diplopia, dysphagia—"

"Excuse me, Dr. Dotella, but could you put these symptoms in layman's terms?"

"Yes, of course. The victim experiences a kind of creeping paralysis. His speech becomes slurred. He experiences double vision, muscle weakness, difficulty in swallowing, a drooping of the upper eyelids."

"Could this victim appear drunk to an onlooker, Doctor?"

"Absolutely."

"Is it possible for someone to be bitten and not know it?"

"Yes, if their attention was elsewhere. There is usually only minor pain, easily dismissed. The lack of local symptoms often lures the victim into thinking that envenomization has not occurred. He goes on his way believing himself fine until hours later when the systemic symptoms of paralysis begin to show."

"So Steven Boudreaux could have been bitten many hours before he began to experience these symptoms?"

"He most likely was."

"Dr. Dotella, why weren't the fang marks of this coral snake discovered at the time of autopsy?"

"The delicate fangs of coral snakes are much smaller than those of other poisonous species. They do not produce easily identifiable marks. I myself did not see them until the photos were substantially enlarged."

"So they were missed at the autopsy?"

"It's not surprising. A coral snake's bite often doesn't

even result in a swelling or redness at the site. I doubt it occurred to the medical examiner to look, since the cause of death had already been determined to be drowning.''

"Dr. Dotella, could Steven Boudreaux's double vision and muscular weakness from the venom of the coral snake bite have been the cause of his falling into the lake and drowning?''

''Absolutely.''

"What about the blow to his head?''

"Steven Boudreaux was probably already so dizzy from the venom that the blow had little or no additional effect.''

"Would Steven Boudreaux have died from the venom in his system if he hadn't first drowned?''

"Without medical attention, death by respiratory arrest was certainly a possibility. With that amount of venom in him there is just no doubt in my mind that he was already half-paralyzed by the time he hit the water. Once he went under, it was the paralysis from the snake venom that prevented him from saving himself.''

The courtroom erupted once again in excited whispering. Logan smiled. "Your witness, Ms. Arbour.''

Tallie took Dr. Dotella over his testimony in minute detail, trying to find a weakness. But at the end of two hours, it held up as solidly as the man's reputation. Tallie gave up.

Logan rested the defense case on the tails of Tallie's failure. He knew there was no other evidence he could offer the jury that would be more compelling than Dotella's testimony. He wanted that testimony fresh in their minds as they retired to deliberate on the fate of Nikki.

On the fate of them all.

BY LOUISIANA LAW, Tallie Arbour got the first chance to address the jury in closing arguments, and the last. Logan had only one opportunity to reach them.

There was total silence in the courtroom as Joanna watched Logan walk over to face the twelve men and women sitting in judgment of the facts. No one coughed. No one whispered. No feet shuffled. The air was charged as if everyone were holding their breath.

Joanna knew that when the jury had entered the courtroom that morning, they had been ready to find Nikki guilty. Since then, Logan had presented them with Steven Boudreaux's character and Dr. Dotella's testimony. As impressive as both had been, Joanna's lawyer instincts told her that the jury was wary, still feeling its belief betrayed by Leonce Lacour's testimony.

They needed an explanation.

"Ladies and gentlemen." Logan's marvelous, resonant voice rang out like a bell. "Steven Boudreaux died from drowning. His drowning was not caused by a blow to his head. It was caused by the deadly coral snake venom that paralyzed his body and rendered him incapable of saving himself when he slipped beneath the waters of the lake.

"How did he get bitten? No doubt it happened that afternoon when he rolled in the leaf litter along the bayou with Vi Venia. He probably never even knew he was bitten. By the time he arrived at Moon Lake that night, the venom in his system was taking hold. He was dizzy and disoriented from its curarelike effects. He was losing control over his muscles, his breathing.

"Ladies and gentlemen, there are a lot of things we don't know about the night Steven Boudreaux died. And because we don't know, they concern us. Not because we *have* to know to render a fair and just verdict. But being human we want to know. We want to have those loose ends tied.

"So let's consider a possible scenario that fits the facts. We know that Steven was feeling the effects of the deadly snake venom when he went to Moon Lake that night. Could he have staggered out from behind the dark trees—smelling of the beer he'd spilled on himself, droopy-eyed, mumbling like a drunk—and grabbed at someone? We've all heard how abusive Steven Boudreaux was when he was drunk. What if this person he grabbed knew that? What if she thought he was attacking her? What if she struck out blindly at him in fear?"

Joanna watched the jury's faces and saw the dawning light of understanding coming to rest in their eyes. Logan had related this scenario to them purposely, she knew. He had given them the explanation they had been looking for, the one he had not been able to present to them through Nikki's direct testimony.

Logan was nodding his head as he looked at each one of the jurors in turn. "We may imagine that's exactly what happened. But we don't know. And you know what, ladies and gentlemen? It doesn't matter. It had nothing to do with Steven Boudreaux's death. He died from drowning after being bitten by a snake. Whoever struck him for whatever reason had nothing to do with his death."

Logan stepped back until there were several feet between him and the jury. He faced them squarely.

"The state said it would prove Nikki Gideon killed Steven Boudreaux. It didn't. The law of this land now says you can release Nikki from this terrible ordeal to which she has been so unjustly subjected. And not only can you, I know you *will* set this innocent free."

Joanna listened as Logan's deep baritone fell to a single, clear, ringing note in the final crescendo of his closing argument.

Win or lose, Joanna was certain that no one in the world could have defended Nikki better. She loved Logan so absurdly, so ridiculously, so completely at that moment that her heart sang with the sweetness of it.

THE JURY RETURNED to the courtroom within an hour.

Logan studied the twelve faces, trying to read the minds behind them, to discern what had made them decide so quickly. He was disturbed to note that none looked toward the defense table and the defendant whose life they held in their hands.

Judge Wooten turned to them. "Ladies and gentlemen, have you reached a verdict?"

"We have, Your Honor."

It was a fortyish woman with a plump face and frame who

stood up as their foreperson to answer. Logan recognized her as one of the few childless people on the panel, one whom Joanna had selected because of her quick mind and kind eyes. He prayed Joanna's instincts had been right.

A uniformed officer of the court took the written verdict from her and passed it solemnly to Judge Wooten. Wooten's face revealed nothing as he scanned it. He instructed the officer to read it aloud for the record.

Logan's hands were perspiring, his heart pounding.

Time seemed to stretch into an eternity as the officer cleared his throat and repeated the criminal docket number and charges that had been filed against Nikki. And then came the verdict.

"We, the jury, find Nikki Gideon not guilty."

The weight of the world seemed to suddenly lift from Logan's shoulders.

He whirled around and gathered both Joanna and Nikki into an enormous, exuberant hug, unable to contain his rush of relief and joy.

Shari, who was sitting just behind them in the first row of spectators, vaulted over the railing and joined in the hug with a very uncharacteristic and unladylike whoop, which Logan adored.

Judge Wooten rapped for order. Logan was past caring.

He was vaguely aware of the spectators—many of whom were Delacroix—bursting into spontaneous applause.

JOANNA STEPPED ONTO the gallery off of Logan's bedroom to see the muted glow of the sky at twilight. The city was like a sauna. It was one of those subtropical evenings where the air kissed the skin and stirred the soul with longing.

It had been quite a day. Logan had taken them to the lovely garden room of the Commander's Palace that afternoon to celebrate the verdict. Both Nikki and Shari had been in tearing spirits. Joanna had never felt so relieved, her heart so light, expectant.

She had patiently waited for Logan to say something—anything—about the future that lay in store for them. But he hadn't said a word. And when he had finally driven Joanna and Nikki to his home, he had immediately left them. And he hadn't returned.

That had been three hours ago. Plenty of time for Joanna to get his message. And she had gotten it. Nikki's ordeal wasn't all that had come to an end.

Logan had never spoken of what might exist for them beyond the completion of the case. Now she knew that was because nothing did.

Somewhere in the drawing darkness of the sultry night a neighbor's stereo was playing the blues. The sweet, sad notes drifted on the velvety air to pluck at Joanna's heartstrings and bring tears to her eyes.

She knew the precise second that Logan came into the bedroom behind her. It wasn't that she heard him or indeed had used any of her normal senses to detect his presence. But she was certain he was there nonetheless. It was as though her heart was now attuned to the beat of his whenever he was nearby.

She had rehearsed everything she had to say. She prayed she was strong enough to say it. By the time he joined her on the gallery, she had blinked back her tears. She turned toward him with a polite smile and hello.

"You packed your bags," he said, not returning her greeting, an odd note of surprise in his voice.

Her eyes drifted toward the two suitcases that waited near the door. "There's no reason to crowd you out of your home another minute. Nikki and I will be going back to the North Shore tonight."

"Tonight?" he repeated.

"I want to get things squared away so that Nikki and I can be on our way to California as soon as possible. Lord knows she had a hard enough time trying to make friends and fit in when she first came to Bayou Beltane. Now that she's been accused and tried for a murder…well, you must see how impossible our living in Louisiana has become."

"Joanna, I—"

"But where are my manners?" Joanna interrupted

quickly. "I haven't even properly thanked you for everything you've done. Not that words will ever be adequate to the task. But I must try. You've been wonderful, Logan. Truly wonderful. Because of you, Nikki has another chance at life. I thank you. With all my heart, I..."

Joanna paused as the tears came into her eyes and a lump clogged her throat. She bent her head as she fought to compose herself. Immediately, she felt Logan's arms circling around her, drawing her close to him. She told herself to pull away, to not prolong the parting. But she couldn't move. It felt too perfect to be held by him, to be surrounded by the warmth and strength he offered. Even if it were for just a moment more.

She felt him kiss the top of her head, firmly, almost fiercely.

"Joanna, listen to me. Please. You don't have to go back to California. New Orleans is not like Bayou Beltane. I know Nikki could be happy here. Shari can help her fit in at school."

"Logan, Nikki's name has been in every news—"

"Forget the press! I'll officially adopt Nikki, change her name to Weston. The New Orleans papers and TV never ran her picture. When she goes back to school in the fall, no one will ever know she was the girl on trial. She can put it all behind her. Don't you see? We'll be here to help her do it. You, me, Shari, all of us, together, a family."

Joanna leaned back in his arms to see his face, the implication in his words making her heart suddenly stumble to a stop. "Logan, did you just ask me to marry you?"

He reached into his pocket and pulled out a ring. It was of beautiful antique gold, with a large round sapphire in the center and two smaller white diamonds on either side that sparkled in the dim light.

"This was my grandmother's. She told me that if I ever got married again I was to give my intended this ring, for luck. Three generations of brides have said yes to the men who offered them this ring. And they all had happy, long-lasting marriages. That's why I went to get it from her this afternoon. I didn't want to take any chances. Joanna, this time has to be for keeps.''

He looked directly into her eyes, his voice deep, gentle and just a shade less than steady. "Don't leave me, darling. I love you. Marry me. Please, marry me.''

Joanna's heart filled as she felt the tears stinging her eyes. But this time they were tears of pure joy. "Yes, Logan. Oh, yes.''

He slipped the ring on the third finger of Joanna's left hand. It fit perfectly. And then she was in his arms and he was kissing her, and a bright new world of beginnings was opening up for them all.

DELTA JUSTICE

continues with

SOMEONE TO
WATCH OVER HER

by Kelsey Roberts

Charly Delacroix didn't agree that she needed a
keeper. So her father, Justin Delacroix, swore
that handsone, protective Marshall Avery was
only a personal trainer and his presence had
nothing to do with the injury that had taken her
out of active duty with the police—or the
whispered threats she kept receiving by phone…

Available in April

Here's a preview!

DELTA JUSTICE

Contract: Paternity   Jasmine Cresswell
September '97
Letters, Lies & Alibis   Sandy Steen
October '97
Finding Kendall   Anne Logan
November '97
In the Bride's Defense   Kelsey Roberts
December '97
Every Kid Needs a Hero   Candace Schuler
January '98
Son of the Sheriff   Sandy Steen
February '98
Overruled by Love   M.J. Rodgers
March '98
Someone to Watch Over Her   Kelsey Roberts
April '98
For the Love of Beau   Margaret St. George
May '98
French Twist   Margot Dalton
June '98
Legacy of Secrets   Judith Arnold
July '98
Desires and Deceptions   Penny Richards
August '98

SOMEONE TO WATCH OVER HER

"WHO *ARE* YOU?" Charly said.

There was just a brief flicker of something in his eyes before he flashed a bone-melting smile. "I'm your trainer."

"Don't treat me like a fool, Avery. You appear out of nowhere and all these weird things start happening to me. I'm not pointing the finger at you, I just want to know what your game really is. And don't try to tell me you're nothing but a jock with a passion for current events and police shows."

"You want to know what my passions are?" he murmured as he leaned across the console. His eyes were riveted to her mouth.

Charly suddenly found it difficult to breathe. The heat she was feeling had absolutely nothing to do with air temperature and everything to do with him. "I can guess," she said evenly.

"Why trouble your imagination when you can have the real thing?" he suggested.

She had expected a kiss, was even braced for it. She wasn't at all prepared for the gentle nibble he gave her lower lip. Nor was she prepared for the way his eyes were locked on hers, daring her to protest.

Charly never backed down from anything. Flattening her palms against his chest, she tilted her head back, forcing him to relinquish her lip. As soon as he did so, she brushed a kiss on his open mouth that was little more than a whisper. It was meant to provoke.

But it backfired. Big-time. Marshall's hands glided up along her throat until her face rested in his palms. He shifted her beneath his mouth, taking control and mastering her with a mere kiss. Now, not a mere kiss—it was seduction.

He tasted hot and faintly of mint as his tongue flicked out to toy with her lip. The action was so simple yet so erotic that Charly swallowed the moan rumbling up from her stomach. How had she gotten herself into this mess in the first place?

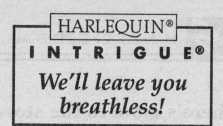

HARLEQUIN SUPERROMANCE®

...there's more to the story!

Superromance. A *big* satisfying read about unforgettable characters. Each month we offer *four* very different stories that range from family drama to adventure and mystery, from highly emotional stories to romantic comedies—and much more! Stories about people you'll believe in and care about. Stories too compelling to put down....

Our authors are among today's *best* romance writers. You'll find familiar names and talented newcomers. Many of them are award winners—and you'll see why!

If you want the biggest and best in romance fiction, you'll get it from Superromance!

Available wherever Harlequin books are sold.

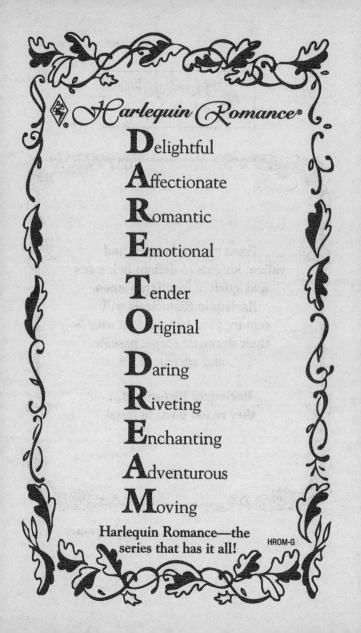

Harlequin Romance®

Delightful

Affectionate

Romantic

Emotional

Tender

Original

Daring

Riveting

Enchanting

Adventurous

Moving

**Harlequin Romance—the
series that has it all!**

HROM-G

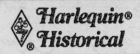

Harlequin® Historical

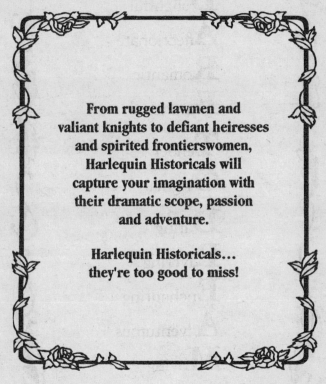

From rugged lawmen and
valiant knights to defiant heiresses
and spirited frontierswomen,
Harlequin Historicals will
capture your imagination with
their dramatic scope, passion
and adventure.

Harlequin Historicals…
they're too good to miss!

HARLEQUIN®

AMERICAN ✦ ROMANCE®

LOOK FOR OUR FOUR FABULOUS MEN!

Each month some of today's bestselling authors bring four new fabulous men to Harlequin American Romance. Whether they're rebel ranchers, millionaire power brokers or sexy single dads, they're all gallant princes—and they're all ready to sweep you into lighthearted fantasies and contemporary fairy tales where anything is possible and where all your dreams come true!

You don't even have to make a wish...
Harlequin American Romance will grant your every desire!

Look for Harlequin American Romance
wherever Harlequin books are sold!

HARLEQUIN PRESENTS

HARLEQUIN PRESENTS
men you won't be able to resist
falling in love with...

HARLEQUIN PRESENTS
women who have feelings
just like your own...

HARLEQUIN PRESENTS
powerful passion in
exotic international settings...

HARLEQUIN PRESENTS
intense, dramatic stories that will keep you
turning to the very last page...

HARLEQUIN PRESENTS
The world's bestselling romance series!